"*Striking Distance* by Debra Webb is a fast-moving, sensual blend of mystery and suspense...I thoroughly enjoyed it."
—*New York Times* bestselling author Linda Howard

"...brims with tightly woven suspense around every corner, and twists and turns abound. Webb moves effortlessly between two very diverse romances and masterfully keeps the reader on the edge until the last page."
—*Romantic Times BOOKclub* on *Striking Distance*

"Webb reaches into our deepest nightmares and pulls out a horrifying scenario. She delivers the ultimate villain for our computer-driven world—a techno sadist. Fortunately, she also gives us a battle-scarred hero who is still willing to fight and a loyal heroine who believes in justice."
—*Romantic Times BOOKclub*

"A chilling tale that will keep readers turning pages long into the night, *Dying To Play* is a definite keeper."
—*Romance Reviews Today*

"Lots of action and an out-of-the ordinary hero add up to an unforgettable adventure!"
—*Romantic Times BOOKclub* on *John Doe on Her Doorstep*

"A page-turning blockbuster."
—*Romantic Times BOOKclub* on *Executive Bodyguard*

"An engrossing thriller with a dynamic heroine."
—*Romantic Times BOOKclub* on *Man of Her Dreams*

"A chilling page-turner."
—*Romantic Times BOOKclub* on *Full Exposure*

Dear Reader,

It's hard to believe that the Signature Select program is one year old—with seventy-two books already published by top Harlequin and Silhouette authors.

What an exciting and varied lineup we have in the year ahead! In the first quarter of the year, the Signature Spotlight program offers three very different reading experiences. Popular author Marie Ferrarella, well-known for her warm family-centered romances, has gone in quite a different direction to write a story that has been "haunting her" for years. Please check out *Sundays Are for Murder* in January. Hop aboard a Caribbean cruise with Joanne Rock in *The Pleasure Trip* for February, and don't miss a trademark romantic suspense from Debra Webb, *Vows of Silence* in March.

Our collections in the first quarter of the year explore a variety of contemporary themes. Our Valentine's collection—*Write It Up!*—homes in on the trend to online dating in three stories by Elizabeth Bevarly, Tracy Kelleher and Mary Leo. February is awards season, and Barbara Bretton, Isabel Sharpe and Emilie Rose join the fun and glamour in *And the Envelope, Please*.... And in March, Leslie Kelly, Heather MacAllister and Cindi Myers have penned novellas about women desperate enough to go to *Bootcamp* to learn how *not* to scare men away!

Three original sagas also come your way in the first quarter of this year. Silhouette author Gina Wilkins spins off her popular FAMILY FOUND miniseries in *Wealth Beyond Riches*. Janice Kay Johnson has written a powerful story of a tortured shared past in *Dead Wrong*, which is connected to her PATTON'S DAUGHTERS Superromance miniseries, and Kathleen O'Brien gives a haunting story of mysterious murder in *Quiet as the Grave*.

And don't forget there is original bonus material in every single Signature Select book to give you the inside scoop on the creative process of your favorite authors! We hope you enjoy all our new offerings!

Enjoy!

*Marsha Zinberg*

Marsha Zinberg
Executive Editor
The Signature Select Program

# DEBRA WEBB

# VOWS
## *of* SILENCE

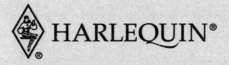

# HARLEQUIN®

TORONTO • NEW YORK • LONDON
AMSTERDAM • PARIS • SYDNEY • HAMBURG
STOCKHOLM • ATHENS • TOKYO • MILAN • MADRID
PRAGUE • WARSAW • BUDAPEST • AUCKLAND

ISBN 0-373-83702-X

VOWS OF SILENCE

Copyright © 2006 by Debra Webb

www.eHarlequin.com

Printed in U.S.A.

Growing up on a farm in small-town Alabama provided many wonderful experiences for my fertile imagination. But it's the lifelong friends who make my Southern history so cherished. One friend in particular was my classmate in school. She married the man of her dreams the same summer I married mine, and went on to have two lovely daughters just as I did. Together we have made the journey from naive young country girls to wives and mothers. We have suffered loss and risen above tragedy. We have made memorable marks in our communities. From birthday parties to PTA fund-raising events, we have worn dozens of hats and wouldn't trade a single moment for anything in the world. This book is dedicated to my friend, my second sister, Joyce Campbell Alley.

Cheers, Joyce!

Dear Reader,

Though Ashland, the town in my story, is fictitious, I grew up in a small town in Alabama much like it. I lived on a farm with a family that was very close. We shared so many wonderful experiences together. Look in the bonus features at the back of this book for one of the more frightening moments from my childhood.

Another wonderful part of growing up in the South was the friends I made along the way—lifelong friends like Joyce, Candi and Evelyn. Friends who would do anything to protect each other and who would keep a secret for a lifetime if necessary. *Vows of Silence* is about that kind of friendship, one that transcends all else. I hope you'll follow this journey with Lacy, Cassidy, Melinda and Kira and find out just how enduring—and at times dangerous—true friendship can be.

As always, I cherish your input. Please check out my Web site at www.debrawebb.com and contact me from there. I'd love to hear from you!

Until next time,

*Deb*

# Chapter 1

"They found the body."

Lacy Jane Oliver froze mid-turn at her perpetually cluttered desk, the receiver clutched to her ear. *They found the body.* Her mouth went incredibly dry as vivid snatches of memory, snow falling from a dark, starless sky and murky waters flashed through her mind.

"When?" she heard herself ask. Her voice sounded alien to her own ears, and Lacy was quite certain her heart had stilled in her chest. It's been ten years, she didn't say. She didn't have to. Cassidy knew every bit as well as Lacy did how long it had been. How could either of them ever forget?

"Day before yesterday," Cassidy answered without inflection. "The chief informed Melinda this morning that the remains had been ID'd. Of course you know that she'll be their prime suspect. The fact that she was in the hospital at the time won't keep them from investigating that avenue," she added with a resigned sigh.

Lacy's chest tightened as her seemingly failed heart now slammed mercilessly against her rib cage. "Oh God," she murmured. Though Cassidy was an attorney, it didn't take one to know that Melinda, the wife of the deceased, would be the number-one suspect.

"I've already called Kira. We're both taking the next available flights. We'll meet in Atlanta, then fly home together."

*Home.* Despite having lived away for more than ten years, Ashland, Alabama, was still home…for all of them.

"I'm on my way," Lacy said quickly, instantly ticking off a mental checklist of all she would need to do to get away from the office for a few days. "I can probably be there before either of you."

"Good. Melinda will need you."

Dead air hummed between them for two beats.

"Remember, Lacy," Cassidy finally said in a tone that made Lacy uneasy. "We've come together during every crisis each of us has endured. This time, especially, we have to do the same. Every move we make must be our routine…exactly what people would expect. We all took the same vow. We're in this together."

A strange calm settled over Lacy. "I remember. See you soon," she murmured before hanging up the phone.

The vow…*silence.*

Ice suddenly filled her veins. Lacy could almost feel the snow and the sharp slap of the wind against her face. Then the biting fury of that winter night had stopped so very abruptly, as if even the wind had known that something was amiss. There had been nothing but silence…and the vow they had made to one another.

To stand by one another, protect one another…no matter the consequences. *Equally guilty.*

\* \* \*

Not much had changed about Ashland, Lacy noted as she slowed her Explorer to the posted speed limit upon entering the city limits of her hometown. She had opted to drive from Atlanta to Ashland, Alabama, after she discovered that the next available flight going in that direction was two hours away. Add to that the actual flying time, luggage pickup and rental-car hassle, and driving direct had won hands down. Lacy had driven like a bat out of hell, which pretty much summed up her churning emotions at the moment, and had managed to make the road trip in record time.

The ever-lingering odor of sulfur hung in the early June air and offended her nostrils. The old paper mill, a couple of textile factories, and a mobile-home manufacturer lined the western end of Norman C. Ashland Boulevard.

*Ashland.* Lacy shuddered as the name ricocheted through some dark, rarely visited recesses of her mind. She would not think about that right now. She had to focus on keeping her cool and supporting Melinda.

*Melinda.* God, what she must be going through right now. And the kids. Chuckie was fifteen, but Chelsea was only twelve, too young to understand any of this and too old to be blessedly oblivious. Lacy prayed with all her heart that somehow this whole nightmare would just go away.

Yeah, right, she mused with self-disgust. Murder doesn't just go away.

*Murder.*

Why couldn't the bastard just stay buried? Even in death, he still tormented Melinda. And her, Lacy admitted. Not one night had passed in the last ten years that she hadn't thought of that low-life son of a bitch. Not a single one. And now he was back to haunt her days.

And maybe ruin all their lives.

Lacy slowly maneuvered the narrow streets bordering the town square. The reconstruction-era courthouse stood proudly as the centerpiece of Ashland's growing municipality. Leaves fluttered at the sudden, rare summer's breeze invitation to dance. A few broke loose from their lush limbs and floated to the ground only to rustle along the aging sidewalks. A collage of shops, old and new, ranging from a turn-of-the-century drugstore with soda fountain to stylish contemporary boutiques, flanked the streets surrounding the courthouse. Other than a fresh coat of paint here and there, and a flashy new business sign, the town's center looked much the same.

Lacy smiled when she caught a glimpse of three old men sitting on a park bench on the east side of the square whittling away at stubs of wood. She wondered if they could possibly be the same three from her childhood.

She shook her head at her mind's foolish meandering. No way. Her childhood felt a lifetime away now. Besides, she hardly knew anyone here anymore. She rarely visited her parents, once a year at the most, and then only on Thanksgiving or someone's birthday. Never at Christmas.

Never, *ever* at Christmas.

She shuddered again. What was Christmas anyway? Just an opportunity for toy and gadget manufacturers to get rich by intimidating unsuspecting parents into buying products their children didn't need. Of all people, Lacy should know. It was advertising executives like her who paved the way for just such blatant thievery. Christmas had become little more than a gimmick. Besides, Lacy Oliver had little time for family or holidays anymore. She was a senior partner at Baldwin, Hall and Oliver, one of Atlanta's top advertising firms.

She didn't need anything Ashland had to offer.

But she had to be here now for Melinda's sake.

For all of their sakes. To protect their secret.

Lacy guided her SUV into the driveway of Melinda's two-story Colonial-style home. Bride-white siding and classic black shutters enveloped the two-story home that reigned amid a backdrop of mature oak and maple trees and meticulously maintained shrubbery. Long, sturdy columns stood as sentinels guarding the welcoming entrance.

After shifting into Park, Lacy turned off the ignition. For a while she simply sat there and stared up at one long window on the far right of the second floor. The master bedroom. She swallowed. The image of Charles lying naked in that ivory porcelain tub with a small, round bullet hole in the middle of his chest and another higher on his shoulder loomed large before her eyes. Then her mind fast-forwarded to the glint of moonlight on his silver Mercedes as it slipped into the murky depths of the natural lake that bordered a good portion of the town.

Lacy blinked away the horrible images. Remembered hysteria climbed into her throat just as it had done that cold, dark night ten years ago. Disbelief, fear, desperation all twisted inside her the same way it had then.

What had they done?

She clenched her jaw and reminded herself of what was really important now. They had to protect Melinda, and one another. The bastard had deserved to die. Lacy refused to acknowledge the little voice that always, *always* nagged at her battered conscience. She would not regret what she could not change. The world was a better place without Charles Ashland. For ten long years he had been a missing person whom no one missed at all, save for his parents, who were blind to his evil ways as parents will be with their own flesh and blood.

But now he was back and poised to destroy the lives of everyone involved. Everything Lacy had worked for, all she had hoped and dreamed of was about to go down the toilet. Self-preservation nudged at her waning determination to no avail. No matter how she justified their actions, the bottom line still hammered away at her self-rationalized defense—murder was wrong regardless of how much the victim deserved to die.

How had she fooled herself into pretending that what they had done was somehow right? Nausea roiled in her stomach. How in God's name had she allowed this to happen? Everything had spun out of control so quickly. There had been no time to think, only to react. Now the past, their desperate act, had caught up with them. The secret they had watched disappear beneath the glassy black surface of the water that long-ago night, was now fully exhumed in the bright, unforgiving light of day.

Charles Ashland, Junior, was dead.

The intricately detailed wood-paneled entrance to the Ashland home suddenly opened and Lacy got her first glimpse of Melinda's pale and drawn face. That picture slammed into Lacy with such force that she jerked with the momentum of it.

Melinda needed her.

The thought shored up her crumbling resolve, solid-ified her emotions. Melinda and the children had to be top priority now. Her movements deliberate and sure, Lacy opened the car door and got out. Without taking her eyes off Melinda, she walked up the sidewalk and steps and straight to her friend. Fear glittered in Melinda's wide hazel eyes. The red, swollen rings around them told Lacy that she had cried all day. Her lips were set in a thin, grim line, bracketed by furrows of fatigue. Just like always, her long blond hair was pulled back into a clasp at her nape. And, just like always, Lacy wanted more than anything to protect her.

"What are we going to do?" Melinda murmured, then trembled.

Lacy pulled Melinda into her arms and held her tight for one long moment without answering. She closed her eyes and wished things had turned out differently. Lacy called to mind the happy little girls they used to be. She envisioned the jump rope swinging high over their heads, pigtails flying, laughter echoing. They had been friends forever. Nothing could change who they were…or what they had done.

"We'll do whatever we have to," Lacy whispered roughly. Tears burned behind her clenched lids as she held her friend closer to her heart. This was way bigger than the four of them—children were involved. Innocent children. How could fate be so very cruel as to resurrect this evil into their lives? She held on to Melinda and tried not to consider the answer to her own question.

Lacy took a deep, calming breath as she drew back. "Where are the kids?"

Melinda brushed at the tears sliding down her cheeks. "Chuckie's away at school. Summer session just started. I went first thing this morning to talk to him. He doesn't…" She cleared her throat. "He doesn't want to come home while this is going on…he…" Renewed tears filled her eyes. "He doesn't even want to talk about it. Chelsea…she's with the Ashlands." She shook her head slowly from side to side. "She adores them, you know. They picked her up early this afternoon in case I had to go to—" she swallowed back a sob "—the chief of police's office when I got back from visiting Chuckie. They don't want him to come home, either. I think maybe they've spoken to him about that already." She shrugged and lowered her head in defeat. "They don't tell me anything."

Lacy gritted her teeth to hold back the retort she wanted to make. She had forgotten the Ashlands' insistence that Chuckie be enrolled in the same private military academy his father had attended until his high school years. It hadn't mattered what Melinda wanted. Fortunately this should be Chuckie's final year away. Charles had started high school with Lacy and the others his sophomore year. His son, apparently, would do the same. And, of course, the Ashlands thought Chelsea was better off with them, too. Melinda was too common, too weak…too unlike them. But she was the mother of their grandchildren, so they tolerated her. Barely.

"What do *you* think?" Lacy said instead of the litany of comments she wanted to make about snobbery, arrogance, and self-centeredness.

Melinda shook her head. "I don't know what I think." Her gaze connected with Lacy's. "Maybe they're right. Lord knows I can't think straight right now. I'm scared."

Lacy took Melinda's hands in hers and squeezed. "Cassidy and Kira will be here soon. We'll take care of this." She displayed a confident smile that she in no way felt. "Somehow," she added with feigned reassurance.

Melinda winced. "I'm sorry." She stepped back from the doorway. "Come in. I know you're exhausted from the long drive. I wasn't thinking."

And how could she? Lacy defended. Melinda's whole life was unraveling around her. Charles, the bastard, was reaching out from the grave and tormenting her and her children once more. Lacy stepped into the foyer and waited as Melinda closed the door behind her. Lacy took that moment to scan the house into which she would just as soon not set foot ever again. But she had no choice.

The elegantly curved staircase hugged one wall of the two-story entry hall, then flowed onto the upstairs landing. Its sleek oak banister gleamed beneath the sunlight that dappled in from the second-story windows. Conservative, linen-colored walls and rich, ornate trim work defined the generous space that was both inviting and pretentious—the mark of an Ashland family home. From what Lacy could see, Melinda hadn't changed much about the place. Lacy knew money wasn't a problem. Hell, she couldn't imagine what had kept her in this house, period. Lacy would have moved long before now. She supposed it had something to do with the children. Maybe Melinda didn't want to take them from the only home they had ever known.

"Would you like tea or…something?" Melinda offered hesitantly, interrupting Lacy's intense reverie.

She blinked. "Maybe later." Smiling, she looped her arm around Melinda's to guide her toward the family room. "Let's just sit and chat until the others arrive."

Melinda paused, halting their forward movement. "About the investigation?" Renewed fear and a dozen other emotions that Lacy couldn't quite sort flickered in the worried gaze that searched hers.

Lacy patted her friend's arm in an effort to calm both their fears. "About anything but that," she suggested with as much nonchalance as she could marshal.

Melinda breathed a sigh of relief. "Good. I don't want to talk about it...not yet."

Lacy started forward once more. "Tell me how Chuckie's doing in school. I'll bet Chelsea's broken a dozen hearts already."

Melinda's face burst into a smile bright enough to chase away most of the darker emotions clouding her eyes. "You should hear her play the piano. She's amazing." Melinda sighed. "And Chuckie's doing great. I can't believe how much he's grown this past year. Wait until you see him, Lacy. He's tall and handsome just like..." Melinda's exuberant expression instantly crumpled.

*Charles,* she didn't have to say. Lacy remembered all too well how handsome Charles Ashland had been. It was only his heart that was mean and ugly.

Lacy changed direction and headed toward the kitchen, Melinda in tow. "Maybe I'll have that tea now after all." They both needed something to do.

"I'm glad you're here."

Lacy slipped her arm around her friend's slumped shoulders and squeezed gently. "Me, too." They were all feeling the weight of their past sins, Melinda in particular.

The kitchen hadn't changed, either. Same fruit-and-Tuscan motif. Lacy slid onto a stool at the island bar as Melinda busied herself with adding water to the teakettle. Acres of weathered white cabinetry and tasteful Italian tile decorated the enormous gourmet kitchen. A huge rack, heavy with shiny pots and pans, cooking utensils and dried herbs and flowers hung over the island. Charles had spared no expense when he built this house to showcase his children and his less-than-socially-worthy wife.

Melinda's family had crashed and burned financially when she was sixteen, but that hadn't changed her standing with her true friends. But it sure as hell had turned the Ashland family upside down when Charles announced two years later that Melinda was having his child. They had married the day after high-school graduation, the entire grand event paid for by the reigning royal family. It hadn't mattered that Melinda's was a good family, it only mattered that their stock portfolio wasn't up to par. But blood was thicker than water. The child she carried made Melinda acceptable, however marginally.

If only they had known the kind of man Charles really was beneath those devilishly handsome looks and all that smooth-talking charm.

But they hadn't. Every girl in town had a crush on the prince of Ashland…Melinda just happened to be the one who didn't get off without the life sentence.

Lacy shivered at the memory of the terrible bruises, concussion and fractured rib Melinda had suffered at her husband's hand. Not to mention the years of emotional abuse. It wasn't bad enough that she'd lost her father mere days before high-school graduation and then her mother when Chuckie was just a baby. She'd been all alone at the mercy of the Ashlands after Lacy and the others left. She'd suffered far too much.

"Sugar or cream?"

Lacy snapped back to the here and now. "I'm sorry. What did you say?"

"Your tea," Melinda gestured to the steaming cup. "Do you want sugar or—"

"Sugar is fine," Lacy said quickly. She had to stay focused. She couldn't keep zoning out like this. Too many lives depended on the events of the next few days. A clear head was a must. With monumental effort, she slowed her pounding heart and concentrated on leveling out her breathing. If the panic building inside her got a foothold, she would be in serious trouble.

"Chelsea's going to try out for the junior-high cheer-leading squad next year." Melinda placed the tea and sugar in front of Lacy. Her eyes shone with motherly pride. "The gymnastics coach says she's a natural. Chuckie's too academic minded to be concerned with sports, but Chelsea loves it. Dance, cheerleading, you name it. Just like we used to do," she tacked on with a futile attempt at a smile.

"That's great." Lacy tried hard to pay attention as her oldest and dearest friend doted on her children, but the past kept nudging her. Voices, images, emotions. *He's dead. My God, what happened? He's dead! I didn't do it. Are you accusing me? It doesn't matter who did it. It only matters that it's done. We're all in this together.*

*Equally guilty.*

Lacy sipped her tea and struggled to zero in on Melinda's nervous chattering. A sheen of perspiration moistened Lacy's skin despite her best efforts to tamp down the mounting panic. She resisted the urge to swipe her palms against her thighs.

*He's dead.*

*Oh, my God. What do we do?*

"You just won't believe how tall he is, but basketball is the farthest thing from his mind," Melinda gushed. "All he wants to do is read or work at his computer."

*Hold that damned door open.* Lacy started, her pulse tripping, as the cold, harsh order reverberated in her head as if it had only just been issued. They had half carried, half dragged Charles's body down the stairs and into the kitchen. When Lacy had tried to back through the door leading to the garage, she had knocked it shut. She could feel the dead weight of his body even now. He was so heavy. So…lifeless. Even the shower curtain they'd had him wrapped up in couldn't disguise the feel of death. *The door, Lacy, hold the damned door,* Cassidy had barked.

Lacy's hands trembled. She tightened her grip on the dainty white porcelain cup and forced her fingers to still. The hollow thud of the closing trunk lid echoed in her head. She tensed at the remembered sound. They had shoved Charles into the trunk and closed it. Cassidy had driven his Mercedes to the lake, Lacy followed in her rental car…the hastily packed suitcase from Charles's room in her back seat.

One final glimpse of silver had winked at her as the Mercedes disappeared beneath the water's murky surface. And then he was gone.

Lacy forced down another sip of her tea, her throat so fiercely dry she could barely swallow. They had thought of everything. When the police investigated and the suitcase and missing clothes from his closet were noticed it would make it look as if Charles had suddenly left town. He had a reputation for drinking and womanizing. No one would ever be the wiser. Cassidy had carefully chosen the deepest and most obscure area of the lake accessible by car. The unexpected and unusually heavy snowfall later that night had hidden any tracks they might have left. When the thaw came, sending the winter blanket melting into the lake, any leftover tracks had eroded as well. Even Mother Nature had been on their side.

*We won't speak of this again. It's done. We're in this together. Equally guilty.*

It was the perfect cover-up…the perfect crime. Until some fisherman had to go and get himself drowned in the swollen waters of the lake after torrential rains last week. The rescue operation had dredged up more than the poor fisherman.

The cup clattered onto its saucer. Hot tea splashed over Lacy's hand, and spilled onto the counter's smooth white surface.

"Damn." Lacy dabbed at the pool of brown liquid with her napkin.

"It's all right, I've got it." Melinda quickly mopped up the mess with a hand towel. "Did you burn yourself? I'll get the aloe."

Lacy licked the stinging patch of skin at the vee of her thumb and forefinger. "It's nothing." She blew out a disgusted breath. She had to pull herself together. "Sorry about the mess."

Melinda frowned, searching Lacy's face, then her eyes. Resigned to what she found there, Melinda murmured, "We're in really big trouble, aren't we?"

Manufacturing a confident expression, Lacy made a sound of denial in her throat. "'Course not. We're going to be fine. When Cassidy gets here, she'll know how to fix everything. She's a damn good attorney, one of the best in San Francisco. She'll keep us out of trouble."

Melinda clasped the damp towel, desperation etching itself across her worried features. She shook her head slowly from side to side in defeat. "For ten years I've been free." She stared down at her hands. "It wasn't nearly long enough, Lacy. I don't want to go to prison and not be able to finish raising my children." She paused to compose herself. "Charles made my life a living nightmare our entire marriage. He took and took and took…" Her voice trailed off as she shook her head again. "I don't want him to take any more."

Lacy placed her hand over Melinda's. "We won't let that happen." She swallowed the last of the uncertainty clogging her throat. "*I* won't let that happen."

Tears shining in her eyes, Melinda nodded her agreement. "You're right. Cassidy will know what to do. We'll be fine."

Lacy blinked back the moisture gathering in her own eyes and glanced around the haunting kitchen. Snippets of memories best forgotten flitted like a slide show amid the other whirling thoughts in her head. She could feel the panic surging once more, threatening her own frail composure like the angry waves of the ocean pounding the shore during a violent storm.

"Come on, let's get out of here." She scooted off her stool and tugged Melinda toward the door. "We need to find some neutral territory."

"What about the others?" Melinda reminded, hesitant to leave the house.

"We'll leave them a note."

Lacy had to get out of this house. She couldn't stand one more minute of the voices…the images…the memories.

She had to find someplace where she could think. Someplace away from the scene of the crime.

Away from the reality of what they had done one desperate night all those years ago.

# Chapter 2

O'Malleys was crowded at five o'clock in the afternoon. The bar that extended the length of the establishment was lined with patrons glad to have the workday behind them. Brightly lit beer signs and the same dancing neon leprechauns added whimsy to the Irish decor Lacy remembered from her senior year in high school. O'Malleys was the place to be even if you were underage and Coca-Cola was the only thing you could order.

Authentic items picked up on the family's annual trips to their homeland embellished the walls. The barrage of windows that faced the street were shuttered in true Irish style, lending privacy as well as ambience. No big-screen TVs would be found here, only the small one at the bar. People came to O'Malleys for the imported beer, the conversation and the occasional darts contest. Two things could be counted on at the most popular pub in Ashland—lots of noise and enough people that blending into the crowd would be effortless. No one ever paid attention to what anyone else was doing. It was a kind of unspoken rule.

An Irish folk selection emanated from the jukebox as Lacy and Melinda settled into a booth at the back of the dimly lit establishment. "Two beers, please," Lacy told the waitress, who appeared reluctant to leave their table without an order. The place was too busy for the help to dawdle, she supposed. And getting the waitress's attention again might not be an easy feat.

When the perky young woman scurried away in a flash of Kelly-green short shorts and long tanned legs, Lacy directed her attention across the table to Melinda. "This is better, don't you think?"

Melinda surveyed their boisterous environment. "When we were teenagers it was better." She smiled faintly. "Now it's just loud."

Lacy laughed, a weary but relieved sound. Man, they were getting old. She'd turned thirty-three last month. Melinda, the youngest of the group, was next in line. She was an Independence Day baby. How had so much time passed so very quickly?

"We're not that old," Lacy protested, more in an effort to convince herself than her friend. "We could still party with the best of these guys if the urge came over us." She glanced at the twenty-somethings clustered around the bar. Fashionably thin and dressed in the latest fads, they weren't really that different from Lacy and Melinda ten years ago.

Before that night.

Lacy swallowed, her muscles constricting with the effort. *He's dead. We're in this together.*

The waitress plunked two chilled mugs of foamy beer before them. "Anything else?"

Shaking off the memories she'd come here to get away from, Lacy lifted her mug and took a sip of the refreshing beverage. She licked her lips as the cool liquid slid down her parched throat. "We're good," she replied, dismissing the long-legged waitress with the impossibly large breasts she had only just now noticed. She shook her head as the woman hurried to a table where three men waved their empty mugs, tongues practically lolling out of their mouths more from the tremendous boobs headed their way than the lack of hops in their glasses.

"What's wrong?" Melinda ventured cautiously.

Lacy glanced down at her own minimal chest then at her friend. "Those breasts can't be real." She arrowed her gaze in the direction of the waitress. "Hell, they don't even jiggle, and she can't possibly be wearing a support bra under that skintight tank top."

Melinda watched the woman flit from table to table. "You're right." She frowned, considering. "You know, I think that's Wade Hall's youngest daughter. I'll bet her daddy sprang for a boob job in hopes of getting rid of her. All of her sisters are married already. You know how it is around here. If you're still single when you turn twenty-five, they think you're an old maid and an embarrassment to the family."

"Well," Lacy said, and shrugged, still tracking the perky waitress's progress, "they certainly detract from the crooked teeth and slightly crossed eyes."

A bark of laughter burst from Melinda, the sound almost painful. Lacy smiled, thankful for even that bit of relief from the tension. "It's true," she insisted, restraining her own building mirth and hoping to encourage Mel's. "I wonder if her daddy even considered an orthodontist and an ophthalmologist before he coughed up the dough for the tits?"

Melinda laughed outright then, and once she got started, she couldn't stop. When the non-jiggling waitress bounced past once more, Lacy erupted into her own fit of elation. She laughed until tears streamed down her face. It felt too good to stop. Each time her eyes met Melinda's, the convulsive laughter started all over again.

"This is definitely not the scene I expected."

Lacy's head shot up at the sound of Cassidy's crisp voice. The fourth member of their group, Kira, stood right behind her. "You guys made it!" Swiping at her damp cheeks, Lacy scooted out of the booth and stood to give Cassidy and then Kira a hug. Melinda did the same.

"Was there any doubt?" Kira drew back and smiled at Lacy. "Girl, you look good."

"So do you." Lacy surveyed her friend with approval. "I love your hair longer."

Kira touched her shoulder-length, corkscrew curls. "The curls I hated growing up are all the envy now." She winked. "Besides, Brian likes it this way." A cell phone chirped and Kira dug into her purse. "Speak of the devil, this will probably be him."

Lacy vaguely remembered that Kira had gotten engaged to a Brian earlier this year. She couldn't recall Kira looking better, or happier. Despite being black in small-town Alabama, Kira had been accepted without condition considering the Jacksons were quite wealthy. Even a mere twenty years ago that had been a major feat. Kira turned her back and lowered her voice but Lacy heard the sudden tension in her tone. The change dragged Lacy out of the past. Apparently Brian wasn't happy about Kira's unplanned trip south.

Trying not to be nosy, Lacy shifted her attention back to the leader of their little posse. Cassidy. Still striking in her own right, Cassidy's dark auburn hair remained short, with not so much as a strand out of place. The unusual color of her hair and the sparkling green eyes provided a vivid contrast to her pale, porcelain skin and sharply defined features.

Guilt suddenly swamped Lacy. It had been too long since they'd all gotten together. Years. Three to be exact. Not since the memorial service for Charles, and then the visit had been excruciatingly brief. Seven years after his inexplicable disappearance he had been deemed deceased by the powers that be. The girls had assembled in support of Melinda and her children...and they hadn't been back together since.

They should never have allowed so much time to pass. She sighed and gave Cassidy's arm a squeeze. "Cass, it's been too long. You look terrific."

"Life is good, what can I say?" Cassidy cocked her head and fixed Lacy with an analyzing expression. "You didn't tell me you made senior partner at your firm."

Lacy felt a flush of embarrassment rush up her neck. She should have done a better job of keeping up with her friends. "This has been a busy year. I don't think I've written anyone."

"You do have e-mail, don't you?" Cassidy looked more hurt than accusing. "Everyone else in the world does."

The road had been long and hard for Cass. Though smart and beautiful, this deep in the Bible belt there were some things that came as close as you could get to the unpardonable, despite family wealth. Choosing not to go along with the set standard of sexual preference fell slap into that category in these parts. But in San Francisco it was a whole different world. Cassidy was no longer an outcast. She was a partner in a prestigious law firm.

"Besides," Lacy teased placatingly, "I couldn't let you get too far ahead of me."

Cassidy smiled briefly, then turned to Melinda. "How are you holding up, Mel?"

"I'm managing," she said, but her voice wavered in spite of her brave smile.

"Are you guys staying?" The big-breasted waitress wanted to know, no doubt already counting on a larger tip with two additions to the table. She eyed Kira suspiciously.

Lacy tensed. Had nothing changed in this damned town? The color of one's skin shouldn't dictate the quality of service.

"We'll have what our friends are having," Kira replied as she dropped her phone back into her bag. "Unless you have a problem with that."

The waitress shrugged one bare shoulder, and her expression instantly shifted to indifferent. "Whatever."

Kira turned back to her friends and added offhandedly, "Anything that could have you two howling with laughter considering our current predicament and is legal in this state, I definitely want some of." She scooted into the booth they'd vacated and Melinda settled in next to her.

Lacy didn't bother explaining the "joke." Especially considering Kira had gotten a boob job herself shortly after graduating from college.

"I think the episode we witnessed is called hysteria," Cassidy commented as she and Lacy slid into the booth across from Melinda and Kira.

As usual, she was too close to the mark. "We decided not to talk about the investigation until you two got here," Lacy explained. "Mel wasn't ready."

"I'm still not," she muttered, intent on her nearly empty mug as if it were a crystal ball containing all the right answers.

"Have you been interviewed by the police?" Cassidy demanded, ignoring Melinda's comment and cutting right to the chase. "Do you have an attorney yet? You're going to need a good one just to show the D.A.'s office you don't intend to take any unnecessary grief."

"I did that already. Got my attorney I mean. But Chief Summers didn't really question me," Mel said thoughtfully. "He came by the house this morning and told me that an investigation was in progress and that he would keep me informed."

"That's all?" Cassidy prodded, clearly suspect.

Melinda nodded. "He was actually the one who suggested that I contact my attorney to find out the legal ramifications of—" she swallowed tightly "—of this new development. He said it would be in my best interest."

"Summers?" Lacy stiffened. "Do you mean Rick Summers?"

"You remember him, don't you?" Melinda massaged her left temple as if an ache had started there. "I think he had a crush on you back in high school."

Lacy wasn't sure a crush was an adequate description of what she and Rick had shared. She had never been able to put that night completely out of her mind. Rick Summers wasn't the kind of guy a girl could forget that easily.

"He's the one who came by the hospital when…" It was Kira's turn to falter this time. "Oh, Jesus." Kira closed her eyes and let go a heavy breath. "We're screwed."

A chill sank clear through to Lacy's bones.

*Charles Ashland, Junior, was dead. Murdered.* It was no longer their secret.

Kira was right. They were screwed.

Tense silence cocooned the group for a long, awkward moment as if they were on a deserted island instead of in the middle of a crowded pub.

How could this have happened? Lacy shuddered inside. They were all good girls. Happy kids, excellent students. Never once had they ever been in trouble. They'd grown up carefree and with life served up to them on a silver platter. Except Melinda. Her parents had lost everything when she was just starting her junior year. Then, after graduation, when Lacy and the others had gone off to their preppy private universities, Melinda had stayed home and married the town's golden boy because she'd gotten pregnant.

Nothing had been right since.

The waitress paused at their table long enough to plop down two more frosty mugs of beer. No one made any effort to thank her or even to sip their drinks.

Nothing would ever be right again.

Between their hectic schedules at college and Melinda's two pregnancies, the four hadn't seen much of one another those four or five years immediately following high school until the reunion. And even the reunion hadn't been on time. The committee had decided a Christmas reunion would insure higher attendance. Most of the alumni returned home during the Christmas holiday.

Maybe it was fate...or the devil himself. That reunion had brought them back together in more ways than one. They had done what had to be done and then they had been united in their vow of silence.

Lacy had come home several times since then. She'd made it a point to stop by and see Melinda, but everything was different after that long-ago night. Too many secrets...too much pain.

"They're going to charge me with murder, I know it." Melinda's hand shook, and she immediately tucked it beneath the table and visibly grappled for control.

"They can't."

All gazes flew to Cassidy.

"They'll use the money, the property, his drinking and the other women." Cassidy morphed into hotshot attorney right before their eyes. "They'll use the physical and mental abuse if they get wind of it. Anything they can dig up, they will. And they'll have enough motivation for a dozen murders." She drew in a calming breath, released it slowly. "But they don't have a murder weapon, and they don't have a single shred of evidence against *you*."

"Will that keep us in the clear?" Kira said slowly.

Cassidy smiled, one of those sly, barely a cut above sinister, lawyerly kind of smiles. "They can't even arraign anyone without sufficient evidence, no matter how strong the motive. Any judge would throw it out. Hell," she added, "any district attorney worth his salt wouldn't even pursue it under the circumstances."

"Thank God," Melinda said softly, her relief palpable.

"So what do we do?" Lacy feared that things would never be quite that simple. Nothing ever was—at least not where Charles Ashland, Junior, was concerned.

"We lay low." Cassidy looked from one to the other. "We provide moral support for each other as we always have, but our primary objective is to insure that no one lets down their guard and makes a mistake."

"A mistake?" Kira's eyebrows drew together in question. "What kind of mistake?"

"No one knows our secret." Cassidy studied each of them in turn. "Only the four of us know what really happened. The water and other elements have long since destroyed any fingerprints or trace evidence we might have left on or in the car. There's nothing to find in the house." She turned to Lacy. "The suitcase was taken care of?"

She nodded quickly. A frame of memory—her digging relentlessly into the cold, hard earth as the snow fell around her—flashed through her mind. "There's no way anyone would ever find it." Not where she'd buried it.

Again Cassidy looked from one to the other, her pointed gaze settling lastly on Lacy. "I also assume that any other evidence was handled as carefully."

For the space of two beats, Lacy had the distinct impression that everyone at the table was waiting for her to confess having knowledge of some other pertinent detail or item.

"Can I get you ladies anything else?"

The tension shrank to a more tolerable level with the intrusion. "I'm fine," Lacy muttered. She had to get past this silly paranoia.

"No more for me." Melinda shook her head, her face as pale with worry now as it had been earlier when Lacy had first seen her at her door.

"We're fine," Cassidy assured the waitress, who quickly left in search of thirsty patrons.

"So you're saying that all we have to do is stay calm and this will blow over," Lacy suggested.

"That's right. We keep our mouths shut and this investigation will die a natural death."

"But it could drag on for weeks," Kira said abruptly, her words echoing Lacy's precise thought.

Cassidy leveled a firm glare on her. "We'll do whatever we have to do for however long it takes."

"But—"

"We're in this together," she said, ruthlessly cutting Kira off. "Equally guilty. We stick together until it's over. Like we always have in the past. No buts. If we do anything differently, then people will get suspicious. Call your respective offices, let them know it could be days or weeks. Agreed?"

The hesitation was gone. Kira nodded. "I can work from here to some extent. So I guess I'm agreed."

Cassidy turned to Melinda and waited for her to voice her understanding, as well.

"Agreed."

"Lacy?" Cassidy shifted in the booth to look directly at her.

"Of course." Lacy blinked, the words they'd chanted all those years ago reverberating inside her.

*...never tell a soul...complete silence...forever...and ever.*

"Well, if this isn't just like old times."

The deep male voice vibrated through Lacy like a lightning bolt.

*Rick.*

Her head went up. She couldn't help the way her greedy eyes lingered on him in the seconds that followed as greetings were exchanged by all around her. There was no way Lacy could be in the same room with Rick Summers and be unaffected.

He had matured into a heart-stopping, handsome man. But then he'd always been extraordinarily good-looking. All the girls had thought so. His black hair was shorter than before, but it suited him. His body looked lean and hard still. Lacy remembered how the taut muscles of his chest had felt beneath her inexperienced fingers. And the way he'd gentled his eager hands so that his touch had been tender despite the lust raging through his young body. No other man had ever touched her quite that way.

"Lacy." He was looking at her now and she couldn't ignore him. Not then…not now…probably not ever.

"Hello, Rick."

"It's good to see you." His voice was deeper, huskier than before, but there was no mistaking the underlying tension there. His expression grew harder, more intense the longer he looked at her. Was he remembering as she was?

"It's nice to see you, too." Lacy broke away from those disturbing gray eyes and sipped her warm beer.

"Is there anything I can do for you, Melinda?" he asked, his tone sincere.

Melinda managed a decent attempt at a smile. "I don't think there's anything anyone can do," she offered listlessly.

Had the question come from any other cop on the force, Lacy would have been certain an ulterior motive existed. But Rick genuinely meant what he asked. He wouldn't beat around the bush. He would say what was on his mind.

"In a few days we'll talk," he went on. "But not now. I know you have your hands full dealing with all this. In the meantime, you be sure and let me know if you need anything at all."

"We're here, Chief Summers," Cassidy said bluntly. "If Melinda needs anything, we'll take care of her."

He nodded, acknowledging the game point to Cassidy. "Of course. I'll keep you informed of our progress on the investigation."

He looked at Lacy one last time before he turned and strode away. She inhaled sharply, almost gasped.

"You okay?"

Lacy met Cassidy's concerned gaze. "Yeah, sure."

"This won't be the last time the chief or one of his

deputies wants to talk to us." Cassidy's focus moved from one to the other. "We have to be prepared to hold our ground. No one, and I mean *no one,* is to be caught off guard. Don't allow anyone—not even your own family—to question you alone. We're in this together. We've all known this day might come. We'll take each necessary step *together.* As long as we're united, no one and nothing can touch us."

"Thank you, Cassidy," Melinda said, tears glistening in her eyes. "I don't think I could get through this without you—without all of you."

"Right now we should all go home and get some rest. We need to stay on our toes. But we have to keep each other informed of our whereabouts. And Melinda—" she turned her full attention back to her "—I don't want you left alone at all."

"I'll take her home and stay with her," Lacy offered, anxious to be away from all this subterfuge.

"All right." Cassidy dropped a bill on the table for the beers and a tip. "I'll relieve you at ten tonight."

Melinda heaved a tired sigh. "Really, Cassidy, I'm not a child. I can be alone."

She shook her head. "It's too risky. They'll target you, Melinda. They'll consider you the weak link."

She looked confused and uncertain, then with a nod relented, "You're right, I suppose."

"Hey," Lacy interjected with as much enthusiasm as she could muster. "It'll be like old times. Remember how we loved sleeping over?"

Melinda smiled weakly.

But it wouldn't be like old times, Lacy admitted to herself. Nothing would ever be the same again.

Charles Ashland, Junior, was dead.

And now the whole world knew.

* * *

Lacy followed Melinda into her house. She would rather walk on broken glass and then tread across hot coals than come back to this house, but she had to. If Cassidy said it was necessary, then it was. They had to pretend that everything was normal—appearances were important right now. And Melinda definitely didn't need to be alone. She looked like hell. Lacy caught a glimpse of herself as she passed a hall mirror, not that she looked any better.

"Are you hungry?" Melinda led the way into the kitchen. "I'm suddenly starved."

"When did you eat last?" Lacy had a bad feeling that it hadn't been today.

Melinda washed her hands in the sink and reached for a nearby towel. "I can't remember. Sometime yesterday, before the call."

"That's what I thought." Lacy opened the fridge door and surveyed the contents. "How about I make a loaded chef salad?"

"You don't need to do that," Melinda protested. "You're a guest. Let me take care of dinner."

Still standing in the vee created by the open door, Lacy lifted a skeptical eyebrow at her friend. "A guest?" She harrumphed. "Get real, Mel."

"God." Melinda dropped into a chair at the table. "I'm not sure I can get through this, Lace."

Lacy shoved the door shut, and crouched down in front of her friend. "Look, we'll get through it. No one has to do this alone."

"But what if Cassidy's wrong? What if they have that stupid inquest my attorney told me about and something goes wrong?"

Lacy shook her head adamantly. "*Nothing* is going to go wrong. Cassidy knows what she's talking about."

Melinda ran a hand over her face and then smoothed back her hair. "I know you're right. It's just so hard. I'm so afraid."

Lacy took Melinda's hands in hers. "We all are, Mel. But we're going to be all right. Cassidy wouldn't be so sure of herself if she had any doubts at all. You know her better than that. She's a tiger when it comes to the law, and she's totally honest and irreverently blunt."

"What about Rick?" Melinda moistened her lips and blew out another breath of worry and helpless frustration. "I'm scared to death he'll suspect something."

Lacy managed a halfhearted laugh. "That's his job. He's supposed to suspect everybody until he solves or closes the case."

An old anger and hurt turned Melinda's hazel eyes as hard as granite. "The son of a bitch deserved to die. He's not worth all the worry he's causing now. The only good that came of him are my two kids." She closed her eyes to fight the tears brimming. "I couldn't live without my kids."

"I have an idea," Lacy offered, desperate to relieve her friend's hurt. "Why don't we go pick up Chelsea and go out to dinner in Huntsville. It's only an hour or so from here and we won't have to worry about running into anyone who might say the wrong thing. Hey, we could drive all the way to Marion and have dinner with Chuckie."

Melinda smiled. "That's a good idea, but I think we'd have to call in advance to have dinner with Chuckie."

The telephone rang, making them both jump.

"Christ." Melinda pressed her hand to her chest. "That scared the hell out of me."

Lacy let go a shaky breath as she stood. "It shaved a couple years off my life too."

Melinda crossed the room and picked up the cordless receiver. "Hello."

Lacy watched the turmoil of emotions that skated across her friend's face as she tried as politely as possible to protest whatever the person on the other end of the line was suggesting. Already etched with grief, Melinda's face turned an even whiter shade of pale. This wasn't good. Lacy's pulse leaped, sending the blood pounding through her veins. Surely nothing else had gone wrong.

Melinda pressed the disconnect button and braced herself against the counter.

"What's happened?" Lacy was at her side in four strides.

"That was Mrs. Ashland." Defeated, Melinda lifted her head. "She's coming over to pack a couple of bags for Chelsea. She thinks my daughter will be better off with her and the senator until this is completely over."

Rage erupted inside Lacy. Just because they were rich and powerful the Ashlands thought they could do anything. "We won't let her keep Chelsea! The old man's only a senator not a god. We can just say no." Charles, Senior had always dabbled in politics, but just over a decade ago he'd launched a serious political career, culminating in his taking a senatorial seat.

Melinda made a sound, not quite laugh and not quite sob. "Tell me, Lacy, how do you stop an Ashland in his own town?"

All emotion drained from Lacy's body, leaving her numb and weak-kneed. Melinda was right. You couldn't stop an Ashland…not in this town.

# Chapter 3

Gloria Ashland had always been one of the town's beautiful people. Time hadn't changed that. Lacy glared, welcoming smile plastered in place, at the woman for a long moment before stepping back and allowing her and her friend entrance into Melinda's home. The idea that Senator Ashland had been asked to run on the Democratic ticket for the vice presidency in next year's election was downright scary.

"Where's Melinda?" Gloria asked sharply, skimming Lacy and immediately flashing disapproval.

"She's in the family room."

Gloria headed in that direction, a flurry of Gucci and Dolce & Gabbana. What a bitch, Lacy fumed. Well, giving Mrs. Ashland grace, Lacy released a weary sigh. The woman had just been forced to relive the loss of her son all over again. Lacy's lips tightened into a grim line.

But then, Gloria Ashland had always been a bitch, even when her son was very much alive.

"I'm Renae Rossman. You remember me, don't you, Lacy? I served as mistress of ceremonies at your debutante ball."

Lacy closed the door behind the woman who had just spoken. Fifteen or so years younger than Gloria, Renae was even more striking than Lacy remembered. And she remembered her all right. A former Miss Alabama, Renae had married Wes Rossman when she was only twenty-one. The rumor was that she had dropped out of college and married so abruptly because she was pregnant, but nine months later that rumor remained unproved. Only about ten at the time, Lacy could remember wondering why such a pretty lady, blond haired, blue eyed, and built like a runway model, would marry such an old man. Wes was at least twenty years older than Renae. Eventually Lacy had come to understand that he was a very rich man, and money talked. He was connected as well. He'd served as the senator's campaign manager in his every political race. Their ties ran deep.

Turning to face the woman, Lacy affected her most charming smile. "Why, of course, I remember you, Mrs. Rossman." She offered her hand.

Renae clasped Lacy's hand briefly but firmly. "Call me Renae. The 'Mrs.' always makes me feel old. You're looking well." Remorse flickered in her eyes. "I regret these circumstances have brought us together again."

*Again?*

Lacy supposed she was referring to the memorial service the Ashlands had held for Charles shortly after he was officially pronounced dead. Lacy, Kira and Cassidy had surrounded Melinda then, as well, providing an insulating barrier between her and the harsh reality of their own actions. A shiver raced through her at the memory.

"So do I." Lacy turned away from the beauty queen's scrutiny and hurried to the family room. She'd left Melinda alone too long with Gloria. Cassidy would not approve. With good reason, Lacy chastised herself. Melinda was vulnerable right now.

"You know I only have the child's best interest at heart," Gloria was saying as Lacy and Renae entered the room. She sat alone on the sofa, her back ramrod straight as she perched on the very edge. "She and Chuckie mean the world to the senator and I."

Melinda stood behind a wing chair opposite the sofa. She gripped the back of the chair, her fingers digging into the elegant brocade, whether for support or protection, Lacy couldn't be sure.

"I know you mean well," Melinda offered, her voice trembling. "But I would prefer Chelsea be with me. I'm her mother. She needs to be with me."

*You tell her,* Lacy cheered silently.

Gloria sighed dramatically, then pressed her handkerchief to her flushed cheek. "Tell her, Renae, about the reporters."

Lacy went on instant alert.

Renae sat down on the sofa next to Gloria and took her hand in hers in a comforting gesture. "They've gathered at the courthouse," she explained quietly.

The woman's voice oozed Southern charm. Lacy could hear her Miss Alabama acceptance speech now, all warm and chock-full of false humility. There was something oddly unsettling about the woman, something Lacy couldn't quite put her finger on. Renae's words filtered through her distracted focus and Lacy went as cold as ice.

"What do you mean?" The question came from her, but Lacy didn't remember forming the words.

"The news of—" she moistened her lips and swallowed "—the discovery has apparently garnered the attention of the media, local and state. There are at least a dozen reporters hanging around the chief of police's office. As soon as they've exhausted their efforts there, they'll come *here*." Her focus shifted from Melinda to Lacy and back. "I don't think Chief Summers will be able to stop them. This story has too many possible ramifications with Charles, Senior, having just been asked to run for vice president."

*Damn.* Lacy hadn't even considered the media circus that would no doubt descend as soon as the news reached the right ears.

"God, I hadn't thought of that." Melinda stared at the back of the chair she clutched. "It'll be a nightmare— even worse than before."

Lacy moved to her friend's side. The damned chair was probably the only thing keeping her fully vertical at the moment.

"Then you see that I'm right," Gloria offered, her eyes shining with self-satisfaction. "With the security we have at home there's no way a reporter is going to get near Chelsea if she's with us."

Melinda nodded her surrender.

"Why don't we go up and pack those bags?" Lacy suggested softly. Even she could see the justification in the move. Melinda nodded again, and with her leaning heavily on Lacy, the two walked slowly toward the hall.

"Chelsea's going to be fine," Lacy assured her. "You know Gloria will take good care of her." She laughed drily. "She'll probably spoil her outrageously."

Melinda paused at the bottom of the stairs. "What

if they won't give up, Lace? What if they keep digging until—"

Lacy shook her head firmly, hoping to convey the certainty of her words. "They won't."

Rick studied the mass of paperwork before him. He had cleared his desk and then spread the Ashland file so that he could review it all at once.

"I'm gone, boss."

Rick scrubbed a hand over his stubbled chin as he glanced up at his deputy. Brad Brewer, his right-hand man, leaned through the open door. He looked like hell. Rick knew, without the aid of a mirror, that he looked just as beat. Neither of them had bothered to go home last night and the lack of sleep was catching up on them.

"Yeah, Brewer, thanks for hanging in here with me." It was nearing midnight. Everyone had left hours ago, except the two of them.

"In the morning I'll stay on the Birmingham office until I get that preliminary forensics report for you."

Rick nodded though he imagined that the senator had already pressed for a speedy turnaround. "Thanks, Brewer. See you in the morning."

The deputy's steps echoed down the empty hall, then faded as he exited the Law Enforcement Center. Rick blew out a breath of frustration and exhaustion and turned his attention back to the puzzle before him.

Dozens of interviews had been conducted with friends, work associates and family members when Ashland first went missing ten years ago. Rick scowled at the stack of neatly typed reports. Preston Taylor, the chief of police in Ashland for as long as Rick could remember until retiring six years ago, had personally performed each interview. The guy wouldn't let anyone else work on the case, not even a deputy as eager and ambitious as Rick. Taylor had insisted that he was the only man with the finesse to do right by the town's most prominent family.

Rick had to admit that Taylor had been thorough if nothing else. Bank records, phone records, appointment book—it was all there. Every step Ashland had taken for a month before his disappearance was recreated in the neat stacks of investigative reports. There had been no evidence of foul play. No indication that Ashland had felt any pressure or unusual stress prior to his disappearance. His finances were in excellent condition and the future only looked brighter for the lucky jerk. He had more friends than you could stir with a stick. And, apparently, plenty of female company besides the little wife.

Any of the women with whom he'd been involved could have put those bullets in him out of sheer jealousy, but only one woman had anything to gain by his death.

Melinda Ashland.

Rick picked up the most damning report and reviewed Taylor's notes. About a year before his death, Charles and Melinda had taken out multimillion dollar life-insurance policies. It wasn't as if they weren't already heavily insured, but the additional policy had left Melinda Ashland a very, very rich woman by anyone's standards. The required wait hadn't been a problem, either, since there were plenty of assets without the insurance money. All that added up to serious motivation.

The interviews with Nigel Canton, Ashland's business partner, garnered Rick's attention next. The co-owned investment firm had made both men wealthy in their own rights. Ashland and Canton had signed an agreement giving the surviving partner first dibs on the business over any heirs of the deceased. The price was a meager ten percent of the firm's worth. Friends of the two men—and clients of the firm—had attested to the growing animosity between the men in the final months of Charles's life. Especially where Canton's wife was concerned.

The fact of the matter was, Rick mused, both Nigel Canton and Melinda Ashland had a great deal to gain from Charles's death. But staring that undeniable fact right back in the face was the indisputable reality that there wasn't a shred of evidence that either of them was involved. To seal that fate, both had alibis. Not necessarily airtight alibis, but alibis all the same. Hell, Melinda had been a patient in the hospital at the time. He supposed there was always the slim chance she had slipped out when no one was looking.

Yeah, right. That's not slim, Summers, that's frigging anorexic. Even though one nurse's statement indicated she'd found her room empty at some point that afternoon, Taylor hadn't put much stock in that idea since mobile patients often walked the floors of the hospital.

There was Melinda's brother Kyle Tidwell. He'd hated Charles, for what he'd done to his sister but, according to the reports, his alibi had also been airtight. Then there was the senator. Though he loved his son, Charles, Junior had been a major embarrassment to him.

Another frown inched its way across Rick's forehead. There was that other little nagging detail of the one-hundred-thousand-dollar withdrawal Charles made the day he disappeared. He'd liquidated a couple of CDs and withdrew the money in cash. A suitcase and some of his clothes had been missing. Every indication at the time, Rick had to admit, was that Ashland had simply skipped town. But now they knew differently. Rick rubbed at his eyes with the heels of his hands. What the hell had happened to that money? Ashland hadn't been a gambler, and he didn't have a drug problem.

He was a drinker and a womanizer. And somehow he'd pissed off somebody badly enough to get himself killed.

The forensics boys from Birmingham had arrived today to go over the Mercedes. But Rick wasn't expecting them to find anything. He'd already had a look himself. No murder weapon, no nothing. Except a couple of slugs and the bare skeletal remains of a man wrapped in a nondescript beige shower curtain in the trunk. Any fingerprints or trace evidence would have been damaged if not completely washed away by the years in the water.

Rick wondered if a man like Ashland, one who'd been born with a silver spoon in his mouth, had suffered any regrets in his final moments before violence stole his existence. Rick studied the glossy photograph of Charles Ashland, Junior, taken ten years ago with his young family. Judging by the cocky grin on the man's face, he probably hadn't known the meaning of the word *remorse,* much less felt the emotion.

Rick tossed the photo aside and pushed away from his desk. He needed sleep. He turned off the light to his office and strode down the long corridor that led to the exit. As far as Rick was concerned there was nothing in Ashland's file that was going to give him any answers. If there had been, Taylor would have solved this case ten years ago. Rick knew where the hidden secrets lay.

The image of Lacy Oliver zoomed into high-definition focus in his exhausted mind. Lacy and her friends knew something. Whether they were protecting someone or merely hiding some seemingly insignificant detail—they knew something.

Rick had every intention of finding out what *it* was.

And he knew just the route to take to get what he wanted.

Lacy jerked awake at the sound of a knock at the front door. She straightened, and the book she'd been reading fell to the floor. She blinked and struggled to get her bearings. She was at her parents' house. After leaving Melinda's, she'd come home and forced herself to read in hopes of falling asleep. Another knock echoed down the entry hall. Lacy got to her feet and started in that direction.

Had her parents cut their two weeks in Bermuda short? She shook her head. That didn't make sense. They wouldn't knock, they'd use their key. Lacy combed her fingers through her hair and then tightened the sash of her robe. She licked her dry lips and drew in a deep breath.

Maybe it was Kira. She might be feeling in need of some company.

A third knock rattled the hinges, startling Lacy although she'd known the sound would come again before she could reach the door. Whoever was out there was certainly impatient, she thought irritably. Tiptoeing, she checked the peephole. Lacy stumbled back at what she saw.

Rick Summers.

*Damn.*

What the hell was he doing here at this time of night? She glanced at the old grandfather clock and grimaced. A quarter past midnight. Boy, did he have some nerve showing up at her door in the middle of the night.

A chill raced up her spine and spread across her scalp. What if something had happened to Melinda?

Lacy unlocked the door and jerked it open. Her heart slammed mercilessly against her rib cage. God, please let Melinda be okay. Surely Cassidy would have called...

Her parents! The Bermuda authorities would have contacted the authorities here in the event of an emergency.

"I wouldn't have stopped at this hour if I hadn't seen the light." Rick angled his head in the direction of the living room. "I hope I'm not disturbing you."

"Is something wrong? Has something happened?" she demanded, unable to bear the crushing pressure of not knowing.

Understanding dawned in Rick's silvery eyes. "No...no, it's nothing like that. Everything's fine. I just wanted to talk to you."

Lacy sagged with relief. Nothing had happened. Thank God. His words suddenly penetrated her haze of euphoria. "Why do you want to talk to me?" Wariness slid over her, making her heart beat fast again. "It's late." And she was alone, she didn't add.

"Do you suppose I could come in?"

Lacy couldn't speak for a moment. Uncertainty suddenly warred with the almost overwhelming urge to lean into his arms. She remembered all too well how strong they were. He could hold her...make her forget for just a little while.

But he was the chief of police. It was his job to investigate the case of Charles's murder. This wasn't a social call.

Lacy hugged herself, suddenly aware of the cool night air against the silk of her robe and her skin. "Can't it wait till morning?" she asked hesitantly.

His smile was subdued but all charm and persuasion

nonetheless. "It could. If you'd rather wait and come into the office around eight, that'd be fine. I just thought we might handle this on a more informal basis."

Lacy stared up into those steady gray eyes and silently admitted defeat. The same tension and throbbing lust that had plagued them back in high school was there still. She could feel his pull as surely as she could feel her own pulse racing. Steeling herself for whatever was to come, Lacy stepped back and allowed him to enter. Better on her turf than his. Cassidy wouldn't approve.

"Your folks are away?"

"Yes," she replied as she closed the door and turned back to him. For one charged moment she allowed herself to take in the complete picture of Rick Summers ten years older. Taller than most men, he was lean and hard. He filled out the pair of faded jeans he wore very nicely. The white, button-up shirt and the loosened tie hanging at his throat set him apart from the average good-looking, small-town guy one might run into in Ashland. But Rick wasn't just any old average guy. He was the man who had taken her virginity all those years ago in the back seat of his daddy's Pontiac. And now he was the chief of police investigating Charles's murder.

"They're in Bermuda for a couple of weeks," she answered belatedly, trying her level best not to sound breathless with her heart thundering beneath her sternum.

His gaze slowly washed over her, heating her skin and making her feel restless. "You look good, Lacy."

The sound of his voice, soft, warm, a little rough from lack of sleep and probably too much coffee and barking orders, curled around her, made her tingle inside. The beard shadowing his jaw only made him look sexier. "We can have a seat in here," she offered. Her hand shook when she indicated the living room. She tightened her fingers into a fist and led the way.

Rick followed Lacy into her parents' living room as he had longed to do a million times back in high school. He squashed that line of thinking. They weren't kids anymore. He had to keep his head on straight here, had to focus.

Dammit. He should not have stopped. She'd been asleep in spite of the light being on. Few people prowled all hours of the night as he did. But it came with the territory. Not all aspects of law enforcement could be accomplished during daylight hours.

He almost groaned at the gentle sway of her hips. When she'd opened the door, she'd looked a little tousled, and a whole lot sexy. Rick had decided a long time ago that Lacy Jane Oliver had been put on this earth to drive him mad with the want of something he could never have. Not completely anyway. And now she was back, reminding him of all he'd lost—not that he'd ever really had her the way he'd wanted her. But that didn't stop the immediate ache in his loins the instant he'd laid eyes on her at O'Malleys.

Hell, he'd had to banish her from his thoughts to get any work at all done tonight. Even then, she'd lingered just beyond conscious thought. Heating his blood, increasing his ache for her on a level over which he had no control.

He was a fool.

And she was a suspect.

Halfway across the living room, she stopped and turned to face him, the gossamer robe outlining her slender body. All that rich, mahogany hair draped her shoulders, whispering against the silk fabric when she moved.

"Would you like coffee?"

Rick swore silently. It irritated the hell out of him that he hadn't been alone in the room with her for three minutes and already he was falling victim to her beauty, to the need he could never quite vanquish.

"No, thanks. I've had too much already."

Her dark brown eyes registered satisfaction, as if she'd known his answer before he spoke. "Would you like to sit?" she inquired politely, too politely.

There hadn't been anything polite at all about the way she'd urged him on that night…all those years ago when she'd been his for just one unforgettable moment.

"No, I think I'll stand," he said tightly. After all this time, the notion of touching her was still almost more than he could bear. Yet she stood there, watching him, seemingly unaffected, and he couldn't even pull his thoughts together.

Wariness crept into her watchful eyes at his hesitation. God, he hoped she couldn't read him that well. "All right then," she said. "What can I do for you, Chief Summers?"

Chief, not Rick. So that was the way it would be. He almost laughed out loud at his own stupidity for hoping it would be otherwise. Hell, it had always been that way. She waited, perfectly still, her spine rigid, the wall of windows and expensive draperies an elegant backdrop to the sensual picture she made. The filmy white fabric looked stark against her olive skin, displaying a great deal more than it concealed.

"Is this about the investigation?"

He noted the movement of her lips as she spoke. They were full, ripe with color without the aid of cosmetics. He wanted to taste them, to see if the woman was as hot and sweet as the girl had been. Rick licked his lips. "Yeah," he finally managed to grind out. "I want to run a couple of possibilities past you. Get your take on the scenarios."

She was nervous now. He could see it in her eyes, her posture. "I'm listening."

Rick surveyed the room, right then left, taking his time so that her tension would escalate. How often had he imagined how her home looked on the inside? Hell, he'd driven by every single day until she moved away. "Nice place."

"Thank you." She tunneled the fingers of her right hand through her hair, pushing the silky stuff away from the face that still haunted his dreams.

Drawing out the wait, he moved to the mantel and studied the photographs of the girl he'd known back in high school. Being an only child, there were plenty to look at. He tried to remember a time when he hadn't been crazy about Lacy, but as far back as he could recall he had been.

But she hadn't noticed…except that once.

"You and your friends were visiting when Charles disappeared," he asked, his voice sounding too harsh after the long moments of silence.

Lacy ordered her heart to slow. She had to stay calm. "You already know the answer to that—you came by the hospital when we were with Melinda." That's right, she told herself, think rationally. Don't let him trick you into saying anything you'll regret. "You know we're always there for each other. Not one of us has ever let the others down."

He shifted from his intent study of the barrage of family photographs, and his penetrating gray gaze collided with hers. "He beat her pretty badly, didn't he?"

Panic broadsided Lacy. She clenched her jaw to hold back the shudder that followed. "What are you talking about? It was an accident. Melinda fell down the stairs." That was the story Melinda had told. She'd always covered up her husband's abuse. Just another aspect of the past that haunted Lacy.

Rick moved toward her, one step, then another. "We both know that's not the way it happened. He's dead, why pretend now? I can just imagine how angry it made you—all of you—to find out he'd hurt her that way. Who knows how many other times she'd suffered at his hand."

Lacy shook her head and held his regard, as difficult as that proved. "I don't know what you're talking about."

An insanely sexy half smile tilted his full mouth. Dammit, she didn't want to notice that. Another step disappeared between then. Lacy stiffened in an effort to lock down her responses, but her defenses were no match for the chemistry still volatile between them.

"You can't fool me, Lacy. Charles Ashland, Junior, was a bastard. Admit it."

He was too close, and coming closer. "Melinda loved him," Lacy insisted in a firm voice. A tremble vibrated through her, threatening her shaky bravado. "He was a good father."

"But he was a lousy husband."

Rick stood toe to toe with her now, his broad chest close enough to lay her cheek there. Lacy lifted her head and unwanted heat roared through her. "I wouldn't know," she said, her voice cracking. "I wasn't married to him."

Another wicked tilt of his lips. "You won't win, Lace. I'm not that easygoing good old boy I used to be. I've got your number. You and your friends are in this up to your pretty necks. Tell me what you know and I'll find a way to protect you."

Fury swept through her, banishing her fear. Lacy

crossed her arms over her chest and glared back at him. *Protect her.* What about the others? "Go to hell, Rick."

"Now, now, there's no need to get nasty." He massaged his beard-darkened chin, the sound rasping over her nerve endings, making her shiver with new awareness despite the anger rising inside her.

"I'm only giving you the opportunity to come clean with me. What are you so afraid of? Charles is dead—he sure as hell can't hurt you. In my opinion he got what he deserved."

Something snapped inside Lacy then. "You're right," she said, her voice too calm, and so low that she barely recognized it as her own. "He's dead. And I'm glad he's dead. I only wish he'd died sooner." A new surge of fury streaked through her. For the first time in ten years, she felt liberated. "Is that what you wanted to hear, *Chief?*"

The scant inch of space between them sizzled with heat and visceral desire. Lacy refused to visibly acknowledge it. Instead she stared directly at him, her own eyes purposely void of the emotions whirling inside her. Let him take his best shot. She was tired, physically and mentally. She'd had enough.

He looked away first. "Dammit, Lacy, you can't go around telling people you wanted him to die." He swore again then glowered at her, his expression dark with anger and something else she couldn't readily identify. "That single statement is motive."

"Isn't that what you wanted?" she pressed. "Didn't you come here tonight to finagle a confession from me?"

He plowed a hand through his short dark hair. "Hell no." A muscle started to tic in his square jaw. "I came here to get you to come clean with me about what you know. You're hiding something from me, Lacy, I know it. The four of you have a secret, and I'm damned well going to find out what it is and how it plays into Ashland's murder."

He was angry now, almost as angry as she was. "We all signed statements ten years ago as to our whereabouts that day. Check your records, I'm sure you'll find them." She spun away. This conversation was over. "It's late. You should—"

Long fingers curled around her arm and swung her back to face him before she took her second step. His expression was savage, intimidating. A new kind of fear shimmered through her. "I will get the answers I need, Lacy, one way or another." He yanked her a few inches nearer, his full mouth close. "I won't stop until I do."

"Is that a threat?" Hard as she tried not to, she trembled.

He released her abruptly, but that fierce gaze held her a moment longer. "It's a promise."

Without looking back, Rick stormed out. She heard the front door close behind him. Lacy brought one shaky hand to her mouth and choked back the sob that swelled in her throat. Oh, God. She had to call Cassidy. He might not have any evidence, but his instincts had hit right on the money. Forcing herself to breathe, breathe deeply, Lacy made her way to the telephone. Before she could pick up the receiver, it rang. She frowned. Her parents? Cassidy?

Fear snaking around her chest once more, she snatched up the receiver. "Hello." She had to calm down. She closed her eyes and cursed her loss of control.

"Lacy Jane Oliver?"

The slow, barely audible whisper tightened the strong hold of fear clutching at her, paralyzing her. Lacy opened her eyes, then blinked. Her mind raced to identify the strangely terrifying voice, but it was no use. She didn't recognize it. Couldn't even tell if it was male or female. "Yes," she breathed the simple response.

"You should be very, very afraid."

Adrenaline fired through her veins. "Who is this?"

*"I know your secret."*

# Chapter 4

Lacy waited at Mama Betty's for the others to arrive. She'd selected a table far from the breakfast crowd. She sipped her coffee, scrolled through her PDA, anything to prevent looking as nervous as she felt. It had taken every ounce of courage she possessed not to call Cassidy last night. *The call* had come in after midnight, almost immediately after Rick had left. With Cassidy having spent the night at Melinda's, calling her would have meant alerting Melinda to the situation. Melinda needed her rest more than any of them.

A hollow feeling dragged at Lacy's stomach.

Rick was on to the fact that they were hiding something—so was someone else obviously. How could anyone know their secret?

It was impossible!

Forcing herself to smile when her attention accidentally landed on an arriving patron she didn't quite recognize but who, apparently, remembered her, Lacy reminded herself to breathe and downed another swallow of her third cup of strong, black coffee. She'd had two at home before coming here. She was wired to the max.

The bell over the door jingled again and, thank God, this time it was Cassidy, with Melinda right behind her. Dread welled inside Lacy all over again. She hated so badly to even bring up Rick's visit and the bizarre call, but what choice did she have? Her nerves jangled as involuntarily as the bell over the door when someone shoved it inward. What if the caller really did know what they'd done? And what if Rick persisted in his assertions?

How much time would it take before his instincts drove him to dig deeper, to push harder? To find something…maybe even a witness who had seen them leaving Charles's house at dark on Christmas Eve ten years ago.

Lacy tried to swallow around the muscles contracting in her throat. More important, how much longer could she hold out? Pretending what they'd done was justified? If she failed all their lives would be destroyed and it would be her fault for not being strong enough.

Cassidy slid into a chair directly across from Lacy without a word, but her expression said it all. What's happened now? And why the hell do you look so guilty?

"You didn't sleep last night, did you?" Melinda asked, settling into the seat next to Cassidy and breaking the awkward tension.

Lacy resurrected the smile that kept dying too quickly each time she rammed it into place. "I slept okay. How about you?" Her friend looked as if she hadn't eaten or slept for a week. The dark circles beneath her eyes gave them an even more sunken appearance. Her face looked as white as a sheet, the skin thin and fragile. This had to be tearing her apart inside—the not knowing, the wondering if someone would figure out the truth and take her kids away from her permanently.

Or if someone, like her best friend, would fall apart and ruin all their lives?

Melinda lifted then dropped her shoulders in confusion or maybe indecision, as if the answer to Lacy's question took all her energy and left her slumped with defeat. "I drifted off once or twice." She managed a faint smile. "But I'm okay," she added softly.

"What's going on, Lacy?" There was nothing soft or reassuring about Cassidy's tone. She wanted to cut straight to the chase.

Though Melinda and Lacy had always been the closest of the four, Cassidy read each of them better than anyone else. Her ability to see through bullshit was almost uncanny. And she didn't like beating around the bush.

Another jingle drew Lacy's gaze back to the diner's entrance. "Here comes Kira. Let's wait for her." She didn't know why she put off the inevitable. But she'd take any excuse to gain another few seconds to steel for the reactions of the others.

Cassidy didn't like to be kept waiting any more than Lacy liked being the cause of the irritation motivating her icy countenance just now, but there was no help for it. Kira, looking annoyed as she came inside, appeared to be attempting to end a cell-phone conversation. Finally she drew the cell phone from her ear, fiercely punched the end-call button and shoved the phone back into her bag.

"Looks like Brian made his hourly call," Cassidy commented drily. "The guy torments her with his constant checkup calls." Cass turned back to the table.

"I don't see how she puts up with him. He's a stalker waiting to happen."

"Are we having breakfast or has something happened?" Kira wanted to know as she took the only other vacant seat at the table for four. Any irritation with her boyfriend had been erased from her expression. "You sounded worried when you called," she said to Lacy.

Cassidy looked pointedly at her. "Maybe now we'll find out the reason."

Guilt pinged Lacy but she'd be damned if she would let it show. As much as she loved Cassidy she was treading on Lacy's last nerve and this whole thing had scarcely begun. They could be stuck in purgatory for weeks. Maybe the others were dealing with it better than her…except for Melinda, of course, but something had to give. She couldn't take the pressure. It didn't matter that she dealt with enormous stress every day on the job…this was different.

"I was afraid to talk about it on the phone," she began quietly. *Take it slow,* she reminded herself. "If we're suspects, they could be listening in on our phone calls." Being seen together in public wasn't a problem. They'd grown up here, people expected them to come together in support of each during a crisis.

Both Kira's and Melinda's eyes widened with renewed concern.

"Jesus, Lace," Cassidy huffed with a roll of her eyes, "you've been watching too many crime dramas." She looked from one worried woman to the next. "Tapping a phone line takes a court order. A court order takes justification and time." She shook her head slowly side to side. "Our friendly chief of police hasn't had either. No judge in his right mind is going to allow such an invasion of privacy without evidence. Besides, we just got here yesterday. We really don't have to worry about anything of that nature just yet."

Lacy felt her tension ease marginally. She'd been so damned worried and keyed up all night, she'd tossed and turned, barely managing a wink of sleep. The image of Rick Summers rushed into her thoughts and she pushed him away. He wasn't the primary reason she hadn't slept last night. *It was the call.*

"So what happened, Lacy?" Cassidy prompted. "What's got you so uptight this morning?"

Lacy clasped her hands in her lap, thankful for the cover of the table so no one would see the nervous gesture. "Rick Summers came to see me last night." This got the whole table's undivided attention. She should get this part out of the way first. "He outright accused us of keeping something secret related to Charles's murder."

Melinda gasped and Cassidy draped her arm around her shoulders in a comforting gesture.

"Take it slow," Cassidy said to Lacy, "and tell me exactly what he said."

"Would you ladies like coffee?"

As if too afraid to make their own decisions, Melinda and Kira looked to Cassidy. "Black," she said. "And one of those doughnuts." Cassidy jerked her head toward the covered dish on the counter.

"Same here," Kira said, following suit, her smile appearing almost genuine.

"Just coffee," Melinda said, "with cream."

The waitress left and Lacy gave Cassidy the details she remembered with far too much clarity. "Rick suggested that Charles had hurt Melinda, that he'd possibly hurt her many times. He didn't come right out and say it, but I think he believes we're involved in what happened to Charles."

There was dead silence from the three women seated around Lacy as she went on. "He warned that he wouldn't quit until he knew the truth. He is certain we're hiding something. He tried to strong-arm me into coming clean, as he put it." Lacy shook her head. "He even promised to protect us if we told him the truth."

Lacy had expected the fear and the worry she saw on the faces of her friends, but what she hadn't expected was the accusation she saw in Cassidy's eyes.

"Why did he come to you?"

The question took Lacy aback. No one, not even Melinda, knew about the night she and Rick had shared…or the attraction she'd felt for him back in high school. That she still felt something made her furious, especially considering the current circumstances, but some part of her understood intrinsically that she could not share that snippet of her past with her friends. And that felt even more wrong. They'd always shared every-thing…even murder. But Rick was the enemy now.

Before she could stop herself, Lacy looked away. Perfect. How much guiltier could she act?

"I don't know." She forced herself to reconnect with Cassidy, whose suspicion seemed to mount. "Maybe because Mel and I were always so close. I guess he thought I would know her deepest, darkest secrets. Or maybe he thinks I killed Charles to save her. Whatever the reason," she said bluntly, allowing her annoyance to show, "he intends to find out what we're hiding. He made that point very clear."

"First of all," Cassidy explained, her expression relaxing, going from suspicious to knowing, "he has his first murder case and absolutely no evidence. Summers is like any other cop, he doesn't want to look bad to those who keep him in office. He needs a suspect.

Melinda is the logical choice since she's the spouse. He's going to follow that line of reasoning until he has something better to consider. Let's face it, in cases like this, more often than not the spouse is the perpetrator."

Cassidy made the whole thing sound so simple, so logical. But her deduction didn't appear to make Melinda feel any better. She stared at the table, as if meeting the eyes of her friends was suddenly too difficult.

Before Lacy could say something to smooth over Cassidy's insensitive remark about spouses and perpetrators, the waitress arrived with their coffee.

"Thank you, that's all," Cassidy said, dismissing the waitress before turning her attention back to the table. "We're Melinda's best friends, so, of course, we're suspects as well." She made a scoffing sound in her throat. "Well, the closest thing to suspects he's got right now. You have to realize that he's desperate to solve this as quickly as possible. All persons of interest are going to be under close scrutiny. He'll apply pressure wherever he thinks he can."

Cassidy continued in that vein, but Lacy's attention was diverted by the man who entered the diner next— Brad Brewer, one of Rick's deputies, judging by his uniform. He climbed onto a stool at the bar, placed his order, then promptly settled his full regard on their table. She looked away too quickly. She cursed herself for letting the whole world see how guilty she felt. Why hadn't she smiled at him? She remembered him from high school. Football. Handsome, popular with the girls. But now he was a cop and that made him a potential enemy. It also made her as nervous as hell.

She hated this! She studied her half-empty cup and wrestled with the need to squirm in her seat. She might as well warn the others. "Brad Brewer just walked in.

He's wearing a deputy's uniform and looking directly at us." This whole thing was insane. How could they just keep pretending that all was as it should be?

Kira's sharp intake of breath punctuated Lacy's announcement, giving her something else to be confused about. Then again, maybe Kira was feeling just as uneasy as Lacy.

"Ignore him," Cassidy ordered. "You have to stop letting these guys get to you. I'm telling you they're on a fishing expedition and you're giving them far too much bait. They don't have anything on us. They won't have anything unless one of us stupidly gives it to them."

Cassidy was right. Lacy closed her eyes a second and fought to regain her composure. She had to get a grip here. The cops had nothing on them. They had nothing period. The only way anyone would know what happened was if they broke their silence.

"No one knows anything," Cassidy added firmly, echoing Lacy's thoughts. "All we have to do is keep it that way until this case is closed."

As awful as all of this made her feel, it was the single tear that streaked down Melinda's face that stabbed the deepest into Lacy's heart. She wished she could take back the words. Her friend had been hanging on so rigidly to her composure until now. She shouldn't have even told them about Rick's visit.

"We'll stick with the plan we've all agreed to," Cassidy reiterated. "We all took the same vow. We're not going to change our course now regardless of any one person's personal demons."

Lacy looked at Cassidy as another memory from ten years ago broadsided Lacy. Kira and Cassidy staring at her with suspicion in their eyes when she'd come back

downstairs after checking to insure they hadn't over-
looked anything in the bedroom where they'd found
Charles. They wanted to believe Lacy had killed him.
She could feel it then, and she could feel it now.

"Was that comment directed at me?" She hadn't con-
sciously made the decision to ask the question, but there
it was. She wasn't going to let it go this time. She'd done
so ten years ago…not this time.

"Lace, this isn't about you," Cassidy returned coolly.
"This is about all of us. Keeping everyone in emotional
turmoil isn't going to help."

"Why don't we just put our cards out on the table this
second," Lacy challenged, any chance of staying calm
gone now. She lowered her voice to a harsh whisper.
"Let's all tell where we were that day. No more dancing
around the facts." She leaned into the table, stared each
one straight in the eye in turn, fury overriding her better
judgment. "Let's just get it over with once and for all.
Clear the air. We all need to know what really happened."

Melinda's hand went to her chest and her ragged
sigh was all that followed Lacy's bitter words. The
silence echoed deafeningly, obliterating the sounds
around them, narrowing the scope of their world down
to the suddenly too tiny table.

Regret for causing Melinda more discomfort crashed
into Lacy, but even that stinging emotion wasn't enough
to fully quell her flash of anger. She was sick to death
of the suspicions directed at her. She hadn't killed
Charles, even though she would have liked to on too
many occasions to count.

Cassidy took Melinda's hand and then reached
across the table for Lacy's. Kira immediately did the
same, taking Lacy's then Melinda's to complete the
circle. A circle they'd clung to as kids…to protect one

another no matter the circumstances. Lacy closed her eyes and struggled for calm. She had to get a hold of herself. These were her friends. She had no right to lash out like that. The suspicions she felt were probably just her imagination, her own guilt coming back to haunt her.

"We're all in this together," Cassidy said with uncharacteristic softness. "It doesn't matter who killed him. He's dead and that's the only thing that matters. We all wanted him dead, and we all participated in covering up what happened. We are all equally guilty. No one is more or less to blame. And each of us will do whatever it takes to protect one another. Shall we reiterate our vow?"

"I swear." Kira was the first to speak up, her eyes glittering with fear.

Melinda nodded solemnly. "I swear."

Lacy wanted to believe they were doing the right thing. She wanted desperately to trust Cassidy's judgment, just like they always had, but part of her couldn't pretend away the truth any longer. One of them had killed a man. All of them had covered up the murder, making sure the evidence would never be found. What they'd done was wrong....

But it was too late to back out now.

It was done, end of story.

"I swear," she said with a reluctance she could no more hide than she could stop breathing.

Kira offered up a big, however shaky, smile and a subject change. "Melinda, I'll be keeping you company today. Anything special you'd like to do."

She sounded upbeat and as calm as the proverbial cucumber, but Lacy didn't miss the little quiver in her voice or the way she kept glancing over at Deputy Brad

Brewer. Cassidy had to have noticed it, too—she never missed anything—but she didn't say a word. Instead she picked at her doughnut.

Enough. Lacy had to stop looking for conspiracies among her friends. She had to pull it together.

"Lacy, you'll relieve Kira at about seven?" Cassidy inquired.

"Sure." Yes, she definitely intended to do her part. She'd caused enough trouble this morning. It was time to suck it up and do what had to be done.

Melinda shook her head, the move so weary no one would have noticed had she not groaned at the same time. "Really, I feel like such a burden to you guys. I'll be okay by myself. You don't have to stay with me night and day."

Cassidy turned to Melinda, her expression unexpectedly gentle for a woman so stern in nature. "Melinda, you're not a burden to any of us. We want to protect you. You're vulnerable right now. Let's not keep going over and over the issue. We have to be careful. We don't want you alone if the chief shows up at your door like he did Lacy's."

Melinda nodded, surrendering. "You're right. I know." She tried to smile, but the effort failed miserably. "I just don't want to put anyone out."

"We love you, Mel." Lacy felt a genuine smile spread across her lips. This was the one good thing in all the insanity, a friendship that had endured through the years. She had to stop selfishly obsessing about her own feelings. "You couldn't possibly put us out."

Just as some of the tension lifted, Cassidy had to toss out another directive. "You steer clear of Summers," she ordered Lacy. "I don't know why he's singled you out, but he'll have his reasons. I don't want you inadvertently giving him any additional fuel to fire his suspicions. He can't possibly have anything more than a hunch."

"I believe he used to have a crush on Lace," Mel put in thoughtfully. "He stared at her all through art class, as I recall. It's a miracle he ever finished a project. I remember thinking how sweet the whole thing was."

Lacy refused to entertain the memories the comment stirred. She couldn't look back. Getting caught up in what she and Rick had felt all those years ago would be a mistake. She had to stay away from him just like Cassidy said. And no one could know what had happened between them…not right now anyway. She already felt as if she'd been singled out as the *one* in this nightmare by those she trusted the most.

"Whether he had a crush on Lacy or not," Cassidy allowed, "we don't need him trying to use that against us. No one knows our secret. We have to keep it that way."

The voice of last night's caller slammed into Lacy's brain. She had to tell them about the call! How could she have forgotten? Maybe because it was easier to forget than to analyze what the caller's words no doubt meant. God, she hated to stir up more conflicting emotions.

"There's something else," she said quietly, dread welling all over again. Would the fact that she hadn't already mentioned the call look suspicious to Cassidy? *Stop it!* she ordered.

The collective attention of those seated around the table settled heavily on her and Lacy would have gladly cut off her right arm not to have to bring this up. She'd caused enough hard feelings this morning. But she couldn't pretend it hadn't happened. Not when it could be the real thing…a true threat.

"After Rick left last night I received a phone call."

Lacy moistened her lips, wished her throat didn't feel all tight and parched. "The caller asked if I was Lacy Jane Oliver." Lacy cleared her throat, could hardly breathe. "I said yes, thinking it could be a call about my parents. I was…worried they might have been in some sort of accident."

"But the call wasn't about your parents?" Cassidy guessed, her guard going up once more to conceal whatever her true feelings might be. Even her tone gave away nothing. But Lacy could feel the doubt expanding between them like a bottomless void. She was suspect of Lacy's story even before she heard it.

Refusing to be dragged back into that whole paranoid frame of mind again, she forged ahead. "No. He or she—" she shook her head "—it was hard to tell if it was a man or a woman. The voice was so low and distant, almost distorted, like a bad cell-phone connection. Anyway, whoever it was said I should be very, very afraid. For a split second I thought maybe it was a prank but then he said *I know your secret.*"

Another long beat of nerve-racking silence passed before any of them found their voices again.

"But that's…" Kira looked at each of them in turn. "That's impossible. No one knows."

"Could someone have seen you guys…?" Melinda moistened her trembling lips. "You know…"

"No one saw us," Cassidy said flatly. "If someone had seen or had known anything we'd all be behind bars serving out our sentences." She leveled her most intimidating stare on Lacy. "This is a hoax. You say the call came in right after Summers left?"

Lacy nodded. "Almost immediately."

"Damn him," Cassidy swore. "He's trying to scare you. He can't get away with that."

"What do I do?" Lacy argued. "Tell him that his creepy calls about my secret are not going to work?"

"You don't tell him anything," Cassidy cautioned. "That's exactly what he wants you to do. Ignore it."

"But what if it's not him?" Melinda leaned in close. "From what I've seen so far, Rick is a good chief of police. I can't imagine he would stoop to this kind of underhanded tactic. Someone had to have seen what you did."

Cassidy glanced around the diner as if worried that they were being watched. Deputy Brewer seemed to be focused on his breakfast. "Melinda," she said, turning her attention back to the woman at her side, "you're overreacting. No one saw us. If they had, they would have talked years ago. Don't forget that Senator Ashland offered a sizable reward for any information on his missing son."

Lacy had forgotten about that. Rumor had it that Charles, Senior, had even hired a private investigator in hopes of locating his son, but the man had found nothing. She wasn't sure whether the four of them had simply been smart or extremely lucky.

Either way, Cassidy was correct. If someone had seen anything, they would certainly have cashed in on the reward ten years ago. But would Rick really go to such extremes to scare her?

"Remember," Cassidy reminded, "this is his first murder case. He's going to be working twenty-four/seven to solve it. Aside from Melinda, we—" she motioned to Kira, Lacy and herself "—are the most logical suspects. We all hated Charles for what he did to Melinda."

Some of them hated him for other reasons as well, but Lacy kept that comment to herself. Nothing good could come of bringing up that past. Hurting Melinda further was the last thing she wanted to do.

"More coffee, ladies?"

The waitress's question jerked Lacy back to the here and now. Apparently the whole group had been lost in their own thoughts.

"None for me," she said, placing her hand over her cup.

"Come on, girls," Cassidy urged, "let's eat and enjoy. How often do we get together anymore?" She smiled broadly for the waitress. "The doughnut was great, but I'll have the Betty special."

"Me, too," Kira piped up.

The Betty special consisted of two eggs, ham, biscuits, pan-fried potatoes and gravy. Lacy was sure she couldn't handle a bite, much less a meal like that, on top of the worry churning in her belly.

"Just toast and orange juice," she said when the waitress looked her way.

"Pancakes and more coffee," Melinda announced, joining in. She smiled at the waitress and then said to those seated around the table, "My husband left me practically the same day we married. Why should I be sad now? Nothing's changed, not really."

The startled waitress hustled off to place their order. Lacy worked up a smile for her friend, but she was as surprised by Melinda's odd comment as the waitress had been. If Kira or Cassidy thought anything of it they didn't say a word. Maybe they thought it was for the best.

And perhaps it was. Lacy felt confused and uneasy with the whole situation. She'd struggled with what they'd done for ten long years. Having to face it now only sharpened the intensity of her regret.

But there was nothing she could do. It was done. Charles was dead and they were responsible. Assuaging her conscience would ruin not only her life, but also her friends' as well. She wasn't prepared to do that. Melinda's children needed her.

The bell over the door broke into its tinny clatter, drawing Lacy's attention in that direction. She'd tuned out the sound during the tenser portions of their meeting, but now, as the four of them grew somewhat relaxed again, her surroundings came back into full focus.

Rick Summers entered the diner and walked over to where his deputy, Brad Brewer, sat. The two men spoke for a few seconds before Rick's attention drifted across the room to settle onto Lacy.

Every instinct warned her that he wasn't here for breakfast, not really.

He was watching them…waiting for one of them to take a misstep.

As his intent gaze bored more fully into Lacy's, she knew without doubt that she was the one he expected to falter.

And he intended to be right there waiting for the fall.

# Chapter 5

"You gonna order, Chief?"

Rick dragged his attention from the four women seated across the diner. "In a minute."

Brewer looked from Rick to the objects of his distraction. "Even before you told me what you wanted me to do, I had a feeling you didn't ask to meet me here for the sake of a decent breakfast."

No point arguing that. Rick had seen Lacy come into the diner. Mama Betty's sat on the east side of the town square, directly across from his office. Since his office came with only one window, that was generally where his focus rested whenever he had something on his mind.

He'd known that Lacy's friends wouldn't be far behind her. The foursome had always traveled in a pack. Some fifteen years out of high school hadn't changed that fact. But it wasn't their cliquish behavior that nudged

his curiosity. Nope. It was the likely subject of this morning's get-together—his visit to Lacy the night before.

"You notice anything unusual?"

"Yep." Brad downed a gulp of coffee. "Been some
damn tense moments during their discussion, but they
kept it too quiet to overhear anything."

Brewer had always been able to anticipate Rick's
needs in a given situation. Rick had never appreciated that
fact more than now. Not that he'd actually expected his
deputy to overhear anything this morning. Rick had
gotten just what he wanted: the climate between the
ladies.

Tense.

That meant trouble.

He'd watched these ladies from afar since junior
high school, maybe even before. He'd been infatuated
with Lacy for as long as he could remember, for all the
good it had done him. Not once in that time had he ever
seen these four suffer a falling-out. Always United
appeared to be their motto. Through thick and thin, they
backed one another up.

That was how he knew for certain they were hiding
something.

There wasn't a snowball's chance in hell that Charles
Ashland, Junior, had gotten himself murdered without one, and that would ultimately mean all, of them
knowing it. He wasn't ready to label one of them as the
killer, but they knew something they weren't telling. No
two ways about that.

Lacy's gaze collided with his and heat immediately
seared his blood. Rick didn't look away. He let her
stare. He needed her to know he wasn't backing off. But
the move cost him. Every single muscle in his body
went on edge, tightened unreasonably. It irritated him

to no end that she still held that kind of power over him after all these years.

"Coffee, Chief?"

Rick smiled for Katie Jo, the waitress who always made it a point to take his order no matter where he sat in the diner. "Sure thing, Katie Jo. I'll take the usual to go along with that fine-smelling brew."

She grinned and blushed to the roots of her bottled-blond hair. "Coming right up."

Katie Jo Hawkins had gone to school with him, as well, but she'd been a couple years behind him. She'd already been married twice, but that didn't stop her from looking for the next available prospect before the ink was even dry on the last divorce decree. Well, at least she'd had the good sense not to have any children. The kids were always the ones who paid the highest price when things went sour. Maybe that was why Rick had opted to remain single.

After a three-year stint in the army, he'd chosen to focus on his career in law enforcement. He should have made time for college, but it just never worked out. Still, he'd done all right for himself. Probably folks like Lacy Jane Oliver wouldn't think so, but then he'd never run in her circles. That wasn't likely to change in this lifetime.

The women in question stood and made their way to the exit. He watched just to see if Lacy would look back.

And she did. He'd known she would. She was nervous. In that split second, he saw the uncertainty, the stark fear shining there.

Whatever she had to hide, it scared her to death.

All he had to do was figure out what button to push to make her talk. She was his best bet. Or maybe he just wanted it to be her. He couldn't deny the nagging desire for a little revenge. After all, she'd used him that one time, let him feel she was his for that one moment. Then she'd walked away as if nothing had happened.

Rick shifted his attention to the steaming mug of coffee waiting on the counter for him. Why the hell couldn't he put the past behind him? By the time this investigation was over he had to make sure of one thing, besides solving the case. He had to be damned certain she was out of his system, whatever it took to make that happen.

He couldn't live the next fifteen years the way he'd lived the last.

The morning was practically over before Rick had a chance to get back to the real work that needed to be done—solving a decade-old murder. The mayor had insisted on an impromptu press conference and then he'd had to sit through a post mortem on the damned press conference with the mayor and his pals.

The only good thing that had come of the morning was the preliminary forensics report he'd found waiting on his desk when he returned. According to the report, Ashland had likely been dead the entire ten years he'd been missing. Both bullets found in the trunk of the Mercedes had come from his body. One had chipped a rib and was likely the one that had killed him since the position of the damage would have been in the vicinity of his heart. The other had glanced off his clavicle near the coracoid process, a minor shoulder wound.

The strangest part of the whole situation was the ballistics report. The two slugs discovered with the body were from two different weapons, both .38s.

Why would a killer use two weapons?

Rick tossed the report aside and rubbed a hand over

his jaw. That scenario just didn't fit. The more likely
case was that Ashland had gotten himself shot by two
different people. One bullet he'd survived, the second
one he hadn't.

That left the questions of who and why. But it was
also an opportunity to withhold something perhaps only
the killer would know. He would have to make sure this
information was kept quiet.

He surveyed the reports his predecessor had left,
specifically the statements made by Lacy and her
friends. All four had alibis. They'd been at the hospital
waiting for Ashland to arrive and pick up his wife. All
three had admitted to being furious with him and had
even gone so far as to get out and look for him when he
didn't show on time. Melinda's brother, Kyle Tidwell,
had owned up to the same in his own statement.

The problem was, after ten years, it was impossible
to tell the precise time of the victim's death. Hell, it
wasn't even possible to nail down the day, only the
probable year.

Every last one of the statements in the file was basically useless beyond a point. Witnesses could attest to
the last time they'd seen Ashland alive and comparisons
could be made. But after about two o'clock on the day
Ashland supposedly disappeared, there was no way to
know what had happened.

Unless someone who knew told him.

That was the only chance he had of solving this case.

Rick sifted through the papers on his desk until he
found another folder containing far fewer documents.
Pamela Carter. She had gone missing around the same
time as Charles. There had been talk at the time that the
two had been lovers and, considering the hefty cash
withdrawal, that they'd run off together. No connection

between the two disappearances had ever been made, by Rick's predecessor or any of the private investigators Senator Ashland had hired. Pamela had had stars in her eyes, wanted to marry a rich man. Most folks figured she'd run off to find her future. But Rick had ideas of his own. He'd spoken with the family and drawn a few conclusions based on what he'd learned. But all of it was only their word, supposition.

And then there was Bent Thompson. He'd abruptly left town about that same time. A week or so after Charles had disappeared. A local thug, well, the closest thing to a thug a small town like Ashland had. Thompson had been arrested for assault and battery a couple of times, public drunkenness even more often and there was a time when he was thought to have done a little dirty work for a loan shark operating out of Memphis.

Bent Thompson was the poster child for reasons to stay in high school. He'd dropped out and turned to doing whatever paid the most to get by. His reputation as a hooligan, if not a total thug, was noteworthy to say the least. Anyone who cared to consider what became of him most likely concluding he'd gotten out of town to avoid someone he'd crossed.

As far as Rick knew, Thompson and Ashland had shared no dealings and had scarcely shared the same air space. Much like him and Lacy. Two people from very different backgrounds and sides of town.

Rick shook his head as he considered that the railroad track at Houston Street had always served as a kind of dividing line. Those who lived south of it were lower middle class and below. And those to the north, well, they had the lake and all the money.

You fell into one class or the other and that was

where you stayed. Boys south of Houston Street didn't get the girls from the north side. All they could do was look…except for Rick. He'd gotten to do more than look that one time.

After that he understood why it was better to stick with his side of the tracks—it cost a lot less on levels that had nothing at all to do with money.

Rick shook off the frustrating memories and focused on the files and reports in front of him. The only option he had, as far as he could see, was to retrace the events of ten years ago and see if he discovered anything new, which was doubtful. Every instinct told him that if he didn't break Lacy Oliver, he would never know what happened.

A ruckus in his outer office caught Rick's attention. Senator Ashland, with at least three reporters on his heels, was waving his arms at Rick's secretary.

Rick pushed out of his chair and strode into the middle of the fray just in time to hear the senator say, "I demand to see the chief right now."

Francine, Rick's easygoing secretary, looked a little uncertain and a whole lot frustrated.

"How can I help you, Senator?" Rick nodded to two of his deputies, who immediately herded the reporters toward the exit.

"Chief Summers, do you really believe the wife did it?" shouted the only one of the three media interlopers Rick recognized. Considering the man knew Melinda Ashland every bit as well as Rick did, he had no intention of acknowledging the insensitive question with a response.

"What about a jealous husband?" another cried before he could be hoisted out the door. "How many wives do you think young Charles seduced, Senator?"

Rick ushered the senator into his office and away from the blunt questions. It wasn't as if the senator hadn't heard it all before, but Rick just couldn't stand by and let him hear it here.

"I apologize, Senator," he said when he'd closed the door of his office. "Some of those fellas just don't know when to keep their mouths shut."

Senator Charles Ashland tugged at the lapels of his fancy designer jacket as if he'd just endured a physical altercation rather than a mere verbal bashing. "It's not your fault, Chief," he offered with something less than sincerity. "There are those of us who thrive and those who strive. Unfortunately for the latter, they generally attempt to do so by clinging to the upwardly mobile coattails of the former."

Rick was pretty sure he'd just been insulted, but considering what the man had been through the past couple of days he decided to overlook it. "Yes, sir. Is there something I can do for you?"

Senator Ashland lifted his chin in the arrogant manner for which Ashlands were known and settled his somber attention on Rick. "You may arrest that gold-digging whore who killed my son."

Rick held his tongue for three beats as he moved around behind his desk. He understood that the senator was agitated and had every right to be upset, but Rick also knew Melinda and she was no gold digger and certainly no whore. A murderer, well, now on that score he couldn't say for sure, but his gut wouldn't let him pin that rap on her. If she had anything to do with Charles's death it was accidental not intentional…or was he fooling himself? Did he want to believe that because Lacy was most likely involved?

"Senator Ashland." He gestured to a chair. "Please have a seat, sir, and let's talk about this rationally."

The senator threw his hands up in an argumentative

gesture. "I am perfectly rational, Chief Summers." He might be rational, but his face was beet-red with irrational emotion. "My wife and I have waited for this day for ten years. We knew when Charles went missing that *she* had somehow harmed him. We want her put behind bars where she belongs!"

Rick considered the best way to approach the subject for a moment before responding. Senator Charles Ashland was a powerful man in these parts. Insulting his intelligence or his integrity could lead to complications Rick didn't need in his life right now.

"It's true, sir, that in cases like this the spouse is generally a suspect, but we both know that the chances of Melinda having harmed her husband are very slim. And she was in the hospital as you'll recall."

Ashland shook a finger at Rick. "That's another thing. I spoke to a nurse there who said she couldn't be sure where Melinda was the afternoon Charles disappeared. She was out of her room for some time. Why haven't you been looking down that avenue?"

Rick rested the tips of his fingers on his desk to keep his hands from clenching. The last thing he needed was to make any gestures of aggression. "I can assure you that every avenue is being examined, Senator. If Melinda left the hospital the day of her husband's disappearance, I will know how and why." He'd read the nurse's statement in the file. Taylor hadn't put much stock into the idea, because the nurse couldn't be sure if Melinda was out of her room for twenty minutes or two hours when he'd tried to pin her down to an exact time frame. The nurse had admitted that they'd been unusually busy that afternoon.

Ashland grabbed the back of the chair in front of him. Rick couldn't tell if he needed the chair for support or if he was fighting the need to rip something apart.

"Chief Summers, you have to understand our situation here." The man sagged as if the burden he carried had suddenly become too great to bear. "Those children are all we have left of our son. We're terrified that she'll take them and run if she feels the heat bearing down on her. Can you see our dilemma, Chief? We can't risk losing those children. So far, we've kept them separated from her, but God only knows how long we'll be successful. She is their mother after all." His face darkened with fury once more. "And those other women have rallied around her. I don't trust them. I don't trust any of them. They could all be involved!"

"You have my word, Senator," he promised. "I will do everything I can to make sure your son's murder is solved. I'll also talk to Melinda and make sure she understands that leaving town just now isn't an option."

The senator exhaled a mighty breath. "I guess that's all I can ask of you."

His head bowed, and with uncharacteristic humility, the senator exited Rick's office. Before Rick had a chance to analyze the sudden about-face in his demeanor, Deputy Brewer came in and closed the door. Judging by the look of excitement on his face, he had news.

Rick didn't dare hope for a real break in the case, but he'd take anything he could get at this point.

"You're not going to believe who Deputy Kilgore spotted in town this morning."

Brad Brewer was not an overlarge guy. Five eight, hundred forty pounds. But at one time he'd been fifty pounds heavier and built like a brick wall. The bulk had gotten him labeled as the Refrigerator back in his highschool football days. Right now he looked as if he'd just scored the winning touchdown.

"Don't tell me," Rick said. "Pamela Carter, right?"

Charles's body had turned up, why not Pam's unexpected return? A reunion of the town's missing would
be just perfect.

Brad frowned. "Who?"

Rick shook his head. "Never mind." Pam had
dropped out of school and, like Rick, she'd been from
the south side of the tracks. Brad wouldn't remember
her especially since he hadn't been in the department
at the time of her disappearance.

"Bent Thompson," Brad blurted. "He's back in town.
Some coincidence, wouldn't you say?"

Well, well. The vanishing thug was back. Now that
was a hell of a coincidence, considering he'd disappeared about the same time as Ashland and Carter. The
circumstances had all been so different that the former
chief hadn't connected the three. All three had been
adults and no indication of foul play had been uncovered.

"Tell Kilgore I want him keeping an eye on
Thompson." Sure there was no proof of course that
Thompson's abrupt departure from town ten years ago
had any more to do with Charles's murder than
Pamela's, it was likely a waste of time. Still his being
back certainly appeared rather timely in a strange kind
of way.

"Will do."

Before he could rush out the door, Rick said, "Just
a minute, Brewer."

Brewer turned back, a question on his face. "Yeah?"

"Close the door."

Brewer did as he was told then approached Rick's
desk as if he sensed the conversation needed to be kept
as quiet as possible.

"Do you remember much about Lacy Oliver and her

friends from back in school? Other than the fact that they were the most popular girls in the class."

He shrugged, looked just a little uncomfortable. "Lacy and Melinda were cheerleaders. Cassidy, well, she was just an uptight—"

"Yeah," Rick interrupted. "I remember she wasn't always easy to get along with. What about Kira?" He found it ironic that Brewer hadn't mentioned Kira, since Rick hadn't missed the way the deputy had stared at her on more than one occasion since her return to town.

Brewer looked thoughtful for a moment. "She was a cheerleader, too, the best I recall."

"That's right," Rick said, going along with his obvious ploy of indifference. "She was the first black girl on the squad, I think."

"Color shouldn't have mattered," Brewer said tightly, bitterness cluttering his expression.

"You liked her," Rick suggested, knowing damn well he had before Brewer said a word in denial.

"We knew each other," he said defensively. "You should have known her, too."

Rick dropped into his chair, an idea taking shape. "I did, but not as well as you apparently."

Brewer averted his eyes. "That's ancient history, Chief. I don't know why we're going there."

"I want you to keep an eye on her, Brewer. Talk to her if you can. Convince her that whatever she and her friends are hiding will only make bad matters worse."

"You really think they had something to do with this?"

Rick shrugged. "I don't know if they had anything to do with the murder, but they know something about it. And whatever it is, it could help me prove who killed him. I need those women to trust me. I need them to talk."

Brewer dropped into the chair directly across the

desk from Rick. "Well, I can tell you one thing, it won't happen as long as Cassidy is in charge. She was always the leader. They'll listen to whatever she says, even now. I guarantee it."

Rick sensed a deeper hostility where Cassidy and Brewer were concerned. "What's the deal between the two of you? You holding a grudge for some reason I need to know?"

He didn't look away as Rick feared he would. "I have no tolerance for…people of her persuasion," he said frankly. "Especially the ones who think they know better than anyone else."

Well, there was definitely a story there, but Rick figured he'd just gotten all he was going to get.

"Make sure Kilgore stays on top of Thompson. You keep an eye on Kira and I'm going to pay Nigel Canton a visit. He keeps making up excuses as to why he can't drop by for a friendly chat."

"His alibi is rock solid," Brewer commented. He'd read the case file, just like Rick.

Rick hesitated as he reached for his keys. "That's true. But that doesn't mean he didn't hire someone to do the dirty work for him."

Just another scenario Rick had to flesh out.

As he left City Hall, he considered how few friends Charles Ashland, Junior, actually had. On the surface it looked as if he had been surrounded by companions and admirers. More of his acquaintances could be listed in the enemy category than not. He screwed other men's wives, used cutthroat business tactics and basically pissed people off in one way or another.

But that didn't justify his being murdered.

Rick slid behind the wheel of his truck and surveyed the town—his town—as he maneuvered around the square. Most of the folks here were good people. Friendly and kind. The racism that had at one time choked the spirit out of the community was all but gone now. Churches outnumbered gas stations. The public school system was the best around.

But that didn't change the fact that someone had murdered the one and only son of the town's wealthiest family. Not to mention that the Ashlands were direct descendants of the town's founding father. Even the best towns had some degree of crime—he just hadn't expected his first big investigation as the chief of police to be murder.

Charles's body had been hidden away until nothing in the way of useful evidence remained. Nothing but two mismatched slugs and a generic shower curtain that could have come from anyone's home, including Charles's own house.

Rick had one of his men running a check on anyone who had registered a handgun, a .38, back then. Trying to track down the shower curtain was useless. The brand was sold locally and at a number of stores around the county.

As much as he would love to solve this case with plain old detective work and hard evidence, that wasn't going to happen. His only chance of figuring out what had really happened to Charles Ashland, Junior, was to push Lacy and Kira until one of them broke. They knew something. He was sure of it. No matter how seemingly insignificant that information was, he needed it. A single detail could make all the difference.

The Ashlands weren't likely to be too happy with him when they discovered his plan of action. But the way Rick saw it, his only hope, outside some sort of information from Lacy or Kira, was to retrace Charles's steps during the final days before his death and hope he found something others had overlooked.

One little detail could make all the difference.

He considered the way Deputy Brewer had looked at Kira. Rick knew that look. It was the same desperate longing he likely displayed each time he looked at Lacy. If he couldn't wear down Lacy, maybe Brewer could get further with Kira.

There had to be a way to dig beneath the defenses of that tight little group. He would push and prod until he had done just that.

He wasn't convinced that one or all of Lacy's friends were cold-blooded killers, but they had been involved on some level. And no matter the cost, he intended to know the extent of that involvement.

Guilt pricked him, but he pushed it away. He had a job to do and sentimental feelings had no place there.

It was time to put his personal feelings aside and focus on finding the truth, whether anyone wanted the real truth or not.

Melinda just wanted the investigation over. The Ashlands wanted to prove she had done it so they could have the children to themselves. Nigel Canton wanted nothing to do with any of it. But each of them were guilty in one way or another. Melinda, for more than likely hating the husband who cheated on her and abused her at will. The Ashlands, for looking the other way all those years as their prized son tortured his wife. And Nigel Canton, for being in business with the devil himself and taking advantage of the situation when the opportunity presented itself.

They all had something to hide—good, bad or indifferent. It was Rick's job to find out if any of it had any bearing on his murder case. No matter how long it took he would get to the bottom of exactly what had happened to Charles Ashland, Junior. He would scratch and dig until he had every last detail of the final hours of Charles's life.

There was no way to run from the past.

*It always came back to haunt you.*

## Chapter 6

Lacy sat at her father's desk for a long while before she worked up the nerve to do what she'd come in here to do. The house she'd grown up in didn't have a study, but that hadn't stopped her father from having a big, beautifully carved wood desk near the fireplace in the living room. It wasn't as if they had used the room that often. They'd gathered in the family room at night to watch television. When she'd had friends over, the family room was where they played games, watched movies and sometimes even slept.

The living room was reserved for more formal, adult get-togethers and for greeting unexpected company. Like the morning of Charles Ashland's last day on earth.

Lacy moistened her lips and pulled the middle desk drawer open. Her father's .38 pistol lay there, right where he'd always kept it.

How was that possible?

She knew it was the same one he'd always had because the pearl handle bore his initials. Her mother had special-ordered the weapon for him more than twenty years ago.

But it shouldn't be here.

The memory of the pounding on the front door sounded so real she jumped. But it wasn't real—it had happened ten long years ago.

That morning.

She'd slept really late. She and the girls had had too much to drink the night before. They'd ranted about Melinda's predicament. Had concocted plans to rid their friend of her horrible husband, even going so far as to come up with ways to kill him. They'd toasted his sure and swift demise so many times she'd lost count. Her parents had been off to work already that morning. Somehow she'd managed to drag herself up and to the door just as the second onslaught of brutal banging had begun.

Lacy remembered cringing in pain. Her head had been throbbing like the ticking trigger of a bomb prepared to detonate any second.

She'd expected Cassidy at the door demanding that she get dressed so they could get to the hospital to stay with Melinda until her no-good husband came to pick her up.

But it hadn't been Cassidy or Kira.

She'd found Charles slouched against the door frame when she'd opened the front door.

He'd looked Lacy up and down with a lecherous stare and said, "It must be true what they say about beauty sleep. I didn't wake you, did I?"

Lacy remembered lashing out at him the way she usually did. She'd called him a bastard and a few other things, but he'd only laughed. When she'd told him to go away and attempted to shut the door in his face, he'd pushed it right back at her, causing her to stumble. Then he'd come inside and closed the door behind him.

She'd known she was in trouble. That moment had been coming for a long time. Charles had been flirting with her every chance he got. He'd teased her about being the one woman he hadn't been able to sweet-talk back in high school. She'd hoped he would outgrow his stupidity, but that hadn't happened. That morning he'd leaned in close to her and told her it was finally their time. He warned that he'd waited long enough. She'd smelled the liquor on his breath and it wasn't even noon. He'd followed her deeper into the house. She knew what he wanted.

Fear had sent her flying to the living room and her father's desk. She'd grabbed the .38 and, clutching it in both hands, she'd aimed it at him.

He'd laughed at her, taunted her about being frigid and repeated the trash talk from the locker room back in high school. They'd all laughed at her behind her back graduation night, calling her the only virgin to walk down that aisle. So many had tried, all had failed, he'd mocked.

She'd threatened to shoot him if he didn't leave.

He'd ridiculed her a little more and then he'd left, but not before wrestling her father's gun away from her. He'd known she wouldn't actually shoot him. She hadn't even had the nerve to take the weapon off safety.

She had rushed to lock the door behind him, then she'd slid down to the floor to cry like the weak, frightened victim she had been.

Why the hell had she let him get away with treating her that way?

To protect Melinda. She hadn't wanted her friend to know how he'd goaded her all those years. She was every bit as much to blame for allowing his abuse as Melinda was. They'd both had their reasons for keeping the ugly truth hidden, but they'd both been wrong.

Later that same day they had found Charles murdered. The question was, how had Lacy's father's .38 ended up back in his desk? She hadn't seen it again after Charles had taken it from her…not until years later, when she'd returned to Ashland for Charles's memorial service. She'd been looking for a stamp to mail a sympathy card to the Ashlands. And she'd found the gun right there in the middle drawer where it had always been kept.

She wanted so badly to ask her father how he'd gotten it back, but she couldn't bring herself to do so. He would have wanted to know why she asked.

How had the weapon ended up back where it belonged? Charles couldn't possibly have broken into her parents' home and returned it. That was ludicrous to think. But someone had put it back where it belonged.

Her instincts told her that the others, Cassidy and Kira, believed she was the one who'd killed Charles. Or maybe one or both pretended to believe so in order to make themselves look innocent. Both had had every bit as much reason to want him dead as she had. Charles had made all their lives miserable.

Lacy couldn't help feeling like a traitor even thinking such a thing. But she had to consider all possibilities. Someone had killed Charles. And it damned sure wasn't her. It was past time she'd figured out who.

She'd thought she could live with the not knowing, that it didn't matter who had killed him. He had deserved to die. What difference did it make?

But she couldn't pretend it didn't matter anymore.

The guilt wouldn't fade.

She had to know the truth. Not that she wanted to hurt her friends. She didn't. She would tell no one what she learned. But she had to get to the bottom of what had really happened. It was the only way she would be able to live with herself after this.

Lacy closed the drawer, concealing the weapon Charles had taken from her...the very one that may have been used in his murder. She shuddered. If one of her friends had killed him, they would have recognized the weapon and returned it to her father's desk.

That was the only reasonable explanation.

It had to be one of them.

Melinda had been in the hospital, but did that completely rule her out?

What was she thinking?

Melinda couldn't have killed Charles.

This whole thing was making her paranoid, making her feel things she didn't want to feel.

She'd read the newspaper reports about Charles and the other events that had taken place around the same time he was murdered.

Pamela Carter had disappeared. There was talk that she and Charles had had an affair. That avenue was certainly worth looking into. Maybe Pamela had killed him and run off with the money Charles had withdrawn. Melinda had told Lacy about the missing money. The police had questioned her regarding the large withdrawal, but she hadn't known anything about it of course.

Charles's partner, Nigel Canton, had been investigated just as Melinda had. If there had been anything to find, surely the police would have discovered it. But then again, the same officers of the law hadn't learned the secret they kept. Could she actually count on the police to find the real killer? Did she even want them to, considering it was more than likely one of her dearest friends?

Enough. She pushed up from her chair. She could sit here all day and speculate, or she could get out and find the truth for herself. That way she could protect her friends if she discovered evidence that it was one of them. Who was she kidding? She knew it was one of them. But which one?

She had several hours before she was supposed to be at Melinda's. There was plenty of time for her to look into things, starting with the long-missing Pamela.

Lacy grabbed her purse and headed for her car. She'd have to be careful. The others couldn't know. They wouldn't understand. They would assume she was working against them. In all the years they'd been friends—and their bond went all the way back to before kindergarten—nothing had ever threatened to pull them apart as Charles's murder had.

Cassidy was with Melinda and Kira would likely be working from her parents' home. They all had jobs to take care of. Lacy had e-mailed and faxed several high-priority items already this morning. Cassidy had dumped her entire caseload on a junior partner at her firm and was consulting via phone and e-mail. Kira could more easily do her work most anywhere since she edited for a New York based publishing house.

Bottom line, they were all busy. No one was likely going to wonder where she was. She had her cell phone. If Kira decided she wanted someone besides her mother with whom to share lunch she would call.

As Lacy drove through town on her way to the Carter place, she abruptly noticed the smell of the old paper mill. Funny how when you spent your life someplace you forgot to notice something as cloying as that. On

her way she opted to go past the suite of offices where
Charles had once worked. The same place his partner
had bought out full control. Nigel Canton darn sure had
a motive for wanting Charles dead. The business aside,
Melinda had told Lacy about the affair Charles had
carried on with Nigel's wife, Patricia.

From what Melinda had seen, Nigel hated Charles.

But he hadn't been alone in his misery. A lot of men
in Ashland had hated Charles.

Lacy drove slowly by the two-story building.
Charles's father had forked over the cash for the swanky
architecture. Nothing was too good for his only son. The
building still belonged to Charles, Senior, but he continued to lease the space to Nigel. Perhaps to keep him
quiet about Charles's extracurricular activities?

People talked in a small town. But when the gossip
revolved around the family who all but owned the entire
county, things were kept hush-hush to a large degree.
And no one in his right mind would have testified
against an Ashland. That would amount to economic
and social suicide in this county and probably a few surrounding ones.

Lacy scarcely caught herself before she slammed on
her brakes. Her breath was trapped in her lungs as her
brain denied what her eyes saw. Rick Summers, Chief
of Police Rick Summers, had just climbed out of his
truck in the parking area outside the building's front
lobby. If he looked back toward the street—

He zeroed in on Lacy's vehicle as if she'd shouted
his name.

Somehow her foot pressed a little more firmly on the
accelerator. As the vehicle carried her away, she knew
it was a flat-out miracle she hadn't hit anyone for she
damned sure hadn't been looking where she was going.

Her entire being had been focused on the man staring at her with such determination.

He would know she hadn't driven by Canton's office by chance. He would know she was up to something.

Dear God, he already suspected far too much. What the hell was she doing?

Exactly what Cassidy had told her not to do: handing him more fuel to fire his suspicions.

Rick watched Lacy Oliver disappear beyond the next intersection before he dragged his attention back to the here and now. What the hell was she doing driving by Charles Ashland's old office? Was she watching Rick or checking up on Canton? One seemed about as unlikely as the other.

Maybe she'd picked up on him watching her and had decided to give tit for tat.

He'd have to find out one way or another. He damned sure couldn't have her nosing around in his investigation.

He ran his hand through his hair and heaved a disgusted breath. He needed to have another talk with her. Soon.

He glanced up at the sky. Even at ten o'clock the sun was already beating down something fierce. The towering sugar maples and pin oaks dotting the landscape did little to block the heat rising from the asphalt.

Rick hustled to the front entrance, crossed beneath the navy canopy that offered some respite from the heat. Each of the windows on the front of the building had a similar canopy. Inside, the lobby boasted a library-type setting with lots of magazines and newspapers from around the globe available for waiting clients. The receptionist greeted him immediately and directed him to his destination.

Nigel Canton's office looked as if it belonged in a penthouse on Wall Street. It definitely didn't look like the sort of place one did business in a small town like Ashland, Alabama.

Thick, luxurious carpet. Rich gold walls with brilliant white trim that had to have been hand-carved the detailing was so intricate. The heavy mahogany furnishings and expensive-looking paintings completed the room. Rick was reasonably certain the decor alone cost more than he would make as the chief of police for several years to come.

Nigel, a tall, thin man with even thinner black hair and small brown eyes, looked inordinately bored with the idea that the chief had paid him a visit. He scarcely shook Rick's hand before reclining back into his soft leather chair and clasping his hands on his desk in front of him.

"I don't understand why this visit is necessary, Chief," he said frankly. "I told the police all I knew ten years ago, and nothing has changed since. Quite honestly, I'm not at all surprised Ashland is dead. He made himself numerous enemies in his short life, including his wife and myself."

Well, at least he was honest to a point.

Rick took a seat though one hadn't been offered. The upholstered chair was plush enough that he sank deep into it and could have enjoyed the pleasantness of it under different circumstances.

"Mr. Canton, considering that we now know Charles Ashland is dead, it's imperative that we nail down a broader time frame for all previously taken statements."

He lifted a sparse eyebrow. "In other words you want to know where I was at the time Charles might have been murdered."

"I'm afraid that one would be tough," Rick admitted,

"since we can't establish exact time of death. But what I would like to do is build a broader framework of activity around the time of his disappearance." Rick flipped open his notepad. "You stated that on the day of his disappearance you were here at the office all day."

Canton nodded. "That's correct. The secretary, Rachel Hill, can confirm my whereabouts. We worked on several proposals that day. Neither of us left. We had lunch delivered right here."

Rick studied his hastily scribbled notes a moment longer before dropping the bomb. "Chief Taylor mentioned in his final report that there was some question as to the exact nature of your and Miss Hill's precise relationship." His gaze settled fully onto Canton's. "Can you clarify that relationship for me?"

Any openness Canton had previously displayed disappeared in a flash of annoyance. His expression closed so completely he could have lapsed into a coma and looked more alert.

"We…" Canton cleared his throat. "Our relationship was first and foremost a working one. But, as you may recall, that was a very difficult time for me and we became more intimately involved."

Rick nodded his understanding. "That was during the time you thought your wife and your partner were intimately involved, is that correct?"

Canton's eyes narrowed. "You know it was, Summers. Why rehash those nasty details? I shouldn't have to relive that misery. There's nothing else I can tell you that you don't already know. Why would I have killed him? As you well know, I was forced to continue operations here as if he were still alive for seven long years. I couldn't buy out his share until he was officially pronounced dead. I worked for seven years and gave fifty percent of the company's earnings to a dead man. I should be stricken from your suspect list for that alone."

"There is one thing that Taylor failed to ask you ten years ago."

His patience at an end, Canton snipped, "What? If I cared that my wife was screwing around with the bastard?" His jaw worked a moment before he answered his own question. "Hell no, I didn't care. It kept the bitch off my back, if you want to know the truth. But the humiliation was something else entirely. Discretion never was one of my former partner's finer points."

"Actually," Rick countered, "I was going to ask if you remembered Charles having had any dealings with Bent Thompson."

Surprise captured Canton's expression to the point that his lower jaw sagged. "Bent Thompson?"

The name brought a certain stigma with it. No one wanted to confess even knowing the small-time hood, much less having had any dealings with him.

"I would say no, most assuredly," Canton replied thoughtfully, "but there was that once about a week before Charles disappeared that he stayed late for a meeting. He said it was private, not company business." Canton lifted his shoulders and let them drop in a show of indifference. "I assumed he intended to meet one of his female friends. I wasn't particularly concerned since my wife was out of town." His brow furrowed as if he was working hard to recall the precise events that occurred next. "As I was leaving the office that day, I noticed Thompson parked across the street. Generally I didn't pay attention to who visited whom along this street, but that day the cigarette smoke rising from the open window of his car drew my attention."

Elm Street, the one running parallel to the building, was occupied by a number of businesses, from small medical practices to accounting offices. Some were housed in new upscale buildings like this one and others had merely taken over former homes.

"I'm sure he wasn't the first person to sit outside in his car and smoke, mind you," Canton went on, "but he seemed to blow the smoke in my direction almost as if he wanted me to see him."

Bent Thompson liked to intimidate. Rick could definitely see where he would enjoy making a man like Canton shake in his shiny leather loafers.

"But you can't be sure he was the appointment Charles had that day."

Canton shook his head. "No. I left immediately. Whatever Thompson's or Charles's business that day, I wanted nothing to do with it."

"Speaking of your wife," Rick asked, "where is she?"

Canton rolled his eyes. "She's on vacation in Europe. Her trip was planned weeks ago. Check for yourself if you don't believe me."

Rick stood. He'd gotten all he needed from Canton for now. "I appreciate your time, Mr. Canton." He tucked his notepad back into his shirt pocket. "I may have other questions later."

Canton nodded. "I know the drill."

"If you remember anything else relevant to Bent Thompson or those last few days before Charles disappeared, I'd appreciate it if you gave me a call."

Canton didn't bother standing but he did ask, "Do you think Bent Thompson could have killed Charles for that money that was never recovered?"

It wasn't such a stretch to come up with that scenario,

but Rick wasn't sure of anything just now. "At the moment I'm investigating all the possibilities. I'd appreciate it if you kept this conversation between us."

Canton nodded, but Rick didn't trust the man as far as he could throw him to keep quiet. Good thing Rick wanted just the opposite.

He thanked the secretary as he strolled back through the outer office and he nodded to the receptionist as he exited the lobby.

Rick had accomplished both the things he needed to with this visit. He had let Canton know that he was still a suspect, though he made a valid point regarding what Charles's having abruptly gone missing cost him. Killing his partner and then hiding the body wouldn't have been an advantageous move for Canton.

In addition to making the man feel like a suspect once more, Rick had also slipped Thompson's name into the rumor mill. Bent Thompson had himself a hell of a temper. If word got back to him that Rick was investigating him as a part of Ashland's murder, he might just come calling. That was exactly what Rick wanted him to do. He wanted him mad as hell and talking way too much.

As Rick settled into his truck, his cell phone buzzed. He and his deputies still had radios for backup and dispatch, but cell phones were a mighty handy tool and considerably more discreet when you didn't want folks around you to hear both ends of the conversation.

"Yeah, Brewer, what's up?"

Caller ID was another handy tool on the job.

"One of the boys on patrol just called in a blue Explorer with Georgia plates out on Long Hollow Road. He's pretty sure it was Lacy."

"Thanks, Brewer, I'll check it out."

Rick had his whole force keeping an eye out for the

persons of interest in this investigation. Lacy, Melinda, Cassidy, Kira, Canton, Thompson and the Ashlands all fell smack into that category.

He started his truck and pulled out of the parking lot onto Elm. Long Hollow Road. Who would Lacy be going to see out that way? It wasn't exactly a part of her old stomping grounds and she didn't have any relatives that he knew of out that way.

The Carters.

Maybe he was way off the mark, but the idea was just too coincidental. His first thought was what the hell did Lacy know about Pamela Carter and Charles Ashland, then it hit him. Melinda was Lacy's best friend. She would have told her about her husband's mistresses if she knew.

Only one way to find out.

He headed in that direction. The Carter place was well out of town and way south of Houston, putting those folks on the same side of the town's society line as him. He'd be right at home in that neck of the woods.

It was Lacy who would be out of place.

Pamela Carter's father lived in a small house a good distance off the main road. The dirt trail—calling it a road would have been totally inaccurate—leading to the house was rutted and narrow. Trees encroached on the space as if they'd tried their best to swallow up the only means of entry. The limbs scratched at Lacy's SUV, but she had bigger worries on her mind than the proper care of her vehicle's paint job.

She'd had the good sense to bring along her high school yearbook from the last year that Pamela had been pictured there. Lacy had been a senior, Pamela a sophomore. She'd apparently dropped out of school after that. Lacy's parents had purchased school yearbooks for another two years after Lacy's graduation probably as some sort of fund-raiser.

For the entire twenty-five minutes it took to get to the Carter home, Lacy had considered what she would say. That she was an old classmate of Pamela's and she wanted to catch up was what she'd decided upon. She didn't know the Carters, and she was hoping they didn't know her.

Lacy's father was a retired engineer, so the probability that he'd worked with Mr. Carter was highly unlikely. From what Lacy remembered, the Carter family had eked out a meager living and the roof over their heads by working on one of the larger farms in the county. Pamela had worn what looked like hand-me-downs to school as had the rest of her siblings. Four girls. All married before age eighteen except for Pamela.

The other girls had all been older than Pamela and Lacy vaguely remembered them. In particular she recalled the year their mother had run off with a traveling salesman. Apparently stuff like that didn't happen only in the movies. She might not have remembered Pamela at all had she not disappeared about the same time Charles had, prompting the grapevine to latch on to the idea that the two had run off together.

Of course Lacy and her friends had known that wasn't true. But the part she didn't know was whether or not Pamela and Charles had been together between eleven in the morning and four in the afternoon on the day he died.

She needed to know that. She needed to find out who had been with Charles during that critical five-hour time period. Someone had killed him, maybe even using her father's gun, sometime between eleven and four.

As she parked, Lacy tried her best to remember the state of his body when they'd found him. She'd been too horrified at the time to consider how long he'd been dead. And she'd spent the better part of ten years trying to forget that night. She needed to remember.

Were his muscles stiff? Had rigor mortis set in? What was his coloring like?

She just couldn't remember.

Cassidy was the more rational one in a time of crisis. Maybe she would recall. But asking her would alert her to what Lacy was up to. She couldn't do that. Melinda wasn't there and she doubted that Kira remembered any more than she did. They'd both been pretty shaken.

Lacy climbed out of her Explorer and prayed the Carters didn't own any dogs. When she reached the porch without incident she breathed a little easier.

The wooden boards squeaked as she walked across to the screen door. She could hear a television set playing inside. Whatever color the house had once been, any signs of pigment had long since faded into something grayish and peeling on the ancient and weathered wood siding. The roof was tin, she'd noticed as she drove up to the house. One rusty piece on the right side had come loose and was a bit turned up on one side. She imagined that the area leaked when it rained, especially if the wind blew. The roof had probably leaked like a sieve last week during those heavy rains.

Although it was only June, the Alabama heat had already taken a toll on the neglected yard, leaving patches of brown grass here and there. Even last week's near flood hadn't done much to revive it.

A broken window had been boarded shut, but the yard actually looked well-groomed. It might not win any awards from the local home-and-garden club, but it was livable.

She cleared her throat and rapped against the wood frame of the screen door. It rattled on its hinges as if it might just fall off if she knocked with too much enthusiasm.

"If you're sellin' something, you've come to the wrong place."

She couldn't make out the man through the screen. The sun behind her back made seeing inside difficult. "No, sir, I'm not selling anything," she assured him. "I'm here to talk to you about your daughter."

"If she ain't paid her bills I can't pay 'em for her. Go see one of her sisters."

Obviously, she should have specified which daughter she'd come to talk about.

"I'm sorry, Mr. Carter, it's Pamela I've come to talk to you about."

The silence that followed was haunting. Made her shiver in spite of the sun beating against her back.

"Pamela's been gone a long time, lady. You must not be from around these parts or you'd know that."

"Actually, I moved away almost fifteen years ago. I just got back to town yesterday. I was really hoping to talk to you if you have a moment."

"You ain't some reporter, are you?"

The edge in his voice warned that he'd been bothered by reporters before.

"No, sir. I'm not a reporter. I attended Ashland High with Pamela."

Lacy stepped back as the screen door moved outward. "Well, come on in then, missy."

The house, or what she could see of it, wasn't exactly dirty but it was cluttered. What appeared to be clean laundry was left in a chair. Newspapers were stacked knee-high next to the sofa. The place lacked the usual organization a woman brought to a space.

Lacy perched on the edge of the seat he offered. He settled onto the couch straight across from her.

"What you wanna talk about?" he asked as he lowered the volume on the television set with the remote control.

"I heard that Pamela moved away a few years back and I wondered how I might reach her." It was a flat-out lie, but she had no idea how to go about this without fibbing.

He glanced at the yearbook in her lap, then back at her. "We don't rightly know what happened to her. She just left for work one day and never came back."

Lacy pressed her hand to her chest. "My goodness, Mr. Carter, when did that happen?" She felt like such a hypocrite doing this. But she needed information.

"On Christmas Eve exactly ten years ago," he said somberly. "She left here on her way to work at the Dairy Dip but Ralph Gunther, her boss, said she never showed up for her shift. We never heard from her again."

That had to be horrifying. Not knowing what had happened to your child, no matter how old.

"No one, not even co-workers or former classmates, ever heard from her?"

He shook his head slowly from side to side. "Me and her sisters figured she'd run off with that Ashland fella seeing as he went missing about that same time. She'd been seeing him, but considering his body turned up we must've been wrong."

Lacy moistened her lips. "She and Charles Ashland were involved?"

He nodded, smoothed a broad hand over his dingy white T-shirt. "I raised her better than that, but that Pamela, she had high hopes, you know. If she couldn't find herself a rich man to marry she intended to hook one any way she could. I warned her she'd only find trouble that way."

"Hook one?" Lacy inquired as if she didn't understand.

"Well, I can't be sure," he said with a negligent wave of his hand. "But her sister, Carmen, the oldest, claims Pamela was pregnant by Ashland." His gaze turned distant. "Guess we'll never know."

Lacy felt the blood drain from her face. "But Carmen couldn't be sure unless Pamela confirmed her pregnancy with a test…"

"I guess she was far enough along she knew for sure," he said knowingly. "Had herself a doctor over in Rainsville."

Lacy's heart started to pound. "Maybe she was afraid of what Charles Ashland would do and she just ran away."

Mr. Carter shook his head. "Nope. I don't think she would've done that. She wanted to be one of them." He shrugged. "You know them high-society folks. I guess she figured getting pregnant was a guaranteed way to make it happen. Must've backfired on her since she disappeared so suddenly."

Lacy didn't remember saying goodbye, but somehow she managed to make her way back to her Explorer without throwing up or passing out.

She started the engine and turned around in the half-dead grass. She drove as fast as she dared back down the narrow path that served as a driveway.

She shouldn't have come here. What she'd learned had only made things more confusing. If Melinda ever found out… It was one thing to have affairs, but to get another woman pregnant…

Lacy shuddered and her stomach roiled as she pulled out onto the highway.

Charles was an even bigger bastard than she'd known.

She had to find out who killed him, no matter who it turned out to be.

Who was she kidding? If the police couldn't figure out what had really happened to Charles, how the hell could she hope to? But she had to try. Didn't she? Her insides knotted with anxiety. She had to try. She couldn't keep pretending it didn't matter.

Just then, in her rearview mirror, blue lights flickered. Not a squad car…a truck. She recognized it from earlier that morning.

Rick Summers.

He'd followed her.

# Chapter 7

"You were speeding."

Lacy stared at Rick dumbfounded. She'd barely pulled out onto the road when she spotted his blue lights. No way could she have been speeding.

She finally found her voice. "That's impossible."

She couldn't tell what he was thinking with his eyes hidden behind the dark eyewear, but if the muscle throbbing in his jaw was any indication he was madder than hell.

"You were swerving recklessly," he accused.

"What?" If she'd swerved it was only because seeing those lights in her rearview mirror startled her.

He grabbed the door handle and jerked it open. "Get out of the vehicle, Miss Oliver."

What the…? "You can't be serious?" Was he playing some sort of intimidation game here? "I haven't done anything wrong."

"Get out now or I'll consider your actions failure to consent."

Confusion clouded her ability to think. "Failure to consent to what?"

"A sobriety test."

He had lost his mind.

"It's the middle of the day? You think I've been drinking? For God's sake, Rick—"

"Get out of the vehicle, Miss Oliver."

Flustered and furious, Lacy unsnapped her seat belt and slid out of the Explorer. She slammed the door. "Now what?"

He pointed to the middle of the road. "See that white line?"

She rolled her eyes.

"I want you to walk it."

"This is harassment," she muttered as she stormed to the middle of the road. "You can barely see the damned line it's so faded."

"Start walking, Lacy Jane." He ripped off his concealing eyewear to allow her to see just how serious he was.

Oh, so now it was Lacy Jane.

Rage pulsing in her veins, she started forward, careful to put one foot directly in front of the other as she'd seen it done in the movies.

When she'd taken a dozen or so steps, she stopped and wheeled around. "Satisfied?"

He towered over her. She gasped. She hadn't realized he'd been right behind her.

"Now close your eyes and hold your arms straight out from your sides."

"I will not!"

"You will."

Sucking in a deep breath to slow her building rage, she closed her eyes and stretched out her arms.

"Now touch your nose with your right forefinger."

Shaking with fury, she barely managed the feat. She did the same with her left finger before he could ask. "See?" she demanded as she dropped her arms and opened her eyes to glare at him once more.

"Keep walking," he growled. "I'm not convinced."

This was insane. So mad she could not speak, she faced forward and did as he ordered. She would file a complaint against him, by God. This was harassment pure and simple. He wouldn't get away with it.

"What were you doing at the Carter place?"

"How dare you!" She spun around to face him, almost bumping into him in the process. "Where I go and who I talk to is none of your—"

"Keep walking."

If he hadn't looked so fierce she might have been able to ignore his crazy order this time. But he looked ready to rip off her head and spit down her throat, so she did as she was told.

"Why did you visit Pamela Carter's father?"

For five seconds Lacy refused to answer. Who the hell did he think he was? It was a free country. She could visit anyone she wanted as long as they didn't have a restraining order against her.

"Because I wanted to know if he'd heard from her."

"I could have told you the answer to that," he snapped.

"I didn't want to hear your version of the story. I wanted to hear it from her father."

"I don't know what you're up to, Lacy, but you're getting yourself in deeper and deeper. Pretty soon I won't even be able to bail you out."

She faced him again. This time she was finished

playing his ridiculous game. "You don't want to bail me out, remember? You want to find out who killed Charles Ashland, end of story. The only reason we're having this conversation is because you think I know something."

"And do you?"

She wanted so badly to hit him that it was a literal ache in her limbs. He didn't care who got hurt. All he cared about was solving his damned case.

"I know Charles Ashland had enough enemies that you could line them up around the courthouse square and have yourself a whole load of suspects. Why single out me and my friends?" Outrage rushed through her all over again. This wasn't fair. Melinda had suffered enough. They all had.

"Because you're hiding something from me," he said, putting his face right next to hers. "I can feel it, Lacy. You know something relevant to this case and you've been keeping it a secret for ten years."

Fear surged through her veins. Too close to home. "You see, that's exactly the reason I decided to dig around in this case myself. You've obviously already decided who killed Charles and don't intend to look any further."

The vein that bulged in his forehead gave away his level of fury even before his words did. "I don't know who killed Ashland, but I do know who wanted him dead more than anyone else."

"Who? Melinda?"

He moved his head side to side. "You."

She fell back a step. "This is harassment. You can't do this, Summers. I could sue."

"So sue me." He folded his arms over his chest. "You know we found two slugs with the remains. We've already run ballistics. All we need now is to find a match. I've already got someone running down the names of anyone in town who had a certain caliber handgun registered ten years ago."

A fresh flood of fear washed over her. He didn't have to say what caliber—she knew. "And you would be telling me this because…?"

"Fair warning, Lacy Jane. I will get to the bottom of what happened that day. Cooperation could make things a whole lot easier on anyone who was involved."

"Did you toss the same warning out to Nigel Canton this morning?" She'd seen him there. He'd seen her drive by. She was pretty sure he hadn't dropped by Canton's office to evaluate his strengths as a stockbroker.

"You think I should have?"

She held up her hands for him to just shut up. He had her far too close to the edge now. "I'm going to get back in my car and I'm going home. If you want to press some sort of charge against me, then I suggest you allow me to contact my attorney."

He stepped aside, giving her the go-ahead to pass. She exhaled a lungful of tension and started back toward her abandoned SUV, the engine still running. She couldn't believe she'd let him badger her into walking this far. Thank God, no one had come along and witnessed the fiasco. Then again, maybe she would have been better equipped to pursue a lawsuit if someone had.

"Did Mr. Carter tell you that Pamela was pregnant?"

Lacy stopped dead in her tracks.

"She'd been having an on-again off-again affair with Ashland for nearly two years. You suppose she thought she'd finally nailed him when she learned she was pregnant?"

Lacy turned to face him, her heart racing once more.

He'd known this and still he pushed her for information about what she knew.

"You think," he said, as he started slowly toward her, "that Charles withdrew that hundred grand to pay her off, maybe get her out of his life once and for all?"

Lacy couldn't respond…couldn't move. She could only watch him come closer, his words filling her with equal measures dread and outrage.

"Do you really believe that a country girl like Pamela could walk away from her family and never once look back?" He stopped right in front of her. "Or do you think maybe Charles killed her and dumped her body somewhere he figured nobody would look?"

A chill went through Lacy, making her shiver.

"That's what I think," he said coolly. "I think Pamela and that baby she was carrying are dead, and we just haven't found the body yet."

"I didn't know…" Lacy shook her head. "I swear I didn't. Melinda doesn't know about the pregnancy. She would have told me."

"Like she told you she left the hospital the day her husband disappeared?"

Lacy blinked, stunned by his statement. "That's a lie."

"Is it? I have a witness, one of the nurses on duty that day, who says Melinda was missing for a while. Are you telling me that your best friend didn't share that secret with you?"

"She had a concussion and a fractured rib," Lacy argued vehemently. "She couldn't have just walked out."

"Maybe she had help. Isn't that what friends are for?"

He was fishing again. Like Cassidy said. He didn't have anything. That's why he kept following Lacy around.

"I've told you all I can." Lacy turned her back on him and took the final few steps to her vehicle. She had to get out of here...away from him.

He put his hand against the door when she would have opened it. "I will find out what you're hiding, Lacy. Mark my words. One way or another, I will find out."

She'd had enough. She turned on him and didn't even flinch when she realized just how close he was. "What's the deal, Chief? Is your ego still bruised because I never called you after that night? Are you still mad that I wasn't impressed enough to want more?"

Strong fingers wrapped around her right arm and jerked her nearer when she'd felt certain they couldn't be any closer.

"This isn't about that night."

The utter calm of his tone made her more uneasy than if he'd shouted the words.

"This is about you and what you know."

She lifted her chin and glared directly into determined eyes. "I don't know anything that will help you catch his killer."

"But you know something."

The way his eyes searched hers...the feel of his hand against her skin. Her pulse faltered, made her shake in spite of her determination not to. "I know a lot of things, Chief Summers." She found herself holding her breath.

"Keep in mind." He was closer...somehow. She could feel his breath against her lips and a new kind of ache went through her, one of desire...of desperate need. "That whoever killed Charles Ashland doesn't want me to find out who he or she is. If you know anything at all, that puts you directly in the line of fire. Think about it, Lace—any odd happenings in your life since you got back to town?"

*I know your secret.*

"I have to go." She pulled her arm free of his hold. "Melinda's waiting for me."

He backed off a couple of steps, let her climb into her SUV, before he warned, "All you have to do is tell me the truth, Lacy. I'll take care of everything else. You need to trust me."

When she would have closed the door, he held it open a couple seconds longer and said, "You trusted me once."

Their gazes held for one long beat more before he closed the door and she drove away.

He was right. She had trusted him that one time. She'd wanted him more than she'd ever wanted anything in her life. It was the summer before her senior year and she was the only one in her group of friends who was still a virgin. Until that night, when she'd decided she wasn't going to be one come daylight. And if she was going to give that precious gift away so freely, it had to be with someone who made her quiver with want. Rick Summers. Tall, dark and handsome. He was a walking, talking romance-novel cliché. The good guy from the poor side of town, all full of pride and honor and big dreams for the future.

He'd done it right, she had to give him that. No matter what she'd said back there in the heat of anger. Rick Summers had made love to her as no one else ever had. Maybe that's why she'd never been able to stick with any of her adult relationships. By age twelve her entire future had been mapped out. Graduate high school with honors. Go off to the best university. Get a high-powered position in her chosen field. Nowhere in that plan was hanging around her rinky-dink hometown with a guy from the wrong side of Houston Street. But that hadn't stopped her heart. She'd fallen in love with the wrong guy fifteen years ago.

Now he wanted her again…for totally different reasons.

* * *

Lacy walked the floors of her childhood home until it was time to go to Melinda's. She'd toyed with the idea of disposing of her father's gun, but that wouldn't change the fact that the weapon had been registered to him for at least twenty years. And it might very well make her look more guilty. She couldn't be sure the gun had even been used. Rick's people would find the registration listing and then he would know what she had to hide. Or, at least, part of it. Better to appear as if she had no reason to be worried than to look guilty.

As she parked in front of Melinda's house she considered whether to tell Cassidy what she'd learned about Pamela, but decided against it. Her unofficial investigation would only draw more suspicion her way. Cassidy would only tell her that she was screwing up, drawing the chief's attention. She would tell her again that all they had to do was lay low and this would all blow over.

But not for Lacy. It would never be over until she learned what had really happened.

Which of her friends killed Charles?

She felt sick to her stomach when she thought of what Rick had told her about Melinda having left the hospital. Why would Melinda keep that from her? Was he simply fishing? Had he made the whole thing up in an attempt to make her talk?

She didn't know, but one thing was certain—she couldn't risk that he was using that line of bull to get her to trust him. No way would she ask Melinda.

The moment she entered Melinda's front door she knew something was wrong. Kira was there, too. She wasn't supposed to take over until the next morning.

"Where have you been, Lacy?"

Lacy closed the door behind her and looked from Cassidy, who'd spoken, to Kira and back, her feelings of defensiveness automatically falling into place. "What's going on?"

"I tried to call you to meet me for lunch," Kira said. "Your cell wasn't on."

Lacy frowned, tried to think if she'd had her phone off at all today. "I must have been in a dead zone," she said more to herself than the others. Along some of the county's back roads cell service was sorely limited.

"I saw you driving back into town," Kira went on. "Chief Summers was right behind you."

Now she understood the problem and exactly where this was going. "Where's Melinda?" She looked past her friends, but there was no one else in the entry hall.

"She's upstairs resting," Cassidy explained. "She spoke to her son today and she was so upset afterward that she had to take a sedative."

"Oh, God." Damn those Ashlands. "I'm going to see her."

Cassidy held up a hand for her to wait. "You need to tell us what's going down between you and Chief Summers, Lace. We're all becoming troubled by the way this looks."

Fury detonated inside Lacy. She'd had more than enough today. "Nothing is going down, Cassidy. You know what he's doing. He's putting the pressure on me, trying to get me to talk. I won't."

Kira blinked, clearly uncertain of her stand now that she'd heard Lacy's side of things. "Why is he singling you out?" she asked.

The answer to that was none of their business, had no relevance on Charles's death whatsoever. But she knew how it would look, especially since she'd kept it a secret for so long. "Your guess is as good as mine. Maybe he thinks he can intimidate me. I don't know. But it's not going to work."

"A man like Summers doesn't act without fore-thought and reason, Lacy," Cassidy stated pointedly. "He has a reason for leaning on you. You need to think long and hard and see if you come up with anything that he might consider a weakness."

Lacy had to bite her tongue to keep from yelling *It's sex, okay?* But she kept quiet. In this situation the truth wouldn't help. She understood that with complete clarity.

"I'll go check on Melinda." Kira rushed off as if she feared the worst was yet to come.

"Something's going on with you, Lacy, and I don't understand why you're keeping it from the rest of us."

Maybe Cassidy was right. Maybe keeping them in the dark was wrong.

"I need to know what really happened, Cass. I can't live with this another ten years, especially now. The whole world knows he's dead. I can't pretend it was just a nightmare anymore."

Cassidy searched her face for a long while before she spoke. "You know what happened, Lacy. You were there. Don't pretend innocence. We're all in this together. Equally guilty. The moment one starts believing they're less liable than the others, that's when things start falling apart. We took a vow. Are you going to renege on that solemn promise?"

Lacy ran her fingers through her hair. God, she was so tired. She didn't want to think anymore. "No, Cassidy, of course not. I just need to know for my own peace of mind."

Cassidy leaned closer, as if what she had to say next

was top secret. "Then I suggest you look deep inside yourself. That's where you'll find the answers you seek."

Cassidy assured Lacy that she would talk to her tomorrow and then she left. Lacy watched her drive away, confusion leaving her too stunned to utter more than goodbye and the occasional acknowledging grunt.

She'd been right.

Cassidy did believe she was the one who had killed Charles.

How was that possible?

"Did Cassidy leave?"

Lacy jumped at the sound of Kira's voice. She'd been so focused on watching the street, even after Cassidy drove away, that she hadn't realized anyone had come into the entry hall.

"Yeah. She said she'd call tomorrow."

Kira shrugged. "I know she's being hard on you, Lace, but she's just worried. Anything we say could work against us. We have to be very careful right now and getting all tangled up with Rick is risky."

"It isn't what you think, Kira. He followed me, I didn't invite him or encourage him in any way." Lacy left out the part about visiting Mr. Carter. She couldn't be sure how relevant Pamela Carter's disappearance was to Charles's murder just yet. Considering the way Kira and Cassidy had looked at her with utter suspicion, the less she said the better…for all their sakes.

"We're all nervous as hell, especially Melinda. You should have seen her after she talked to Chuckie. It was heartbreaking. He refuses to come home or even talk about what's happened."

"Do you think the Ashlands are behind this?" Lacy wanted to shake both of them until they came to their senses and saw how lucky they were to have a daughter-in-law like Melinda.

Kira sighed. "I don't know. Melinda didn't want to talk about it and I didn't push. I was a little upset myself after having seen you with Summers right on your tail."

Lacy shoved a handful of hair behind her ear and let her irritation override her other emotions briefly. "You know if we're all equally guilty, then why am I feeling like the guilty one here? You and Cassidy are acting like you've already decided I'm the one and I have to be honest, I don't like that feeling."

Kira grabbed Lacy's hands and held them tightly, her eyes shiny with emotion. "We're not judging you, Lace. We're just worried about you, that's all. Your vulnerability has been showing since we got here. We just don't want you to make a mistake."

Lacy couldn't bear it any longer. She wrapped her arms around Kira and hugged her. She needed to feel the closeness, the unity. But what she felt was doubt, tension, and worse…restraint.

"I'm okay, I promise," Lacy said as she drew back. "You guys don't have to worry about me."

But they were worried. Kira and Cassidy were convinced that Lacy had killed Charles.

Did that mean that the two of them were innocent? Or was it simply a ploy by one or both to shift doubt, as she'd considered earlier?

When Kira had gone, her cell phone ringing before she could even get out the door, Lacy tried to occupy herself for a while then went upstairs and checked on Melinda. She still slept soundly. Lacy suddenly felt damned tired herself. It wouldn't hurt her to go to bed early tonight. Sitting around in Melinda's house, allowing the memories to assault her was definitely not something she looked forward to. And nothing she'd found on the hundred or so television channels had distracted her.

She would just lock up and make herself a bed on the chaise longue in Melinda's room. That way if Melinda woke up she'd be there for her.

With the security system activated, Lacy headed for the stairs once more. It was barely nine, but she was beat.

When she lifted her foot to the first tread the telephone rang.

For all of two seconds she considered letting the machine get it, but it could be one of Melinda's children and besides, the continued ringing might wake her.

Lacy trudged back to the living room and grabbed the receiver before it could ring the third time. "Hello."

"I'm the only one who knows the truth, Lacy."

The voice. Her heart stilled in her chest. The voice from the caller the other night.

"Who is this?"

"I know your secret, Lacy, and you're all going to regret what you did."

# Chapter 8

Bent Thompson's luck had always run bad. Whether it was his mean-as-hell daddy or his mealymouthed mama, or some other relative he'd never heard of who had passed that unfortunate trait on to him he couldn't say. He'd read a lot about DNA in the past few years. Seemed everything about a person, from the color of his eyes to the hair on his ass, could be traced back to his DNA. That being the case, he was fucked from the day he was born.

Not one damned member of his family had ever amounted to anything. Plain old white trash. That's what he'd been called for as far back as he could remember. Same went for his folks.

He'd lived in dumps in various cities around the south. Memphis had been his favorite, but he couldn't go back there. He'd crossed the wrong people.

Some folks liked holding grudges.

Personally, he didn't believe in wasting the energy to hang on to anything unless he had something to gain from it. That's why he'd come back to Ashland as soon as he heard the news.

He'd been hanging on to something that might one day provide him with everything he would ever need.

It wasn't a big deal, nothing complicated. Just a small handgun, a .38 Smith & Wesson. Wasn't even a top-of-the-line model. But it was worth its weight in gold a thousand times over.

This was the weapon used to put a bullet right through Charles Ashland's black heart. At least that's what he'd heard about the way the poor bastard died.

"I don't know why you kept that," his host remarked blandly, snapping Bent from his reflections.

Bent smiled. Some people thought they were immune, never expected anything bad to happen to them, even when they deserved it. Then when their naughty deed came back to bite them in the ass they whined about it. That was the problem with being born anything other than plain white trash. Folks who had something always expected things to work out, expected more. Maybe it was in their DNA. Who knew?

"I kept it," Bent said as he studied the weapon in the nifty Ziploc bag he'd slipped it into ten years ago, "because I wanted some insurance for the future. You know, an investment, sort of like a 401k."

"What do you want from me?"

Now they were getting somewhere. A lot of people had benefited from young Charles's untimely death, the way Bent saw it. His wife had shed a cheating, abusive husband. His business partner was finally rid of the star who always outshone him. His own father no longer had to worry about his son's deviant activities tarnishing his spotless political reputation. Sweet little Pamela no longer had to obsess about someone else having the man she wanted so badly. Then there were the others like Lacy Jane Oliver and her friends and countless husbands around town, all of whom had reason to want Charles Ashland, Junior, dead.

But only one person had killed him. And Bent held the single item that could connect the killer to the victim.

The weapon.

"Let me get back to you," Bent said smugly. "I need some time to decide what the rest of your life is worth. That's what hangs in the balance, wouldn't you say?"

Bent didn't wait for an answer. He pushed out of the chair and walked away. No need to hang around. Time could be a formidable ally. It made folks squirm…made 'em sweat. But Bent had learned patience the hard way—two stints in prison. And even though they were fairly short compared to what he could have gotten, he knew he didn't ever want to go back. Now was his chance to set himself up for life. No more running cons…no more dodging the law.

All these years he'd hung on to this damned little .38 when he wasn't even sure why. He hadn't had any real proof that it had been used in a crime. Hell, he'd been in the same boat with everybody else. He'd figured Charles had run off with Pamela after all. Stranger things happened. But on a farfetched hunch, in light of the circumstances surrounding how he'd come into pos-session of the weapon, he'd decided to take very good care of it. Funny, he'd left town ten years ago for his own reasons, with no idea what a gold mine he'd taken with him in that handy little Ziploc bag.

Imagine his surprise when he learned that Charles

had been murdered, that his body had been found and that no one had a clue what had really happened.

Then he'd known exactly what his little keepsake was worth.

The world.

Lacy left Melinda's the next morning and dropped by her parents' house to shower. She didn't bother with breakfast. She went straight to the library as soon as it opened.

That call last night had shaken her far worse than the first one.

*...you're all going to regret what you did.*

No matter how she looked at it, she and her friends had been threatened. The others could believe that Rick was somehow behind the calls in order to scare Lacy into talking, but she knew better. The caller was real, and his or her threats were real.

Someone knew what they'd done.

She didn't understand how it could be so. As Cassidy said, Mr. Ashland had offered a sizable reward for any information related to his missing son and no one had come forward. So, clearly money wasn't this person's motivation. She shivered as she considered that this was no doubt about revenge.

But who could have seen them?

One of the neighbors as they left in Charles's Mercedes? Someone at the lake? It was dark. She couldn't fathom how anyone saw anything that happened that night. Then again the moon had been big and bright, glinting off the glassy water of the too-still lake.

But why not come forward ten years ago, especially in light of the reward?

Some kind of twisted revenge was the only possibility that made sense.

Rick thought she was hiding something and he wasn't about to give up trying to learn what it was. Some wacko caller appeared to know something. The way Lacy saw it she had only one choice: piece together herself what had happened. The only way to protect her and her friends was to be armed with the facts.

What they had done was wrong, no matter how much Charles had deserved exactly what happened to him…it was wrong.

The question of who had been the one to do what they'd all wanted to do crossed her mind again. Surely Melinda hadn't left the hospital. That had to be another of Rick's ploys to get information. But what about Cassidy or Kira? Cassidy had been awfully quick to pull together a plan when the rest of them had fallen apart at the sight of Charles's body.

Lacy shook off the thoughts. The bottom line was it didn't matter which of them had done the deed—it was done. But for her own peace of mind, Lacy needed to know what really happened. She tried to tell herself it didn't matter, but it did. For reasons she didn't even fully understand. She had to know. And she had to find out who could have seen their desperate act.

She pushed through the double doors leading into the library and walked directly to the information desk. "Where do you keep the old copies of the *Ashland Announcer* filed?" Since it was the only paper the town had, the library surely had all the back copies on microfiche somewhere.

The clerk smiled and pointed to the stairs in the middle of the library's main level. "Take the stairs to the second level and you'll find the electronic files on the right at the rear of the reference section."

Lacy hurried up the stairs, focusing straight ahead. She didn't want to talk to anyone, so avoiding eye contact was necessary.

She found a free desk and sat down before the computer screen. She moved the mouse to shut down the screen saver. The desktop appeared with a table of contents. She was impressed. Everything she would need was right here, only a mouse click away. That was pretty uptown for Ashland.

Going back to around Thanksgiving ten years ago, she slowly surveyed the biweekly newspaper's headlines for anything related to the Ashlands or Charles's investment company.

Several articles appeared regarding the election of Charles, Senior, to the senate. No one had been surprised when that happened. The elder Ashland had been working toward that goal for as long as Lacy could remember.

His granddaddy had been the governor, and his own father had served as Ashland's mayor multiple terms. Politics ran in the man's veins, but Charles, Junior, never once displayed any penchant for that world. He was too busy being a lady's man to bother with anything that might get in the way.

Lacy gritted her teeth and tried her level best not to think badly of the dead, but she couldn't help herself. He'd been a miserable bastard in life and he wasn't proving any kinder in death.

*Ashland Heir Missing...*

Lacy rolled her eyes. This was small-town Alabama for Pete's sake. Did they have to make him an heir? Then again she supposed that this was the closest thing to a royal family that Ashland had. The town was even named after the founding family, some of Charles's forefathers.

She focused on the numerous articles related to Charles's disappearance. Several articles from larger papers were cross-referenced. She made it a point to read every single one. Being thorough was absolutely essential.

Her life, as well her friends', could very well depend on it.

She moved back a screen to read an article she'd almost missed on Pamela Carter's disappearance. There was only one and it was very small. No one had really cared that a mere waitress from Long Hollow Road had gone missing.

Lacy shivered when she thought of the baby Pamela had been carrying. Melinda would be so hurt by that revelation. Maybe she would never have to know. It was bad enough that Charles screwed around, the least he could have done was to take the necessary precautions. Poor Melinda. It was a miracle she hadn't caught some horrific disease from the careless bastard.

None of the articles mentioned the money Charles had withdrawn. Lacy couldn't help wondering what had happened to it. Had he given it to Pamela to shut her up? Had Pamela disappeared and never come back? Lacy had to agree with Rick on that one. The chances of a small-town country girl disappearing and never once looking back, especially if she came into money, were highly unlikely.

Once she'd read the articles directly related to Charles, she moved slowly through the weeks and months that followed. She had nothing but time this morning.

She had reached the September first issue from three

years ago before she discovered anything else related
to Charles. An article announcing the ruling that Charles
Ashland, Junior, was in fact dead, droned on about the
details surrounding his disappearance, what few there
were. Followed by an explanation of what occurred
when one was officially pronounced dead.

Articles about Charles, Senior, and his new run for
the senate were splashed across most issues. A last-
minute, six-figure anonymous campaign donation had
been chalked up to closet Democrats who called themselves Republicans by day. Of course the opposing
party had insisted the donation was most likely nothing
more than an illegal, hidden payoff for future services
to be rendered. Wes Rossman had staunchly denied
such charges. Lacy wasn't exactly pro Charles, Senior,
but she imagined it would take more than the speculated
one hundred thousand or so dollars to buy off an
Ashland.

More enthusiastic pieces relayed the tight race
between Senator Ashland and his Republican opponent
as election day neared. And then, the many hurrahs for
his successful reelection to a new term.

Nothing out of the ordinary.

Nothing useful to her investigation.

Basically nothing she didn't already know.

Lacy rubbed her eyes and tried her best not to admit
defeat too quickly. There were other places she could
look, people she could talk to.

A man hanging around the periodicals sections
snagged her attention. He looked away as soon as she
noticed him. He looked remotely familiar, but she
couldn't be sure. Tall, broad shouldered and heavily
built. He looked…mean, tough, definitely not like

anyone who would hang around in the reference section of a library.

Her pulse reacted to a burst of adrenaline. Was he watching her?

Okay, paranoia had set in again. She had to get a grip on her reactions. Everyone wasn't out to get her. For all she knew, the guy could be there researching how to decorate his living room or nurture orchids.

Determined not to play mind games with herself, she skimmed a couple more issues beyond Christmas three years ago and then decided she'd learned all she was going to.

Nothing.

She exited out of the archives file, grabbed her purse and pushed out of the chair. Her stomach rumbled, reminding her that she'd skipped breakfast. Maybe she'd go hang out at the diner and see if she overheard any gossip. That was one thing you could count on in Ashland. Whatever was going on in town would be hashed out at Betty Mama's.

It wasn't until she'd gotten outside and settled into her Explorer that her nerves jangled once more. Mr. Tough Guy had come out, as well. She stilled, held her breath, as she watched him make his way to a blue Camaro that, if she were feeling charitable, she would call vintage. Definitely not anything from the past decade and a half.

Since he didn't look her way, there was the possibility that she was, once again, overreacting. Not certain she could take the chance, she rummaged through her purse to buy some time. She poked around a while, fiddled with the CD player until she found a selection she liked. And still he just sat there. Okay, now for the big test.

She put her car into reverse and backed from the slot.

Easing out onto the street, she noticed in her rearview mirror that he'd executed a ninety-degree turn and pulled out just moments after her.

A new shot of adrenaline roared through her veins and she ordered herself to stay calm. She would drive around a while, head back toward her house and if he still followed her she would…what? Go to the police? No. She couldn't do that. Not without ending up being questioned herself and appearing even more suspicions.

If he stayed on her tail she'd just have to go to Melinda's. At least there she wouldn't be walking into an empty house with a stranger shadowing her.

She made several unnecessary turns as she took the longest route she knew and each time he followed her as if they were connected by some invisible tether.

Lacy pointed her car in the direction of Melinda's and planted her right foot a little more firmly on the accelerator. Her stalker did the same.

For the first time since she'd spotted him in the library true fear ignited in her veins. What if this was the caller? What if he intended to make her regret her past actions now…this minute?

She turned onto Melinda's street and tightened her fingers on the steering wheel. If she could just get to her friends…

And what? Lead the bad guy right to them? Upset Melinda more than she already was?

No.

Lacy slammed on her brakes and came to a screeching halt right there in the middle of the street, forcing the guy behind her to do the same. She grabbed her purse and cell phone and shoved the car door open.

She was out of the vehicle and striding toward the Camaro before the driver had fully emerged from his.

"Why are you following me?"

"You don't know who I am, do you?" he asked as he straightened out of his car.

Maybe it was the smug way he asked the question, or maybe she was just mad, but she did something she had never done before. She reached deep into her purse and curled her fingers around the canister of pepper spray she had yet to use since the day she'd ordered it off the Internet.

"I don't know who you are and I don't care. Just stay away from me or you'll be the one regretting it. And if you call my house again—"

"Call your house?" He laughed. "You just don't know what you've gotten yourself in the middle of, do you, Miss Oliver?"

She snatched out the canister and aimed it at him. "Get away from me!"

Another vehicle skidded to a stop right next to the man whose demeanor had abruptly changed from amused to threatening.

Five full seconds passed before Lacy recognized the vehicle as Rick Summers's truck. He stormed around the front of his truck and stopped toe to toe with the brute of a man who'd turned to face the newcomer. "Is there a problem here, Thompson?"

Thompson? Where had she heard that name before?

"Oh, no, Chief," said the man, Thompson, as he offered up his hands in a show of nothing to hide. "I just wanted to let the lady know she had a broken taillight before she got herself a ticket." He gestured to the rear of Lacy's vehicle. "I know how you and your deputies despise folks who don't take proper care of their vehicles, especially when it comes to driving safety."

Lacy stared at the taillight. How the devil had that

happened? She walked over to it and touched the broken red cover.

"I'd suggest," Rick said, "that you be on your way, and I don't want to hear of you bothering this lady again."

Thompson laughed. "Don't worry, Chief. I'm sure you can take good care of her."

Lacy stared at the two men as the odd exchange played out. There was no love lost between these two. She shuddered inwardly at the idea that maybe she'd made a serious mistake confronting the man. As she watched him get into his past-its-prime Camaro, back up and then pull around Rick's truck, her knees went suddenly weak. What had she been thinking? She dropped the can back into her purse and leaned against the rear of her Explorer.

"What the hell was going through your head when you pulled over and got out of your vehicle like that?"

"I…" She blinked and felt as if maybe she'd better sit down. "I don't know. I just thought that he…" Realization dawned with the weight of a boulder on her chest. She couldn't tell him why. Then she'd have to explain about the calls, and he would know she had something to hide.

He lifted a skeptical eyebrow. "Seems to me you weren't thinking."

She sucked in a much-needed breath. He was right. She hadn't been thinking, not rationally anyway. "You're right. It was a stupid idea."

Rick set his hands on his hips and made a sound of disbelief. "I don't believe it. You just said I was right."

Lacy straightened, still felt a little shaky but not as much as before. "Don't let it go to your head, it was a one-time thing."

He turned serious so abruptly that she felt herself holding her breath all over again.

"You need to be careful, Lacy," he warned softly. "I still don't know what you and your friends are up to, but every instinct tells me that you're skating on very thin ice. Bent Thompson is not a nice guy. He's dangerous. He's already served two sentences for felonious assault. I don't want you to be the reason he has to serve a third one."

The fluttering sensation in her chest acted as an alarm. She was letting her guard down, wanting to trust him, but she couldn't. As much as she wanted to believe he might still have feelings for her, the idea was foolish. Fifteen years was a long time and he was the chief of police. Solving a murder would be far more important to him than that one night they'd shared so long ago.

"Thank you for your assistance." She squared her shoulders and lifted her chin in defiance of all the softer emotions that seemed determined to make her weak.

When she would have turned to go, he said, "Don't forget to get that taillight repaired."

Something about the way he issued that last warning or maybe the epiphany suddenly clicked in her mind, but she wheeled back around to face him. "You were following me." Saying the words out loud only reinforced the sudden realization that she was absolutely right. He had been following her.

He sauntered up to her, the white shirt looking crisp and professional with the nice, blue tie. Even the well-worn jeans didn't detract from the polished look. It would have helped tremendously if he hadn't aged so damned well. Even more handsome than she remembered, the hot teenager she'd been unable to resist had grown into an equally hot man. The few lines he'd earned around his eyes and mouth merely added to his sex appeal.

Lacy felt her resistance melting just like all those years ago, but she couldn't let him close this time. Too much was at stake.

"I won't bother denying the charge. I'm watching you and your friends. It's my job. A man is dead and I want to know how that came to be. My instincts are still telling me that you know something, Lacy. I need to know what it is."

Fury and maybe a little disappointment swiftly overrode the softer emotions. "You were wrong, Summers," she shot back. "It's not Thompson I need to be worried about, it's you."

She turned her back on him and got into her vehicle. There was nothing else to say. He'd made up his mind about her and she wasn't about to get caught up in the temptation he offered.

As much as she wanted to trust someone, to lean on someone strong, she couldn't trust anyone…not even her friends.

# Chapter 9

Kira brought Melinda. Cassidy selected the place. The Goose Pond Your Time Spa was the only one of its kind in the whole county. It offered the same luxurious options as full-service spas found in much larger cities. The latest in a relaxing sauna, with a number of smaller private rooms rather than one large one, was a favorite of clients, according to the counselor who'd waited on them.

Wrapped in towels and the door closed tightly on their private, steamy sanctuary, there was no way anyone could overhear their conversation and, considering the time of day, they weren't likely to be interrupted by someone mistakenly entering their reserved space.

For the first few minutes after they arrived, they simply relaxed on the ergonomically designed redwood benches and enjoyed the sweltering heat. Lacy wondered if the others were afraid of what she might have to tell them now. She definitely didn't look forward to it. Especially the part about Rick still following her.

Maybe she would keep that part to herself, but the call she couldn't stay quiet about that. It was a definite threat against all of them.

Lacy leaned her head against the damp redwood and drew in a bracing breath. Might as well get this over with. "I received another call last night."

Melinda's abrupt inhalation of balmy air underscored the blunt, however reluctant, statement.

"When?" Kira demanded, her eyes round with worry.

Lacy had expected that question from Cassidy. That their usual leader lay back and listened without saying anything at all set Lacy on edge.

"Last night. Around nine or so."

Confusion lined Kira's brow, but something else, suspicion perhaps, narrowed her gaze. "You didn't mention it this morning when I got to Melinda's."

"Was it the same caller?"

Lacy's gaze connected with Cassidy's. This line of questioning was what Lacy had expected. That Cassidy kept her thoughts on the announcement so completely unreadable, Lacy had not anticipated fully. This troubled her. She just couldn't understand how this wall had formed between them, but there it was, as plain as day.

She nodded. "The same voice." She thought about the voice for a moment. "The sound is distorted, so I still can't tell if it's a woman or a man."

"What did this person have to say?"

Lacy would have given anything not to be the cause of the distress evident on Melinda's face as she asked that question. Lacy took a deep breath and gave her the answer that none of them would want to hear. "He or she said, 'I know your secret, Lacy, and you're all going to regret what you did.'"

"I don't understand," Kira challenged, her expression waffling between confused and accusatory. "Why is Lacy the only one receiving these calls?"

Now there was something Lacy definitely hadn't expected. Was this a contest? Before she could say as much, Cassidy took the offense a step farther, "That's an excellent question."

Tension traveled outward along Lacy's limbs, making the act of remaining seated almost impossible. What the hell were they trying to say? "I don't understand this." She stood, unable to help herself, arms crossed over her chest, and glared at first one supposed friend and then the other. "What are you two insinuating? It's not my fault some freak is calling me with these crazy warnings. I didn't ask for this." She tried her level best to calm down, but she wasn't doing a very good job at all.

"Wait." Melinda pushed up to a standing position, to align herself with Lacy. "She's right. This isn't her fault." She pointed a scolding look at first Cassidy and then Kira. "What happened to being united? To protecting each other? When did Lacy become the enemy?"

"She's not the enemy," Cassidy clarified with blatant impatience, as if they should understand perfectly how she intended her every word and gesture. She motioned for Melinda and Lacy to sit. "We're all overreacting just a little." She said the last with a tad of remorse in her tone. "You're right, Lacy, this isn't your fault."

Feeling vindicated to some degree, Lacy resumed her seat. Melinda did the same.

"Let's analyze this mystery and see what we can come up with," their fearless leader offered.

"Sounds reasonable," Kira added, with a hopeful look in Lacy's direction. "I'm sorry if I jumped down your throat with everybody else. I guess I'm just a little edgy."

Lacy relaxed considerably. She should have known her friends wouldn't turn on her. They were just worried, that's all. So was she. They were all under a tremendous amount of stress here. Stress did things to people, made them act out in ways they generally wouldn't dream of doing. Christmas Eve ten years ago was indisputable proof of that.

"In my estimation," Cassidy continued, "the most likely candidate is Summers." Before Lacy could argue that assessment, Cassidy raised a hand to stall her. "I know we all think he's a nice guy, but he has the most to gain by intimidating one of us into talking."

"But," Melinda cut in, "didn't you say that's illegal? I just don't believe Rick would go that far. He's much too honorable."

It made Lacy feel better somehow to hear that Melinda considered Rick an honorable man. Not that Lacy had doubted it, but she liked hearing it. God, she was so totally screwed up right now. Rick, no matter how honorable, was the enemy. She had to remember that.

"Maybe so," Cassidy allowed, "but, for now, he's the only suspect we've got."

Suspect? Jesus. Lacy couldn't go there where Rick was concerned. He was too proud to lower himself to that level. He might be the enemy in a manner of speaking, she admitted once more, but she didn't believe he would cross the kind of line Cassidy was suggesting. The man, Thompson, who'd followed her that morning—now there was a different story.

"There may be someone else." The others leaned forward in anticipation of Lacy's words. "This morning I went to the library just to review the articles from around the time Charles…died and then again around the time of the memorial service." She didn't miss the subtle change in Cassidy's expression. She didn't like what Lacy had done. "I wanted to see if we were mentioned in any of the articles," she ad-libbed, in hopes of smoothing over her actions. "I considered that maybe that's how this caller connected us to…to the case." She managed a wan smile for Melinda. "Other than the obvious one, of course." It wasn't exactly a lie. She had toyed with the idea that perhaps their closeness to Melinda was the reason for the calls. A con artist would know who to glom onto in a situation like this.

"Did you find anything?" The anticipation in Kira's voice indicated just how hopeful she was that the answer would be that simple.

Lacy shook her head. "No. Sorry. But I did notice this man watching me." Another subtle shift in Cassidy's demeanor accompanied that announcement. "I got nervous considering why we're here." She managed a dry laugh. "I even thought maybe I was just being paranoid. With you guys on my case, I'm feeling a little oversensitive."

"I'm sorry, Lace." Kira offered again as she draped her arm around Lacy's shoulders and gave her a hug. "You know we love you."

Lacy pushed a smile into place with a little more ease this time. "Thanks. I love you guys, too." She took a deep breath and went on. "Anyway, I took a long, winding route to Melinda's street, thinking I would see if he was actually following me or if it was my imagination."

"And?" Cassidy prompted.

"He was definitely following me. The idea kind of made me angry so I stopped in the middle of the street, leaving him no choice but to stop, as well."

The girls started to talk at once then.

"Have you lost your mind?" This from Cassidy.

"My God, Lacy, he could have hurt you!" Melinda chimed in as Kira huffed, "We're going to have to start babysitting you, too." This garnered Kira an annoyed look from Melinda, to whom she apologized profusely.

"I know it was foolish, but I was mad as hell at the idea that he could be the one trying to scare me."

"Obviously you survived the encounter." Cassidy tugged at her towel. "What did your mystery man have to say for himself."

Part of her wanted to tell them the truth, but she was certain it wouldn't bode well and she didn't have it in her to cause more of those accusing looks. "He claimed he was following me to tell me I had a broken taillight."

"You have a broken taillight?" Melinda looked surprised. Maybe because Lacy's car was so new.

"As a matter of fact, I do. Or did. I had it repaired this afternoon. I don't know how it happened, but I do know when. Sometime this morning, while I was in the library."

"That's pretty specific," Cassidy countered. "How can you be so sure that's when it happened? Most of us don't notice things like that."

Any other time that assessment from Cassidy would be right. But Lacy had an explanation. "Because I put my overnight bag in the back when I left Melinda's this morning and I took it out at my parents' house. The taillight wasn't broken then. I went straight from there to the library."

"But that doesn't mean he did it...does it?" Kira looked from Lacy to Cassidy and back.

"You saw him watching you inside the library, right?"

Lacy nodded an affirmative to Cassidy's question.

"I'd say you're right. He probably broke it so if you noticed him and maybe called the police he'd have an excuse. This is a small enough town that giving a description of his car could have gotten him questioned at the very least."

"You have no idea who he was?"

Lacy shifted her attention to Melinda who appeared absolutely horrified with the whole account. "Bent Thompson." She couldn't tell the rest, that according to Rick Summers he was a dangerous man.

"Bent Thompson..." Cassidy echoed thoughtfully.

Melinda pressed a hand to her chest and made a sound of distress deep in her throat, dragging everyone's attention to her. "You're absolutely certain it was Bent Thompson?"

Lacy nodded. "Positive. Do you know him?"

Melinda shook her head. "But his name came up in the investigation when Charles was first listed as...missing. I'll never forget it."

"Came up how?" Cassidy wanted to know.

"Chief Taylor asked me several times if I knew the name. He even showed me a picture of him, but I'd didn't recognize him. He was older than us. We wouldn't have gone to school with him."

Bent Thompson was at least ten years older than they were and definitely not from the same neighborhood or church. There was no reason any of them would have known him.

"Did Chief Taylor ever indicate to you that he considered Thompson a suspect?" Cassidy was sitting up straighter now.

"I think he was maybe one of many on the chief's list," Melinda granted, "but I found out later that he was only considered a suspect because he disappeared about the same time Charles did."

Again Lacy kept the details about Bent Thompson to herself. He'd disappeared all right. To jail, at least shortly after that time. But she couldn't mention that fact without bringing up Rick.

"And now he's back," Kira suggested. "Ironic, don't you think?"

Cassidy studied each of them in turn. "But we all know what happened to Charles. The question is, what does this guy know and what does he want?"

Lacy chewed her lower lip a second. "He didn't mention wanting anything." *You just don't know what you've gotten yourself in the middle of, do you, Miss Oliver?* "He did say something about me not knowing what I'd gotten myself in the middle of."

The silence that followed combined with the humid air made breathing nearly impossible.

"He can't know anything," Cassidy argued, her tone not nearly so certain as usual.

"That night," Lacy began with a covert glance in Melinda's direction, "when I went back up to check the room...after...after Charles was already in the car, I got this feeling like someone was watching me. Could this Thompson guy have been hiding in the house? Could he have killed Charles?" The impact of that possibility hit her full force, the complete ramifications penetrating just then.

Cassidy and Kira exchanged a secretive look. "We

all know who killed Charles," Cassidy said calmly. "We did. End of story. We killed him, and we disposed of the body. Trying to pin it on someone else isn't going to make this investigation go away."

The fury Lacy had hoped she wouldn't have to feel again came rushing back. "Haven't you even once considered another possibility? What if someone else killed him? Who says one of us did it? Just because we talked about it the night before when we'd had too much to drink? Be reasonable. Someone else could have done it! Right?" She looked to Melinda for confirmation. Lacy felt taken aback by the noncommittal mask her best friend wore.

"We agreed not to go there, Lace. We're all equally guilty." The stern lines of Cassidy's face spoke volumes regarding her staunch stand on the matter.

This was insane. Lacy threw her hands up. "Whatever. I'm tired of fighting you guys on this." She leaned back against the sweaty wood wall and ordered her raging temper to slow its rush toward outright, white-hot fury.

"I guess it's possible this man could have been doing some sort of business with Charles," Kira offered, guilt probably prompting her. "Maybe he found him dead, heard us come in and hid somewhere in the house. Maybe that's what happened to the missing money and why you felt like someone was watching you. Maybe Bent Thompson was."

"And maybe the tooth fairy dropped in that afternoon as well," Cassidy challenged impatiently. "We're going down a no return street here, ladies. The next thing you know we'll start arguing and be at each other's throats worse than we already are. We need to let this thing die a natural death. There is no evidence. Whoever this Thompson creep is, he's probably attempting to set us up for some sort of blackmail scam. He likely knows we're friends of Melinda's and he's guessing the rest." She leveled her gaze on Lacy. "If he's even your caller. We don't know that for sure. We're only going to dig ourselves a hole if we keep stirring the stink. We need to back off…let it play out."

"She's right."

Startled to hear those words from Melinda, Lacy's attention swung to her. Melinda cautiously kept hidden whatever she felt, didn't let a thing show on her face or in her eyes. It didn't make sense. But, none of this did.

"What does Lacy do if Bent Thompson keeps following her?" Kira wanted to know. "Or if he starts following one of us? What're we supposed to do?"

"We go to the police and report it like any other citizen. We behave as if we're just like anybody else in this. Outraged, indignant."

Cassidy didn't need to worry about that part. The chief of police already knew about the incident.

That was where the conversation died. Cassidy and Melinda didn't want to discuss it anymore and Kira assented to their wishes. Lacy didn't see the point in pushing the issue. Cassidy had made up her mind. And, apparently, so had Melinda. Lacy tried her best not to feel betrayed by Melinda's actions, but she couldn't help it.

By the time they'd showered and dressed, the chitchat had turned to lighter subjects. Melinda talked on and on about her daughter. She didn't mention the tense conversation that had taken place between her and Chuckie. The only awkward moment had come when Kira's cell rang with one call after the other from her fiancé, Brian.

Despite the lingering feelings of betrayal, Lacy did

feel somewhat more relaxed when they left the spa. Unfortunately, the slight relief was short-lived.

Although reporters from all over the country had flocked to Ashland, so far they hadn't run into any real trouble. The police had pretty much kept them away from Melinda's street and since the group of them hadn't ventured out that much, there had been no incidents with the media.

But today was apparently going to be a bad one all the way around.

The instant they walked out onto the sidewalk, flashbulbs started to snap. A reporter, conservatively dressed in a gray suit but with no manners whatsoever, rushed up to Melinda and demanded, "How does it feel to know that the world is finally aware that you killed your husband?"

Cassidy pushed him out of Melinda's face. "You may direct your questions to Ms. Ashland's attorney, sir," she said firmly.

"Still showing your masculine side, are you, Miss Collins?"

Lacy had always been certain she would never live to see anything rattle Cassidy Collins. Cassidy was always cool, under any and all circumstances. But just then, it was as if an old demon, one far too familiar, had burst, full throttle, back into her life. She froze with the impact of it. No matter that alternate lifestyles were accepted every day in other places, the same could not be said here.

"Let's go, Cass." Lacy grabbed her by the arm. "We don't need to listen to this jerk."

"And what about you, Miss Jackson? Does your fiancé in New York know about your old secret lover here in Ashland?"

The look of utter devastation on Kira's face made Lacy want to lash out at the damned man.

"I've called the police!"

The voice was familiar, but just then Lacy was too damned angry to analyze it.

"Come on, ladies," the ambitious bastard taunted, "you can't give me just one sound bite?"

"I'll give you something," Lacy snapped. "Go to hell!"

"Miss Oliver, come inside."

A hand tugged at Lacy. She shifted her attention from the haughty reporter just long enough to identify Renae Rossman attempting to drag her toward a door to a boutique or store of some sort.

"Please," Renae urged. "All of you, come inside until Chief Summers gets here."

The reporter shouted another remark or two to their backs but somehow they all managed to get inside the shop without further incident.

"Melinda, are you all right?" Renae practically enveloped Melinda in her arms. "Shall I call Gloria or the senator to come pick you up?"

"No." With an adamant jerk of her head side to side, Melinda eased away from the woman. "Really, I'm fine. We're all fine."

Renae patted her arm as if she hadn't noticed the way Melinda recoiled from her. "This is precisely why Gloria felt Chelsea would be better protected with her."

"This is the first time anything like this has happened," Lacy said, unable to keep a defensive tone out of her voice.

Blue lights throbbed outside and for a moment the conversation inside lulled as they watched Rick chase away the annoying reporter and his cameraman.

When he'd taken care of the nuisance, Rick opened

the door just far enough to stick his head inside the shop. "Everyone all right in here?"

Renae moved to the door. "We're fine now, Chief. Thank you so much for your timely response."

He and Renae chatted for a moment more, but Lacy was too busy visually examining Rick's profile to pay decent attention. As he withdrew from the shop entrance his gaze collided with Lacy's. The draw was so strong, so compelling, it made her ache inside.

She had to find a way to sever the connection, which appeared to be growing stronger every day.

When he'd gone, Renae turned back to them. "Can I get you something to drink, ladies? You look parched."

No one bothered to say that it might be because they had just spent the better part of an hour in a steamy sauna and then endured the public ridicule of a ruthless media shark.

When their host had guided them to a lovely seating area done in Victorian pinks and whites, she explained, as she served the finest bottled water from the Fiji Mountains, how she came to be the owner and manager of Finer Things.

Since she and Wes, her filthy-rich husband, had never had children, he'd purchased this lovely boutique for her where she sold the finer things, like delicate, decorative women's handkerchiefs and one-of-a-kind vases, Italian perfume bottles, and handwoven table-cloths. The shop couldn't get that much business, not in a small town like Ashland, Lacy surmised. She supposed that whether the small business made a profit or not wasn't the point. Obviously the exclusive shop kept Wes Rossman's much younger, trophy wife occupied.

As she sat there, Lacy realized that so many of the

people she'd known growing up here were not exactly what they'd seemed when she'd admired them as a child. What was it about this place that had nurtured such hidden unpleasantness in so many lives?

Something in the water? She stared at the bottle in her hand. Good thing this came from far, far away. She just wasn't sure how safe it would be to let anything about the place where she'd grown up get too far beneath her skin.

# Chapter 10

Lacy sat in her Explorer in the dark outside her parents' home. She should go inside—it was past eight already—maybe scrounge up something for dinner.

Rick had been following her again. She'd spotted his truck around town twice after she and the girls had left Finer Things. She'd thought about going back to the library, but she doubted there was anything left to be learned from the archives of Ashland's only newspaper. Going back to see Mr. Carter again would be pointless.

She'd even thought about attempting to talk to one or all of Pamela Carter's sisters, but that could be a mistake. The last thing she wanted to do was stir up more tales about the old affair between Pamela and Charles. Melinda didn't need any more pain in her life. And gossip flew at the speed of light around a place this size.

Approaching Nigel Canton, Charles's former

partner, was out of the question. That left no one on her too-short list. Well, except for Bent Thompson, whom she'd added after what Melinda said about how Chief Taylor had questioned her about him. But even Lacy wasn't brave enough to approach a man like Thompson alone. Rick had warned her that he was dangerous. She'd gotten a taste of just how intimidating he could be when he'd followed her this morning.

No. She wasn't stupid. If she intended to look up Bent Thompson, she needed to do so with at least one support person. Backup, so to speak.

Cassidy was with Melinda tonight…that meant Kira was available. Like Lacy, she hadn't lived in Ashland in so long she didn't really know anyone to hang out with. Lacy wondered if Kira had stayed away all these years for the same reason she had. She wondered what the journalist had meant when he'd implied Kira had had a secret lover. Maybe, like Lacy, she'd kept a secret of her own.

The only way to find out if Kira was at home and willing to do a little investigating off Cassidy's radar was to drive to her house and ask her. That wasn't something Lacy cared to discuss over the telephone. She needed to see Kira's face during the discussion to really know if she was taking it the way Lacy meant it.

She started her Explorer and backed out of the driveway. No time like the present. Besides, she just wasn't ready to go in for the night. Not and risk receiving another one of those creepy calls.

Part of her couldn't help wondering, as did the others, why she was the only one getting the bizarre calls. She refused to believe Rick would stoop to those kinds of methods and apparently Melinda felt the same way.

But who knew?

Who could have been watching them that night?

She heaved a weary breath. Maybe nobody.

The possibility that the caller could be someone hired by Melinda's in-laws abruptly bobbed to the surface of all the other confusing thoughts churning in Lacy's head. But why would they call her? The tactic would be much more effective if they called Melinda.

If she gave the Ashlands any credit at all, she would agree with Renae's steadfast assurance that both Gloria and Charles, Senior, were intensely worried about Melinda and the children, that the two would do anything to put this horrible nightmare behind them. But Lacy had a hard time believing that the Ashlands were worried about anyone but themselves. As they had chatted in Renae's elegant shop, she'd gone on and on about what fine folks the Ashlands were. She spoke almost reverently of Charles, Senior, and how he'd even been talking about passing on the opportunity to run for vice president because of the painful family tragedy.

Lacy wondered if maybe Gloria should be wary of her beautiful, considerably younger, friend. Maybe one rich old man wasn't enough for Renae.

Or maybe she'd gotten way too cynical, Lacy mused.

She braked, then eased into the driveway of Kira's childhood home. The house stood two-and-a-half stories. A grand reproduction of antebellum splendor. Everything about the property, from the prestigious home to the wrought-iron fence and the well-groomed landscape, spoke of money and family pride.

Like Lacy and Cassidy, Kira had never wanted for anything. It felt so strange that the three of them, and even Melinda for the most part despite her family's financial woes those last two years of high school, could have had so much and still felt compelled to commit a crime so heinous and desperate. She shuddered at the idea.

None of them had been or were alcoholics, drug addicts, or financially troubled at the time of the crime. It just didn't make sense that they could have made such a tremendous error in judgment, all in the blink of an eye. But they had been young. She had to take that reality into consideration.

Lacy got out of her car and walked slowly up to the sprawling front veranda. She'd told herself over and over not to dwell on what she couldn't change. Focusing on finding the truth was a far more purposeful use of energy.

But somehow that ugly reality just kept creeping back into her thoughts. Maybe because she ran into Rick every time she turned around, proving Cassidy's and her theory that he was watching her, had something to do with her inability to stay focused.

Too bad the reality of why he was so interested in her didn't change the building momentum of her craving for him on a wholly physical level.

Clearly she was on the path of another of those grievous errors in judgment.

Lacy knocked on the door and hoped she wasn't interrupting a late dinner or maybe a movie.

The door opened right away and Kira's mother beamed a broad smile the second her eyes told her who the unexpected late-evening arrival was. "Lacy!" She engulfed Lacy in her arms. "It's wonderful to see you." Mrs. Jackson drew back. "Won't you come in?"

Lacy summoned a smile. "It's good to see you, too, Mrs. Jackson. Is Kira home?"

Her hand fluttered to her cheeks. "Oh, my, this feels like old times." Then she patted Lacy's arm. "You girls were always rushing off somewhere. I'm so sorry, but Kira's out. Would you like me to have her call you when she gets home? You have her cell number, don't you? I'm sure she wouldn't mind your calling."

"Sure. I'll give her a call or catch her later." Lacy backed up a step. "Thanks, Mrs. Jackson. Have a nice night."

Kira's mom waved until Lacy had settled behind the wheel of her car then closed the door, leaving Lacy in near darkness. The decorative lighting around the landscape was subtle, definitely not for security purposes. But that was the norm. Folks in Ashland expected the best out of others, even when they shouldn't or perhaps didn't practice the ideal themselves. Lacy dug around in her purse until she found her cell and opened it to punch in Kira's number, but an arriving vehicle stopped her.

The car didn't pull fully into the driveway as Lacy had done, instead it remained on the street. Lacy powered down her window in anticipation of Kira's stride up the driveway. She couldn't tell who else was in the car, but it wasn't Kira's rental. The rented sedan sat in the driveway next to where Lacy had parked.

The passenger-side door of the vehicle opened and Kira got out. Lacy frowned as she watched her friend's determined stride. She appeared furious or in a hurry to get away from something.

…or someone.

Just when Lacy would have called out to Kira, the driver's-side door of the car opened and someone else got out. He caught up with Kira about halfway up the driveway. Though the lighting, including that provided by the almost nonexistent moon, was sparse, she could see that it was a man.

Bradley Brewer.

Confusion disabled Lacy's ability to draw in her next breath. That same confusion kept her focus nailed to the couple standing less than thirty feet from where she sat. She had never been more thankful for her vehicle's dark blue color. Obviously neither Kira nor Brad had noticed her.

"I've waited a long time for you to come back, Kira." Brad took her by the arms and pulled her closer. "Don't pretend it never mattered."

"I have to go." Kira said the words, but she made no move to pull away from him.

"When I heard you'd gotten engaged…" He looked away a moment. "I almost came up there…I didn't—"

"My life is in New York now. Nothing you say is going to change that." Her voice was firmer, her chin held higher.

Lacy listened, somewhere between startled and offended, as the two went on this way for two or three minutes more. She found it funny that her friend didn't mention her fiancé. And why hadn't Kira ever told anyone about this situation with Brad? Was he her secret lover from the past? Or maybe she had told the others. Lacy silently railed at herself for going down that paranoid path again. She had to stop thinking the worst of her friends. No one was out to get her. She was still part of the group. Like sisters. They always had been, always would be. Charles's murder had simply put a strain on their friendship, but they were all here, together, for each other…just like always. Besides, how could she hold this against Kira when she was guilty of such a similar offense?

"You know how I feel, Kira."

With that, Brad released her and walked away. He had started his car and driven off into the night before

Kira moved. Lacy sat there in stunned silence until Kira turned and saw her.

She started slowly toward Lacy's vehicle then. "Lacy, I didn't—"

That she fell abruptly silent told Lacy that she'd just realized her exchange with Brad had been overheard.

Lacy got out of her vehicle and closed the door. "I didn't mean to eavesdrop. Your mother said you weren't home and I was about to leave when you and…" She cleared her throat. "Anyway, I thought we could talk."

Kira blinked a couple of times and looked as if she wasn't sure what to do.

The awkwardness lengthened between them and Lacy understood that if she didn't make a move to break the tension it might not happen. Getting past the issue that Lacy had just overheard a private conversation had to be the first order of business. "I don't want to do anything behind anyone's back," she began hesitantly, "but I really think I need to check out this Bent Thompson guy and I don't feel quite prepared to do it alone."

Kira's uncertainty morphed instantly into a mixture of impatience and irritation. She held up both hands in a signal to stop. "You know what Cassidy said. Anything we do will only draw more attention to us." She set her hands on her hips then and copped the usual attitude. "Why are you doing this, Lacy? We all know what happened to Charles. If we're smart, we'll keep our heads on straight until this investigation dies and then we'll get on with our lives. I don't know about you, but I don't want to end up in prison."

Lacy forced back the words she wanted to toss at her friend. Why didn't anyone want to know what had really happened? Instead, she took a breath and spoke as reasonably as she could. "I know Cassidy's right about a lot of things, but this just feels wrong." She offered her hands, palms up. Why didn't anyone get it? "We need to find out what really happened. I'm not so sure any of us killed him. I'm beginning to believe—"

"Just stop it!" The harshness of Kira's words was belied by the unsteadiness of her tone. "I don't want to talk about this. We all know what happened. We're all in this together."

What exactly was she afraid to say? There was something she was leaving out...Lacy could feel it.

"I don't know what happened," Lacy threw back at her. "Why don't you tell me? Do you know who actually killed Charles?" Anger infused her tone, making her come off as hostile rather than desperate and hurt, which was what she really felt.

"You, of all people," Kira snapped, her own anger overpowering all other emotion, "should know."

When she would have walked away, Lacy stopped her. "What does that mean?" When Kira faced her once more, Lacy goaded her friend, "Are you insinuating that I killed Charles?"

Kira closed her eyes a moment and drew in a deep breath. When she opened them once more, she said, "We all killed him, Lacy. Equally guilty. Let's not do this, okay?"

As much as she wanted to stay fired up, to force Kira to say the words, Lacy couldn't bring herself to do it. Some part of her realized that if she pushed the issue, she and Kira would cross a line into territory from which there was no return. Charles Ashland, Junior, had already cost all of them far more than the bastard was worth.

"Maybe I'm the one who's wrong," Lacy admitted. "I guess I can't get past the guilt."

Kira placed her left hand on the one clutching her

right arm. "Lace, this will eventually be over. All we have to do is stay calm and listen to Cassidy. She knows what's best for all of us." She laughed wearily. "She's the one with the law degree."

Maybe her friends were right. All she had to do was calm down and ride out this storm. It would pass. As horrific as it was, it would pass.

"You're right. I'm sorry." She hugged Kira. "I guess I just lost my head, what with all these calls and that weirdo following me." She drew back and smiled for the woman she'd loved since before kindergarten. "We will get through this. Cassidy always knows what's best."

Kira hooked her arm in Lacy's. "Come on. Let's go see if my mom can still make hot chocolate like she used to."

That was an offer Lacy couldn't refuse. Kira's mom had always made the greatest hot chocolate.

She visited with Kira and her mom for hours, until almost midnight. There was no reason to go home to an empty house. Or to risk getting another one of those calls.

No, the night had been far more pleasant this way, and not once had she mentioned Brad Brewer. Deputy Brad Brewer. Kira didn't talk about him, either. Just another little secret. Apparently they all had them. Who knew? Lacy had always assumed that they told one another everything, but that was a foolish assumption considering she'd never told anyone about Rick Summers.

Was it really possible to ever know everything about a person?

Maybe not.

But there was one thing Lacy knew for certain. She was finished believing the worst about the people she loved the most. She was through digging into the past in search of things she really didn't want to know.

She trusted Cassidy. This whole thing would blow over. All she had to do was be patient.

It was past midnight when the telephone rang.

Cassidy was still awake, so she answered after the first ring. Melinda had finally fallen asleep and she didn't want anything to wake her. She was a real mess. Falling apart a little more each day.

Considering how Lacy was behaving, that was not a good thing. The last thing she needed was both of them going off the deep end on her.

"Hello." Cassidy rubbed her eyes with her thumb and forefinger and hoped it wasn't bad news related to the kids. She didn't want anything else tipping Melinda closer to that edge both she and Lacy teetered on.

"Cassidy Collins?"

Cassidy felt her brow draw into a pucker. "Who is this?" The voice sounded strange, gravelly and distorted. She glanced at the caller ID: Blocked Call. Realization dawned at the same instant that the voice came across the line again.

"I'm the one who knows the truth. You're all going to regret what you did."

Cassidy smiled. This son of a bitch thought he could scare her? He was out of his mind. "I don't know who the hell you are, but this is harassment. Fair warning, as soon as I hang up I'm calling the telephone company and requesting that this number be monitored, so maybe you'd better not call again."

The silence that radiated across the line for the next three or four seconds had just about convinced her that she'd gotten through to the jerk, then he or she said,

"I've been watching all of you. I know where you are every minute of every day. I know the *truth*."

The words reverberated through Cassidy as if one of those California earthquakes she hated had just rocked Ashland, Alabama. She bit back the first response that rushed to the tip of her tongue. She knew what this person was up to. She also knew, he, she, whoever the hell, wouldn't stop until he'd gotten what he wanted. She needed to know exactly what that was.

"I know you're dying to learn my identity," the distorted voice taunted. "You don't have to say it. I'll be at Sydney's for another hour. You come in person and I'll tell you what I want…and don't worry, you'll know who I am the moment you lay eyes on me."

The click echoed in Cassidy's ears, made her jump. Her own reaction bothered her big time. She stared at the receiver until the recorded warning that the phone had been off the hook too long snapped her out of the trance of disbelief. She pushed the disconnect button and dropped the receiver back into its cradle.

Whoever this caller was, he or she appeared to know something. But that was impossible. No one could possibly know. Lacy's ridiculous suggestion that someone had been in the house besides them all those years ago flitted through Cassidy's mind but she dismissed it. Anyone who'd actually known anything would have come forward years ago. The senator had offered a huge reward. This didn't make sense.

She got up from the sofa and glanced down at herself. She'd already changed for bed, but she could slip back into her clothes. If Melinda was still sleeping she would be fine long enough for Cassidy to check this out. She knew where Sydney's was. A sleazy bar on the outskirts of town.

# An Important Message from the Editors

Dear Reader,

Because you've chosen to read one of our fine novels, we'd like to say "thank you"! And, as a special way to thank you, we're offering you a choice of two more of the books you love so well, and a surprise gift to send you – absolutely FREE!

Please enjoy them with our compliments...

*Pam Powers*

Peel off Seal and Place Inside...

FREE GIFT SEAL

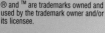

# THE EDITOR'S "THANK YOU" FREE GIFTS INCLUDE:

▶ 2 Romance OR 2 Suspense books

▶ An exciting surprise gift

**YES!** I have placed my Editor's "thank you" Free Gifts seal in the space provided at right. Please send me the 2 FREE books which I have selected, and my FREE Mystery Gift. I understand that I am under no obligation to purchase anything further, as explained on the back of this card.

PLACE FREE GIFTS SEAL HERE

## Check one:

| | ROMANCE |
|---|---|
| | 193 MDL EE3L  393 MDL EE3X |

| | SUSPENSE |
|---|---|
| | 192 MDL EE3W  392 MDL EE4A |

FIRST NAME          LAST NAME

ADDRESS

APT.#          CITY

STATE/PROV.          ZIP/POSTAL CODE

▶ DETACH AND MAIL CARD TODAY! ▶

© 1998 MIRA BOOKS

(ED1-SS-06)

## The Reader Service — Here's How It Works:

Accepting your 2 free books and gift places you under no obligation to buy anything. You may keep the books and gift and return the shipping statement marked "cancel." If you do not cancel, about a month later we'll send you 3 additional books and bill you just $5.24 each in the U.S., or $5.74 each in Canada, plus 25¢ shipping & handling per book and applicable taxes if any.* That's the complete price and — compared to cover prices starting from $5.99 each in the U.S. and $6.99 each in Canada — it's quite a bargain! You may cancel at any time, but if you choose to continue, every month we'll send you 3 more books, which you may either purchase at the discount price or return to us and cancel your subscription.

*Terms and prices subject to change without notice. Sales tax applicable in N.Y. Canadian residents will be charged applicable provincial taxes and GST.

If offer card is missing write to: The Reader Service, 3010 Walden Ave., P.O. Box 1867, Buffalo, NY 14240-1867

NO POSTAGE
NECESSARY
IF MAILED
IN THE
UNITED STATES

## BUSINESS REPLY MAIL

FIRST-CLASS MAIL    PERMIT NO. 717-003    BUFFALO, NY

POSTAGE WILL BE PAID BY ADDRESSEE

THE READER SERVICE
3010 WALDEN AVE
PO BOX 1341
BUFFALO NY 14240-8571

She shouldn't. Dammit. She shook her head. This was not the move she needed to make. What she needed to do was call Lacy and Kira and demand to know who they had told.

Fury whipped through Cassidy. As much as she loved her friends, it annoyed her that they couldn't be stronger. Like her. No matter what happened, she always kept her composure.

Realizing that you were a lesbian at age thirteen in small-town Alabama definitely toughened a girl up. Cassidy shook off that thought. She wasn't going there. She'd left all those feelings behind when she'd gone off to college fifteen years ago. She'd outgrown that kind of small-minded thinking. Being home again wasn't going to drag her back into redneck mentality.

A new burst of fury erupted inside her. If this dirtbag wanted to play hardball, Cassidy would show him how it was done. Blackmail was a crime. She would just have to call this smart-ass's bluff. It could be that lowlife Bent Thompson who had followed Lacy that morning. Well, she knew how to deal with deadbeats looking to make a buck.

Cassidy tugged on her clothes before checking on Melinda just to be sure she was still sleeping. She considered leaving her a note, but this wasn't going to take long. As soon as she set this jerk straight she'd be back and the freaky calls would stop.

As tough as she was, Cassidy had never in her entire life taken foolish risks. She checked her purse to make sure the handy, compact .9mm she carried was where it should be. She smiled. A girl should always hedge her bets. No matter where she traveled, no matter the airline hassles, she always carried her weapon. She was licensed and trained in how to use it.

She carefully closed and locked the front door behind her and walked briskly down to her rented sedan. She depressed the unlock button on the remote and slid into the driver's seat. After shoving the keys into the ignition, she fished her weapon out of her purse and placed it on the seat beside her. She was ready.

As she reached for the gearshift to put the car into Reverse, she automatically glanced into the rearview mirror. The face reflected in there startled her at first, then recognition flared. Realization abruptly dawned but it was too late to change her fate.

## Chapter 11

Half the night passed with Lacy just lying there wishing she could sleep another hour, another minute. But she'd awakened well before dawn and that had been the end of any possibility of rest. Her brain simply refused to stay shut down.

She'd played yesterday's events over and over. The call the night before, the man—Bent Thompson—following her, and then that hateful reporter Renae Rossman had rescued them from.

Closing her eyes, she allowed Rick's words and the way he'd looked at her when he'd ushered that reporter away to filter through her mind once more. He'd warned her about Bent Thompson. As prepared as she had been to look into who the guy was and why he might be following her around, she couldn't deny being a little afraid.

Thank God, Kira had talked some sense into her. She'd expertly avoided the subject of her and Deputy

Brad Brewer and, for now, that was okay. From the way Brad had spoken to her, Lacy had a sneaking suspicion that the two had a secret similar to the one she kept to herself where Rick Summers was concerned.

Lacy closed her eyes again and let the past seep into her thoughts. She knew it wasn't smart, but she just couldn't pretend it hadn't happened.

She'd first noticed Rick when she was a freshman and he was a sophomore. Something had happened between his final year in junior high, where she'd last seen him, and her first day of high school. He'd gotten far taller. His shoulders had widened considerably. He'd looked strong and incredibly handsome…too handsome to ignore. His face had taken on those lean, chiseled manly qualities that marked the guys who would grow up to have their choice in women. The strangest part of all, she realized now, was that he hadn't seemed to recognize his own power over the opposite sex. Rick Summers had been quiet and studious. Not at all the sort of guy one would expect with a build and look like that.

Maybe that was why she'd been so damned attracted to him. She'd watched him every chance she got. The only class they'd ever had together in high school had been art and that was the only opportunity she'd needed. She'd taken the seat next to him before anyone else could and it was in that room with the smell of oil paints and prepared canvases surrounding them that desire had exploded like an angry volcano. Every accidental touch, every stolen glance had played a part.

They'd lived in two different worlds. She'd enjoyed the forbidden fantasy, but the rules of society had kept her from going there. Rick worked at a supermarket after school while she went to cheerleading practice. He drove an old beat-up truck while she drove the sleek convertible two-seater her father had purchased for her. She attended all the right parties, he didn't. It was as simple and as complicated as that.

But the year he graduated, the summer before she started her senior year, she knew she couldn't let him get away without tasting those amazing lips…touching that awesome body just once. Rick Summers, she had decided, would be the one to make a woman out of her. She was sick to death of being the good girl who wasn't having any of the fun all her friends appeared to be enjoying.

She and Rick had made love.

And nothing else she'd ever experienced had even come close to matching the experience.

That night had cost her far more than she'd imagined was possible to lose during the course of a single sexual interlude. He'd been her only lover for several more years to come.

Lacy threw the covers back and sat up. She hugged her knees to her chest and ordered her traitorous body to relax. Need hummed inside her. Right now, the way she was feeling, she would love to feel those strong arms around her again. Would love to feel the weight of his lean body pressing down against hers.

But that would be such a huge mistake. The murder investigation aside, she had burned that bridge long ago. He didn't have to spell it out for her to know that she'd hurt him. Walking away had hurt her, as well, but it would never have worked. She'd known it. So had he. Maybe that was why he'd joined the army. Left. Without even saying goodbye.

Just like now, she'd seen him watching her, and she'd ignored what she had known his eyes were telling her.

She had to stop this! Determined to get her mind off the subject, she got up and went down to the kitchen.

Maybe a big breakfast would do the trick. Her appetite hadn't been that great since she'd gotten here. A little bacon and eggs and maybe some toast would be just the enticement she needed. Nothing like a protein high to get a girl going.

But, first things first. She dumped some ground beans into the brew basket and poured water into the reservoir. The rich smell of coffee drifted up from the carafe and she inhaled deeply and moaned. Oh yeah, she could use a couple of cups of joe. Her parents had always bought only the best blends of coffee beans.

She pilfered through the fridge until she rounded up the bacon and eggs.

"Damn." There wasn't any sliced bread. Her parents had likely let their fresh supplies dwindle those last few days before they left for Bermuda. She should have asked if they wanted her to restock when they called last night. She shuddered at the memory of freezing when the call had come in. The very first ring had sent sheer terror roaring through her veins. She'd been sure it would be the same caller as the night before. But the second ring and the accompanying display on the caller ID had allayed her worries. Out of Area. Not a local call.

Of course she couldn't say for sure that the threatening caller was local. The caller ID always showed "Blocked Call." She just assumed.

It was nice to hear from her parents. She missed them more than she wanted to admit sometimes. If the truth be known, she missed living near them. But she was pretty sure she could never be happy in this town again.

The telephone rang, making her jump. She closed the refrigerator door and took a deep breath before walking over to check the caller ID on the phone hanging on the wall next to the back door.

Melinda Ashland.

Lacy frowned. Melinda? A new kind of fear slid through her. She snatched up the phone. "Hello."

"Lace, is Cassidy over there?"

Lacy glanced at the clock. Six o'clock. "No. Isn't she with you?" Lacy wasn't supposed to relieve Cassidy until seven.

"She's gone. Her car is gone and she didn't leave me any sort of message. I tried her cell phone, but it's apparently not turned on or maybe she's in a dead zone." Melinda sighed. "I don't mind. You know I told you guys that I'd be fine. But this...this is weird."

Lacy bit her lip for a second and mulled over the situation. "Don't worry," she said then. "Knowing Cassidy there's a perfectly logical explanation. I'll change and come right over to wait for her to come back. Maybe she told me to come earlier and I forgot. Is that okay?"

"Don't do that, Lace. I'll be fine. Take your time."

"No." Lacy pushed a hand through her uncombed hair. "I insist. I'll go through Mickey Dee's drive-through and pick up breakfast, okay?"

"Well, okay. I'll get in the shower. If I don't answer when you get here, you know where I keep the spare key."

"Under the rabbit in the flower bed to the right of the steps."

"Yeah. I'll see you soon."

She disconnected and Lacy did the same. She stared at the phone a moment. Why would Cassidy, of all people, leave Melinda alone?

Something was wrong. Dread trickled through Lacy. Very wrong.

She hung up the phone and put what would have been her breakfast back into the refrigerator. Good thing she'd showered last night, because she sure didn't have time now.

As she headed for the stairs, she mentally ticked off the things she needed to do that morning. There were a couple of projects at the office she needed to check on. Find out what the hell had happened to Cassidy, and avoid Rick Summers and anything else related to this investigation.

She had a new attitude this morning.

No more obsessing about the past. Cassidy was right. This would all blow over. What difference did it make who had actually killed Charles? He was dead and no amount of shattered lives would bring him back.

The doorbell rang as Lacy rounded the newel post at the bottom of the stairs.

If Cassidy was at her door, she was going to give her a piece of her mind for making her worry unnecessarily. She'd already worried enough for two or three lifetimes. She was due some relief.

Lacy opened the door. The idea that she should have checked to see who was there before she did so occurred too late. Another leftover habit from small-town life. Never expect anyone bad to show up at your door.

Chief Rick Summers stood on her porch.

"Rick—" She cleared her throat. "Chief Summers, what're you doing here at this time of the morning?" She tried her best to pull the hem of her skimpy tank top down to meet the waist of the hip-hugging sweatpants she used for sleepwear. It wasn't happening. Too many washings and dryings made the soft cotton fit as though it were a size or two too small.

"I need you to get dressed and come with me, Lacy." His gaze roamed over her body but his expression remained unaffected when those gray eyes settled back on hers.

"Are my parents all right?" Fear banded around her chest. She'd just talked to them last night.

"This isn't about your parents." He stepped through the door, forcing her to move back to accommodate him. He closed the door firmly and repeated, "Get dressed. I'll explain everything on our way."

There was something in his eyes, something about the set of his mouth that told her not to argue. She nodded and rushed up the stairs to do as he'd instructed.

As she stripped off the tank, her thoughts whirled in confusion. Was this about Charles? Had they found something else? Some new evidence? Damn. She needed Cassidy.

Lacy tossed the tank to the bed and reached for the phone on her night table. She entered Cassidy's cell number and waited through unanswered rings until her call rolled over to voice mail.

"Damn." She dropped the receiver back into its cradle and quickly snapped on a bra and picked through her open suitcase for a pair of jeans and a blouse that wasn't too wrinkled.

After running a brush through her hair and quickly taking care of other essential needs, she pulled on her sneakers and returned to the foyer, where Rick waited.

He looked as if he hadn't moved, still in front of her closed door.

"Can you tell me what this is about now?" The time it had taken to change had bolstered her courage. She had a right to know why he'd shown up at her door like this.

"I turned off your coffeemaker." He opened the door to go. "There's no time to waste."

That he would completely disregard her questions ticked her off. She grabbed her purse from the hall table but didn't budge. "Tell me where we're going and I won't give you any trouble, but don't expect me to just walk out that door without knowing where I'm going."

"To the lake, Lacy." He indicated that she should precede him out the door. "We're going to the lake."

If he'd said any other place on earth she might have been able to hold her ground. She walked out of her parents' home and straight to his truck without looking back. The idea of what he might be about to show her rendered her mute, defenseless.

She heard the front door close, heard him behind her, but she didn't speak again. She climbed into his truck, snapped on her seat belt and just sat there.

Panic had taken root in the pit of her stomach. Whatever had happened, it couldn't be good. If she opened her mouth now…she might say the wrong thing and Cassidy would kill her.

He drove in silence as he made the turns she recognized all too well.

The lake that bordered her hometown covered a fairly large area but, despite the passage of ten years and the inevitable changes, she knew exactly where he was taking her. Exactly what it looked like…the image was indelibly imprinted on her soul.

As they neared their destination, she got antsy and couldn't just sit there. She had to demand some answers, didn't she? "What's this about?" she finally worked up the nerve to ask as he took the final turn onto the narrow thrust of land that had haunted her dreams for more than a decade.

"Recognize the place?" He cut a look in her direction that made her stomach turn over. "You've been here before, haven't you?"

Before Lacy could dredge up a credible response, she looked toward the place where they'd pushed Charles's

Mercedes into the water that night ten years ago. The air she'd only just drawn into her lungs evaporated, taking the oxygen she needed along with it.

Several official-looking vehicles were jammed into the narrow space that led to the water's dangerous edge. Everyone knew this part of the lake was too danger- ous…no fishing, no swimming…

A police car, a tow truck and a van—white van…with red letters spread across the side.

CORONER.

Why would the coroner return to a crime scene after the body had been taken away?

Why did they need a tow truck? And all those cops?

Her movements on autopilot, as if she were watching herself from a distance, she climbed out of the truck and walked toward the cluster of vehicles.

A morbid grinding sound came from the tow truck as it pulled a dark sedan up onto its flat hauling bed. A frown furrowed Lacy's brow, but she didn't recognize the generic-looking car.

That was good, wasn't it?

Rick's fingers abruptly curled around her upper arm and she felt herself being ushered forward, toward the group of cops standing a few yards away. As they ap- proached, the men separated, revealing what looked like a hospital gurney.

It was a gurney.

Lacy stalled.

Rick held her tighter in his powerful grip, urged her forward.

Her heart banged against the wall of her chest.

What had happened here?

She looked up at Rick but he avoided eye contact. He just kept dragging her toward the gurney, where a large black plastic bag lay. It looked almost like a garment bag, but deep down she knew what it was.

"Give us a moment."

No one argued with Rick's request. They scattered before the cold words stopped echoing in the damp morning air.

In a sort of stunned amazement Lacy watched them go. Why didn't someone tell her what was happening? She didn't understand. She wasn't supposed to be here. This couldn't involve her.

As she started to turn back to the gurney, something about the car being driven away aboard the tow truck snagged her attention.

*Budget.*

The sticker was unmistakable. The car was a rental.

Black dots floated in front of her eyes as her mind fought to deny the first thought that rushed to the front of her brain.

The metal-on-metal sound of a zipper dragged her fading attention to Rick and the gurney. She hadn't even realized he'd let go of her.

But he had.

His long-fingered hands slid the zipper down the length of the large black bag, and then he drew open a flap revealing what the bag held.

Lacy stared at the face that was as familiar as her own. Pain knifed through her heart. Her knees shook. Cassidy's skin looked grayish-blue...her eyes were open but unseeing. Ugly purplish marks marred her slender throat.

She was dead.

That couldn't be.

Every drop of blood in Lacy's body dropped to her feet and she swayed.

Strong hands clamped around her arms and shook her hard. "Look at her, Lacy! Take a good, long look. Your friend is dead and nothing you tell me now is going to bring her back, but it might just save you or one of the others from suffering this same fate."

Lacy sagged against him, unable to hold up her own weight. Her entire body alternately shook violently and stiffened as if paralysis had set in. How could this happen? No…it just couldn't be.

Rick crushed the sympathy that immediately welled inside him. He couldn't let the pain Lacy felt get to him. He had to make her understand how dangerous what she and her friends were doing really was.

"Do you want Kira or Melinda to end up like this?"

She looked up at him, her dark eyes wide in horror, her lips trembling with the need to cry. "What happened? I…I don't understand."

He turned her around to face him, but he didn't let go. He was pretty sure she'd hit the ground if he did. "I don't know what she was doing last night, but someone killed her, then drove her out here in the trunk of her own car. Sound familiar?"

Lacy's knees gave out completely then and he had to hold her against him to keep her vertical. "I don't…I have to call her folks." Her body rocked with the sobs that followed on the heels of her murmuring.

"Someone will take care of that, Lacy." He shifted her slightly and walked her back to his truck. En route he nodded for his boys to finish up the work they'd started. He helped Lacy back into the passenger seat, then rounded the hood to get back behind the wheel.

"Oh, my God." Lacy swiped at her eyes and sucked in a ragged breath. "She's dead. Cassidy's dead."

"Are you ready to talk now?"

She stared at him, pain etched across her face. "What?"

"Someone strangled her, from behind we think, loaded her into the trunk of her own car and brought her here. We haven't found any footprints or any other tire marks. Nothing. Whoever did this was careful. They didn't want to get caught—they only wanted to send a message."

Her eyes red and overflowing with emotion, Lacy blinked in confusion. "A message?"

She was practically in shock. Fat lot of good she would do him then.

"Listen to me, Lacy." He shifted in the seat to face her fully. He had to make her understand how important her cooperation was. "You and your friends know something. Whatever that knowledge is, it just cost Cassidy her life. I need you to tell me the whole truth about the day Charles died. I need you to tell me right now."

She looked at him, her eyes so round with emotion that it twisted his gut into knots of pure agony. "We're all going to regret what we did…"

The whispered words were scarcely audible, but they sent adrenaline rocketing through him. "What did you do, Lacy?" He grabbed her by the shoulders again and shook her just enough to get her attention back on him. "Tell me what you and your friends did." He had to stop this from escalating. Whatever had occurred ten years ago, someone was out for vengeance.

And then she did the last thing he needed her to do. She dissolved into tears all over again. He couldn't help himself. He had to take her into his arms and comfort her.

He'd just forced her to look at the body of her murdered friend. She was devastated. He should be ashamed. But he was desperate.

Desperate to save her from the same fate.

A knock on the window followed by, "Chief," jerked Rick's head up.

Deputy Keith Larson waited patiently outside the driver's side door. Rick powered down the window, keeping one arm firmly wrapped around Lacy as she sobbed against his chest. "Yeah, Larson, what is it?"

Larson offered his cell phone. "It's Brewer. He needs to talk to you. Something about finding human bones over at the Thackerson place."

Human bones?

Just what he needed, another frigging body—or what was left of one.

He hoped like hell this one wasn't the result of a homicide. Two murders to solve in a small town known for serene living were more than enough.

Something his grandmother always used to say suddenly came to mind out of the blue: Skeletons weren't meant to stay hidden.

# Chapter 12

"**D**efinitely human."

Rick stared at the pile of bones the coroner had been inspecting. "Any idea whether the victim was male or female or what might have been the cause of death."

Jacob Griggs scratched his head thoughtfully. "Well, I'd say this is more likely a female, judging solely by the size of some of the bones. Maybe a small male but I—"

"Chief!"

"Excuse me, Jacob." Rick left the coroner crouched over the trace sheet where the bones were scattered and walked toward the site where his two deputies, as well as a couple of forensics techs from the Birmingham lab, scratched around in the dirt. The remains had been discovered on the edge of a corn-field belonging to Lester Thackerson. The heavy rains a week back had resulted in one of old man Thack-erson's trucks becoming mired in mud up to the axle at the edge of the field. They'd had to wait until the soil dried thoroughly before attempting to pull the truck out. All the digging had unearthed more than the truck's rear tires.

"Look at this." Brewer rushed up with a plastic evidence bag containing what looked like a dirt-encrusted wallet. He tapped the bag. "Driver's license. One Pamela Sue Carter."

Tension sharpened in Rick. "Let me have a look at that." He took the bag from Brewer and studied the partially disintegrated license. Sure enough, it was Pam's. His pulse rate jumped into overdrive. "We still have to confirm that the remains are hers." He pinned Brewer with a firm warning. "Not one word of this to anyone until we have confirmation and we've notified her daddy."

"I understand."

"You find anything else?"

Brewer shook his head. "We're still sifting around and finding bits and pieces of clothing. Part of a shoe. What's left of a purse."

"All right. Just keep this quiet."

Brewer hustled off to rejoin the search. Rick shifted his attention back to the coroner, who had gathered the remains into a body bag and was preparing to leave the scene.

First Charles Ashland, Junior. Now Pam. And who the hell had killed Cassidy Collins?

Those friends of Cassidy's had been hiding something and someone knew it. But what?

Ironic, he mused, that the same heavy rains of early last week had resulted in Charles's body being found as well as Pam's. Or maybe it was just plain old fate.

Rick still felt guilty for dragging Lacy down to view her friend's body that morning, but he needed to shock her. Needed her to understand that their secret could get them killed.

There was always the chance, of course, that Cassidy's murder would turn out to be a hate crime or some other random killing, but it was just too coincidental that the murderer had brought her body to the exact spot where Ashland's body had been dumped ten years ago. She'd been locked in the trunk the same way he had.

Whoever had killed Cassidy wanted Rick to know that it was payback. The question was, who cared enough about Charles Ashland, Junior, to want to avenge his death? His parents, sure, but they weren't killers. And, he already knew that they both had alibis last night. One of his deputies had been called to their house when the herd of reporters wouldn't leave peaceably at the request of Ashland's personal security.

Deputy Kilgore had spent several hours outside the Ashland residence, where both Senator and Mrs. Ashland were tucked safely away.

Melinda? Definitely not. She and Cassidy were best friends. Though, the fact that Cassidy had disappeared abruptly from Melinda's home did beg to be looked into more closely. Rick would thoroughly investigate all avenues, but he knew with an absolute certainty that Melinda hadn't done the deed.

Whoever had killed Cassidy had been strong enough to choke her to death without any trouble and then heft the body into the trunk. Definitely not something Melinda could accomplish alone. Then again, adrenaline often provided abnormal strength to those in desperate situations.

He knew for certain Lacy wasn't involved because he'd been watching her house last night. Brewer had been watching Kira's.

Rick heaved a disgusted breath. The fact that Bent Thompson had been following her had him worried for her safety. Now, considering Cassidy's murder, he should be worried about far more than Bent Thompson. Sure Bent would be fully capable of pulling the murder off, but he had no reason to want to hurt Cassidy...unless she figured out he was on to them, which would explain why he'd been following Lacy.

All questions he needed answers for.

There was only one place he would get the answers he needed.

Lacy hung up the telephone in Melinda's kitchen. She summoned her courage and relayed the information she'd just gotten from Cassidy's cousin Julia. "They're forgoing the usual funeral because of the—" Her throat closed. She bit down on her bottom lip to hold back a surge of anguish. She had to keep it together. Cassidy would want her to be strong. "Because of the autopsy. Her folks have decided to have a simple memorial service tomorrow for family and close friends."

Kira and Melinda sat at the island, the expression on their faces the same as Lacy's: bewildered...shocked.

"We..." Lacy moistened her lips and tried to find the right words to say. "We should probably try to get some sleep. Tomorrow's going to be a long day." It was eight or nine in the evening already. She wasn't even sure which one. Lacy only knew that she felt like death warmed over.

"I don't understand how this could happen," Melinda murmured.

Melinda's brother, Kyle, had called to see if she was all right. He was out of town with a death in his wife's family, leaving Melinda pretty much alone. Lacy's folks were coming back home after hearing the news but wouldn't arrive until just before the memorial service. Kira was the only one with a decent support system handy.

But they had one another.

Lacy walked over and put her arm around Melinda's shoulders. "I don't know who did this, but I intend to find out." She said the words with a bit more ferocity than she'd meant to. But she was tired, unable to modulate her tone or even attempt to control her emotions. If she lived a thousand years she would never be able to forget the horror of seeing Cassidy that way…and she would never forgive Rick for putting her through that experience.

"It's got something to do with those calls," Kira said quietly, her entire demeanor a study in defeat or something on that order. "I just know it. We were certain it was just you freaking out, maybe even imagining stuff, but you weren't…it's real."

Maybe it was the stress, but just then, with her friend lying dead on some medical examiner's cold table, the idea that any of them would have thought such a thing about her made Lacy want to scream.

"I can't believe you," she snapped. "Why would I make up something like that?" She plowed the fingers of both hands through her hair. Her head ached horribly. "You're supposed to be my friends and you think I would make up taunting calls like that?"

Kira looked ready to burst into tears again, but Lacy just couldn't help it. She was sick to death of all the subterfuge.

"If we'd been open with each other the way I wanted to maybe Cassidy wouldn't be dead."

"Lacy," Melinda chastised quietly, as if she didn't have the strength to put any real oomph into her words, "don't say that. You know Kira didn't mean anything."

The last thread of Lacy's control frayed and broke apart. "No, I don't know what she meant, Melinda." She glared at first one and then the other of her lifelong friends. "I saw her…" She blinked back the tears burning in her eyes. "I saw what had been done to her…where the car had been left." Her gaze zeroed in on Kira's. "Exactly the same place we stopped Charles's car before we pushed it into the lake. Whoever is responsible for Cassidy's murder, knows exactly what we did."

Kira did burst into tears then.

"God Almighty, Lacy, did you have to say all that?"

Melinda wrapped her arms around Kira and comforted her while Lacy stood back like the enemy and felt at once sorry for herself and furious with both of them.

"All I'm saying," Lacy said finally, feeling like the heel the others must surely think she was, "is that someone knows and we have to do something to protect ourselves."

Kira swiped at her cheeks with the backs of her hands. The cell phone in her purse started to ring again, for the dozenth time. She knew it would be Brian so she ignored him. Lacy was beginning to think Kira's fiancé wasn't exactly a stellar catch. The guy apparently had serious trust issues. The picture of Kira and Brad Brewer outside her parents' home last night slammed into Lacy's head. Or maybe Brian had good reason not to trust his bride-to-be.

Guilt knifed into Lacy. What the hell was she doing? First she couldn't stop the paranoia as to what her friends were thinking about her and now she was doing the same to them.

This had to stop.

"Why don't you tell us what to do," Kira demanded, sliding off her stool and coming to stand toe to toe with Lacy. "You're the one getting the calls. You're the one with Chief Summers following you around."

An ache of disappointment, mostly at herself, settled deep into Lacy's bones. "You're right. I'm the one who got the calls. I should have been the one who was murdered."

"No!" Melinda planted herself firmly between them. "I know you don't mean that." She turned to Kira. "We have to stick together. Isn't that what Cassidy would want us to do? We've always been there for each other. Are we going to fracture during the biggest crisis of our lives? What kind of friends are we?"

Melinda was right. "I'm sorry," Lacy said wearily. "I'm not thinking very clearly. You can't imagine how awful it was to see her like that."

"My question is, what was Summers thinking?" Kira shook her head slowly from side to side. "He's trying to get you to talk, Lacy. He's not going to stop. Not until you cave. We're all depending on you and I'm not so sure you're that dependable anymore."

The accusation stabbed straight into Lacy's heart, but the fighter in her rushed back with a punch of her own. "You think he has any more of a hold on me than Deputy Brewer has on you?"

Disbelief flared in Kira's wide gaze. "You don't know anything about Brad. We…"

"Were involved?" Lacy suggested. "That was easy to see."

"Are you accusing me of something?" Kira

demanded, her arms folded over her chest, and her chin thrust out belligerently.

Lacy took a mental step back. She couldn't let this get so far out of control. They were already on the verge of a major breakdown in their relationship. This whole thing was tearing them apart. "I'm just saying that whatever went on between you and Brad doesn't mean you're up to something behind our backs, any more than this thing between Rick and me means the same about me."

"That's right," Melinda put in quickly. "Rick had a thing for you." She turned to Kira. "And, apparently, Brad had or has one for you. But none of that means anything, given what we have to do. Cassidy said we had to stand strong. We have to stick together and protect one another. They don't have any evidence against us. The case will fall apart. Remember?"

Somehow all of that, which had sounded so logical a few days ago, didn't quite cut it now. Someone knew their secret…that same someone obviously wanted them dead. There was nothing rational or logical about any of this.

"None of us are thinking straight just now," Lacy admitted, too tired to analyze anymore. "Why don't we just call it a night and we'll talk after the service tomorrow?"

"That sounds reasonable to me," Melinda said quickly. "Anything we say tonight we'll likely regret tomorrow."

That was the smartest thing any of them had said all day.

"I can stay with Melinda tonight," Kira offered.

"Why don't we all stay together," Lacy offered. "We'll be safer that way." *And we'll know exactly what the other is up to,* she didn't add. But she didn't have to—

she could see that very conclusion in Kira's eyes. God, she hated the feeling of insecurity and helplessness.

She realized at that exact moment what had really been bothering her for ten long years. She hadn't killed Charles, so it really wasn't guilt—it was insecurity. The dynamics of Melinda's, Kira's, Cassidy's and her relationship had changed that night. The possibly of their secret being discovered had loomed over their heads ever since. All the feelings of safety and future happiness she'd had were shrouded in the ever-present uncertainty of what could happen. Lacy couldn't have been the only one who felt that way. The others had to have experienced their own insecurities related to what they'd done.

"I'm sorry," Kira said, moving away from the group. "If I'm not needed, I'd just as soon go home. You go ahead and stay, Lacy."

Melinda saw her to the door. They hugged and gave final assurances. Lacy stood back and watched. No matter what Melinda said, Lacy was the one left on the outside. There was something she couldn't quite identify that separated her from the others when it came to that night ten years ago. Her every suggestion was taken as an affront.

Would any of them survive long enough to figure out what really happened?

Melinda closed and locked the door behind Kira, then made her way back to where Lacy waited. "Let's call it a night, Lace. I can't bear to be awake anymore. I need to go to sleep and pretend none of this ever happened."

But it had and there was no going back now. Melinda was right, though, she looked ready to collapse. They should end this day, the sooner the better.

Lacy lay in bed in Melinda's guest room that night and listened as Melinda spoke to her daughter by phone. Apparently the Ashlands had felt sorry for her because of Cassidy's murder and had agreed to a late-night call. The relief and tenderness in Melinda's voice spoke of just how badly she missed her daughter.

Melinda hadn't mentioned Chuckie in the past few days. There had to be tension between mother and son considering his father's remains had just been found. Despite the idea that his father had been declared dead three years ago, it was another story altogether to have his brutal murder surface.

The newspapers and most news channels were carrying constant updates on the case. The kids didn't need any of this. Melinda didn't need it, either.

In the beginning Lacy had felt certain she, Kira and Cassidy would get over all of this pretty quickly, but that wasn't the case. Someone wanted to make them regret what they'd done that night and they had succeeded.

Lacy had wished a million times over that she'd stood up to the others that night, that she'd been stronger. But she hadn't been, and now they were paying for what they'd done.

Charles Ashland, Junior, would have the last laugh after all.

Rick tried to find a comfortable way to sit in his truck as midnight approached, but nothing he did made a difference. He wasn't ever going to be comfortable as long as his thoughts were on Lacy Oliver. He'd learned that fifteen long years ago. Too bad he hadn't learned his lesson well enough.

If he had, maybe he wouldn't be sitting here wishing he was in there in bed with her instead of in this damned truck doing surveillance. Brewer was watching Kira's house.

They had all the bases covered, but would it be enough?

Someone clearly suspected that these women had killed Charles ten years ago, and apparently this same person had decided to have his or her vengeance.

Rick hoped Cassidy Collins hadn't died for nothing. If her death could save the others by prompting one or all to come forward, maybe all would not be for naught.

But how did he get that across to Lacy?

She'd been too emotionally wrecked to pressure this morning. But tomorrow, after the service, he intended to interrogate her. If his observations were correct so far, it would be Kira's turn to stay with Melinda. That meant Lacy would be alone. He would make his move then.

He felt like a dirtbag even plotting such a thing with her friend lying on a slab in the morgue. But it was the only way he knew to protect her. She could be the next person on the killer's list.

Or, hell, maybe the whole thing was a ploy to throw off his investigation. He couldn't be sure, wouldn't overlook any variables until he had some solid evidence.

Whether or not finding Pamela Carter's remains would prove beneficial to the case or only open up another can of worms was yet to be seen.

They had determined, based on dental records, that the remains did indeed belong to Pamela. Rick had given the news to her father, who took it as if he'd expected as much.

Preliminary finding on cause of death was a gunshot since a slug had been discovered in the grave site. The slug was at ballistics right now. Rick had pulled a few strings to get a report back ASAP. He needed to know if the .38 slug matched either of the ones discovered with Ashland's body.

That would put a whole different spin on who may have killed Ashland.

Rick didn't want to believe it, but it was looking more and more like Melinda had the most reason to do the deed. And there was that slight discrepancy as to whether or not she had been in her hospital room the entire time in question that day.

There was always her brother. Rick had considered him before, but Taylor's reports had indicated that his alibi was rock solid. But how could he be sure when time of death couldn't be pinpointed? He couldn't.

No one could.

Except the killer himself—or herself.

Rick's cell phone vibrated against the dash where he'd tossed it.

"Summers."

"Chief, this is Kilgore."

Anticipation lit in Rick's veins. Kilgore was standing by in Birmingham with the lab tech for the preliminary ballistics results.

"What've you got for me, Kilgore?"

"It's a match, Chief. No question. One of the thirty-eights used on Charles Ashland, Junior, is the same weapon used to kill Pamela Carter."

And there it was, his first piece of solid evidence.

# Chapter 13

It rained the entire morning before Cassidy's memorial service.

At two o'clock the Episcopal Church of Jackson County filled quickly with mourners and perhaps a few who were simply curious onlookers. The idea of confining the service to the family and close friends had apparently been overridden by the community's need to come out and show its support in one way or another.

Rick and his deputies were keeping the media at bay. Lacy felt intensely grateful for that measure.

She'd lain in bed alone last night, thinking that she was actually more alone at that moment than ever before in her life. There wasn't a significant other; her relationship with her lifelong best friends was falling apart right before her eyes. In addition, she felt like a stranger in her parents' home. Their flight from Bermuda had been delayed for at least two more days due to a rare yet imminent category-three hurricane. They almost never happened in June. Just Lacy's luck one had to occur now when she needed all the support she could get.

Ten years ago she had made the biggest mistake of her life. She'd allowed a Pandora's box to be opened and she couldn't close it. That step had driven a wedge between her and all she'd ever known and all she'd ever hoped to be.

Every single person gathered in this church had watched her, Kira and Melinda take their seats. Lacy hadn't missed the suspicious looks…the whispers behind hands. The whole town suspected that the four of them had murdered Charles Ashland, Junior, dumped his body in the lake and now that long-buried secret had come back to haunt them in the worst way.

She imagined they also wondered which of them would be the next to die at the hands of Charles's unknown avenger.

Lacy shivered when she recalled the way Nigel Canton and Bent Thompson had looked at them as they'd passed down the long aisle to sit close to Cassidy's family.

Had one of them killed Cassidy? Was Nigel or Bent attempting to cover his own part in the events of ten years ago by diverting suspicions toward them using this elaborate revenge scheme? Honestly, outside of Charles's parents she couldn't imagine anyone wanting revenge for his murder. And, God knows, with the security at the senator's house, there was no way he or his wife went anywhere without someone knowing it.

Stop it. She didn't want to think about any of it anymore. She just wanted to get through this.

The Ashlands had even shown up for the service.

Lacy wasn't sure why she was surprised by that since the Ashlands had been friends with the Collinses for as long as she could remember, the same as her own parents had. Her parents were deeply saddened that they couldn't be there.

Lacy stared up at the priest, who spoke of salvation and hope. It felt like a nightmare come true. How could this be real?

How could Cassidy be dead?

Another wave of emotion welled inside Lacy, making her want to wither into a mass of tears. Cassidy hadn't deserved this kind of end. She'd had so much to give. Her life had scarcely gotten started.

Lacy couldn't help thinking that maybe it wouldn't have happened if…circumstances had been different.

They had sentenced Charles to that watery grave for an entire decade and now he was back, wreaking the same old havoc in all their lives.

Only this time, there was no turning back.

Dead was dead.

And Cassidy was dead.

Melinda reached over and took Lacy's hand in hers and held on tightly. Lacy tried to be consoled by the gesture, but she couldn't muster the necessary strength. Things would never be the same for any of them.

Cassidy was gone.

The service droned on for another half hour before people rose and started to file out of the church. Melinda held on tightly to Lacy and Kira as they exited the service together. United, just the way Cassidy would have wanted them. Only this time it was more show than anything. Everything had changed.

Lacy noticed Rick immediately. He stood very close to the steps, ready to move in if he was needed. She recognized several other deputies, like Brad Brewer, stationed about the parking area to control the crowd of media vultures restricted from the event.

For the umpteenth time since coming back home she wished she could run into his arms and hide there. It had been ages since she'd felt the need to seek shelter in the strength only a man could offer, but this afternoon she felt the urge stronger than ever before.

She wanted desperately to feel safe and secure again.

From the church the three of them rode in silence with Kira's parents to the Collinses' home for a more private gathering to honor Cassidy.

Lacy wished she could just go home and go to sleep. She didn't want to face this for one second longer, but she had to do it for Cassidy and her family. They would be hurt if she left too early.

She wandered around the luxuriously appointed great room and took her time admiring framed photograph after photograph of Cassidy. An only child, like Lacy, she would be sorely missed. Lacy couldn't imagine how her parents would survive this kind of terrible tragedy. How did anyone recover from the loss of a child, even if that child was all grown up?

She'd hugged and been hugged by so many people that she felt numb with the condolences. Not that she regretted having taken in those caring words and reminders of moments from the past. She was just tired, that was all.

The beautiful framed photograph of Cassidy standing proudly in the center of a table with a flickering candle on either side of it made Lacy feel incredibly sorry for how off-kilter their time together had been since returning to Ashland. She wished she could take back some of the tension she and Cassidy had experienced during the past few days.

But you couldn't take back some things and that stressful time was one of them. The opportunity was gone.

Cassidy was dead…murdered.

The four of them were no more. Now only three remained.

Lacy couldn't be in this house a second longer. She had to go.

It took her a couple of minutes to locate Melinda. "I have to go," she said, without bothering to tack on an excuse. She couldn't help it. She couldn't breathe…couldn't think.

"But we came with Kira's parents," Melinda reminded softly. "We should—"

Lacy held up her hands to stop whatever else she intended to say. "It's okay. I'll walk."

With Melinda still attempting to persuade her to stay, Lacy hurried out of the house. She couldn't bear it a moment longer.

Her parents' house wasn't that far from here. Maybe seven or eight blocks. She would just walk. No need to disturb anyone else. It was still daylight outside.

Halfway down the driveway, she realized her mistake.

A reporter, the same one from the other day, rushed past the line Ashland's finest had laid down as the boundary the media couldn't cross.

"Which one of your friends do you think will be next, Lacy?"

Why her? Why did everyone have to assume it was her who'd done the deed? Clearly that was what this reporter assumed; otherwise, why would he suggest that her friends would die rather than her?

She kept walking, while the reporter's photographer cohort snapped photo after photo. She held up one hand to block his view, but he was too fast. He danced around her as if he'd done this very hateful and callous routine a dozen times before and enjoyed every minute of it.

"It would make life so much more pleasant if you told the truth, Lacy!" the reporter called after her. For some reason he chose not to follow, just yelled out to her back. "Why don't you let me help you bring the truth to all those who care. They have a right to know!"

Lacy walked faster, made the ninety-degree turn from the driveway to the sidewalk so quickly she almost stumbled.

Big hands steadied her. "Whoa."

Rick.

She shook free of his hold. "I have to go home." At least now she knew why the reporter and his photographer hadn't raced after her.

"Why don't I drive you?"

She wanted to tell him no, that she wouldn't be caught dead riding around with him after what he'd pulled yesterday. But she didn't have the strength to say the words.

She nodded her agreement to the ride.

That he left it at that was better. Silently, he led the way to his truck, which was parked a good distance down the block because of the number of folks who had crowded into the Collinses' home.

He opened the passenger-side door and waited for her to climb in, then closed it behind her. She should have thanked him, but she didn't bother. Instead, she closed her eyes and relaxed against the seat. She wanted to put the horror out of her mind for just a little while.

He'd pulled out onto the street and driven a block or two before he spoke. "About yesterday," he said quietly. "I shouldn't have put you through that."

The urge to rail at him about how terribly he'd treated

her nudged at her but she lacked the enthusiasm to follow through with the inclination.

"I know how close you were. I shouldn't have been so heartless."

If he was looking for forgiveness, he could just forget it. She wasn't about to give him the satisfaction.

So she gave him the silent treatment all the way to the block where her folks lived.

"Oh, God."

A whole horde of reporters waited on the sidewalk in front of her house.

Rick swore.

"Don't stop," she implored. "Just keep driving." She couldn't endure any more.

He drove away without even slowing. She slid as low as possible in the seat. Not one of the vultures circling her childhood home appeared to notice her in his vehicle. Now she felt thankful her parents weren't here having to witness this ruthless invasion of privacy.

The idea that Melinda would likely go home to the same scene gave her pause, but she felt confident Kira would take care of Melinda.

"I'll send one my deputies over to Melinda's house to make sure she doesn't find the same thing at her place."

That he'd read her mind so clearly startled Lacy. But then, that was the logical step, right? The chief of police would think in those terms.

It had nothing to do with him caring how she felt. He'd proved that yesterday morning.

As promised, he made the necessary call. Lacy felt better knowing Melinda wouldn't have to face the same unpleasantness.

God, she wanted this to be over.

She closed her eyes for a while. She couldn't think anymore. The sound of the tires gliding over the damp streets lulled her into a light sleep. But sleep only brought the voice of the caller echoing behind her as she ran from some dark figure.

Lacy sat up, blinked a few times and tried to get her bearings. She recognized the street but hadn't been in this neighborhood in a really long time.

"Where are we going?"

"My place."

It took a couple of seconds for his words to penetrate the haze of fatigue. "Wait." Going to his home would be a mistake. She didn't have to analyze it. She knew it would be. "I should…" What? Go home? Go to Melinda's? There was no place for her to go and feel safe.

"No one will bother you at my place," he assured. "You'll be safe there."

And that was exactly what she needed to feel. How could he know her so well? They'd only been together that one time. How could he sense her needs so precisely?

Rick's house was a small, neat rancher at the end of a street where the city met the thick forest of the green-belt Goose Pond Colony had formed ages ago. Ashland wouldn't be allowed to expand into that natural setting for at least another couple hundred years.

Lacy scooted out of the truck seat when he opened her door, but she was too busy taking in the place to consider the man. The lawn was freshly mowed, the shrubs neatly pruned. No flowers, but then she wouldn't have expected any. Traditional red brick with black louvered shutters dressed the outside of his home. Steps led up to a small porch that provided shelter for the front entrance. A typical six-panel door with lock and dead bolt led into the home.

He flipped a switch and two table lamps in the living

room glowed to life. There was no entry hall. Just a generous-sized living room with well-worn, comfy-looking furnishings. The walls were a deep sand color, the floors red oak polished to a high sheen. A big-screen television sat in one corner of the room.

"Would you like something to drink? I've got soda and beer. Coffee."

The uncharacteristic tension in his voice drew her attention back to the man. It wasn't her imagination. He looked nervous or otherwise uncomfortable. How was that possible? He always appeared calm and rational, never flustered or uneasy.

"Nothing, thank you."

"There's…" He cleared his throat. "There's water too."

She shook her head. If she'd been thirsty she would have denied it. Her entire interest was focused on the place. It smelled like him. Something fresh and yet classic like the softest leather after a brisk rub to release the natural essence.

A massive oak bookcase across the room drew her there to study the framed photographs of Rick and his family. A few were of his deputies gathered for cookouts or holiday celebrations.

He looked happy, secure in his own skin.

What she would give to feel that way again.

"Should I leave a message at your house for your folks, in case they get in this evening?"

Lacy set aside the photo of Rick and his fellow officers she'd been contemplating and turned to him. Did he think that wooing her with kindness would get her to talk, since intimidation hadn't?

Those silvery eyes, the ones she had never been able to forget, rested easily on hers, as if he enjoyed admiring her and was in no hurry to look away.

He really had turned into an amazing guy, every bit as handsome as she would have expected and even more in ways that went beyond the superficial.

Rick Summers was what folks around here would call a good man. Honor, loyalty and all those traits that were growing more and more extinct with each generation.

The kind of man any woman would want to capture. A good catch.

Except she'd walked away. Used him and gone on as if he hadn't counted in the grander scheme of things.

She wondered if he had ever forgiven her for that.

Then again, he hadn't attempted to draw her back for more either. Maybe that was the problem she really had with him. Maybe she'd never forgiven him.

"My folks are stuck in Bermuda for at least a couple more days. The whole island is on lockdown. The storm blew up too fast for an evacuation. Besides, being nice to me isn't going to induce me to talk, Chief," she said wearily. "I have nothing to say. It won't matter what you do, that won't change." She owed it to Cassidy to abide by her wishes. Lacy would die before she would talk now. And that was a very real possibility.

He moved closer. "So, no matter what I do, you'll say nothing to me or anyone else."

The huskiness of his voice seared her with a heat that she longed to feel over and over.

"That's right."

She didn't know how, but the moment had gone from talking about murder investigations to something much more intimate. And it didn't matter how it had happened...she didn't want to go back. She didn't want to feel anything but the sweet heat of this moment.

His fingers dove into her hair, wrapped around her skull and drew her mouth up to his in one fluid motion.

His lips sealed over hers and even her own name left her, leaving her floating and exquisitely anonymous. She couldn't think...could only feel. The incredible taste of him, sweetened coffee, rich and alluring. The feel of his strong hands holding her firmly as he kissed her so deeply.

She shivered as his hands moved downward, tugging at the buttons of her blouse. Slipping down the zipper of her skirt. Both garments dropped to the floor and he hadn't stopped kissing her for even a fraction of a second.

The feel of his hands on her naked skin propelled her into action. She tore at his shirt. She moaned as her fingers touched his hot, bare skin. The surge of want that rushed through her made her knees so weak she had no choice but to lean into his sturdy frame.

He tore his lips from hers to trace a path down her throat with his mouth. Her entire being throbbed with the desire he'd lit inside her. When his tongue touched her nipples, first one and then the other, the rhythmic contractions started deep inside her, propelling her toward climax.

Down, down, down he moved, dropping to his knees, kissing his way down her torso. She shuddered with the delicious tension rippling through her. It felt so good to have him touch her that way. She wanted so much more...didn't want it to stop.

His hands settled on her hips and he braced her against the bookcase. Picture frames crashed into one another and fell over onto their shelves, but he didn't care and neither did she. He dragged her panties down and off and then ushered her legs wider apart. She clutched at the shelves behind her, closed her eyes and let the cascading sensations take her.

He brought her to that ultimate place of pure pleasure

using nothing but his hands and his mouth and she wept with the beauty of it.

She'd waited so long to be touched by him...to be with him this way. No one else had ever been able to erase his memory or to fill her mind and body the way he had.

He lifted her into his arms and held her against his bare chest. She couldn't question anything. Her head found the perfect fit next to his shoulder and she didn't worry what was next.

The bedroom they entered was dark, but the smell of him, the feel of him, made it welcoming, marked it as his own as he had long ago marked her. He placed her gently on the bed, shed his trousers and moved down next to her.

The feel of him all around her was like a shield protecting her...made her feel secure again for the first time in so long she'd almost forgotten how wondrous that sensation could be.

"Rick, I..." She wasn't sure what she wanted to say but she needed to make him understand how special he was to her. No matter what took place between and around them in the bright light of day, this was theirs and no one could take it away from them.

"You don't have to talk." His lips covered hers and he led her to the peak of insanity all over again. Only this time he planted himself deep inside her and they both lost their breaths.

Long moments passed before they could move, but need hummed fiercely between them and it soon took over.

She smoothed her hands along his body as he moved over her. He felt stronger, far more powerful than before. His touch was more skilled but every bit as tender, more restrained by maturity. But nothing had changed about the fire that burned out of control between them.

He made love to her twice, each time draining her so completely she could do nothing but beg for more. When he'd exhausted himself, he lured her to the bathroom where they bathed together and made love one more time.

She went to sleep in his arms.

For the first time since she'd gotten that call, nothing mattered except the way his skin fused with hers.

Safe and secure…he gave both to her…at least for a little while.

# Chapter 14

Rick lay very still and watched Lacy sleep as dawn crept into the room. She'd slept all night without waking once. He'd roused a couple of times, but it had nothing to do with his not being utterly emotionally and physically satisfied from their lovemaking. On the contrary, it was habit. He'd always been a light sleeper and just over ten years in the police business hadn't helped any.

But this, well this was the closest thing to heaven he'd ever experienced. He'd known the connection between him and Lacy was special that first time…when he'd greedily taken the innocence she offered. He hadn't quite forgiven himself for being so selfish. Wasn't sure he ever would.

But last night had confirmed what he'd suspected all along. He'd been in love with Lacy Oliver since he was seventeen. Neither the passage of time nor the reality of a triple homicide investigation was going to change how he felt.

It wasn't as if the signs hadn't been there. He hadn't been able to get serious with any other woman. No matter how his friends and family had tried to "fix him up." He'd always felt something significant was missing. And he'd been right. His heart hadn't been in any of the ill-fated relationships he'd attempted.

Funny thing was, this epiphany was the last thing he needed just now. How could he conduct an investigation with any objectivity if he was in love with one of his prime suspects?

He'd told himself he could set aside his personal feelings, but he'd been wrong. Whatever she had done ten years ago, he didn't care anymore. The only thing he wanted to do was protect her.

There was a killer out there who might very well be looking for revenge. He had to protect Lacy and the others. It was his sworn duty…but more than that, he couldn't survive losing her again.

That was the part that stuck in his chest and twisted like barbed wire. He couldn't bear the idea of her leaving, and that was exactly what she would do when everything was over.

She'd left before, and he doubted she would change strategies now. Her life was in Atlanta. He'd kept up with her to some degree, had watched her career rise the way he'd known it would.

He stilled inside. What would he do if he learned that she had been involved in Charles's murder?

He'd promised himself that he would cross that bridge when he came to it, but that was now. She had to be involved on some level. His instincts nagged at him to pay attention when he wanted to look the other way. He'd pretended that his determination to get her to talk had been about finding the truth, but in reality he'd only wanted to protect her.

He knew that now.

His heart wouldn't let him believe that Lacy could be too deeply involved in murder. But his cop training reminded him that desperate people took desperate measures. She and her friends would have done most anything to protect their own. Who wouldn't?

So here he was, lying in bed, with his arms wrapped around the woman he loved like no other and he couldn't be sure if she had been an accomplice in a homicide.

He eased out of bed, allowing her to gently sink into the pillows. He needed to think. Not that he figured it would do any good, but he had to try.

He tugged on his pants and padded barefoot to the kitchen and put on a pot of coffee, then moved noiselessly back to the bedroom.

She'd gotten up, and was standing in the predawn light of the window staring out at morning's rapidly changing colors. She'd wrapped the sheet around her slender body and he ached to take her into his arms.

"You sleep okay?" He knew for a fact she had, but he had to break the ice somehow.

She turned slowly to face him. Her smooth skin was still flushed with the intense physical activity of last night. Her lips were red and slightly swollen from their frantic kisses. Just looking at her made his mouth water for more and his body harden.

"I should go home." She moistened her lips and glanced around the room, probably to avoid looking directly at him. "My parents might call."

He plowed his fingers through his hair. "I'll take you home whenever you're ready."

She nodded. "Thanks." She scanned the floor, probably looking for her clothes. "I need to get dressed."

He gathered her skirt, blouse and panties from the chair on his side of the bed. "I picked them up after you'd gone to sleep."

The flush on her face deepened. "Good. I'll just…" She gestured to the door. "Find the bathroom and get dressed."

"First door on the left."

She took the clothes from him, careful not to touch his hand and hurried out of the room.

Oh, yeah, she wasn't just leaving, she was already gone.

He grabbed a clean shirt out of the closet and tugged it on. The smell of freshly brewed coffee lured him back to the kitchen. Might as well have some caffeine. The moment they'd shared was over…again.

Lacy closed her eyes, couldn't look at her reflection.

The woman she saw in the mirror was one who'd been thoroughly attended to in every aspect of the phrase *made love to*. But that woman had let her guard down to the very man who could ruin all their lives.

What in the world had she been thinking?

Sadly, she'd had to ask herself that several times over the past few days. Apparently she'd lost all grasp of good sense.

Now she had to face Melinda and Kira with this hanging over her head.

She opened her eyes and forced herself to look at her reflection.

What had happened between her and Rick hadn't been a bad thing. It had been magical…powerful. She'd felt safe and protected for the first time in a decade.

She couldn't regret that. But she had to separate fantasy from reality.

Last night had been fantasy, an illusion of happiness.

Today was reality. Cassidy was dead. The past was hovering over their heads like a storm cloud prepared to rain all over their parade. But the rain was the least of their worries.

The person who'd killed Cassidy wouldn't stop with just her. All four of them had hidden Charles's murder and, apparently, one of them had killed him.

As much as she wanted to abide by what Cassidy had told them to do, she'd decided last night that her own strategy would be the best, in the cold, harsh light of day Lacy knew that Cassidy's way would never stop whoever knew their secret.

Lacy had to figure this out. She had to find out who had made those calls to her. Whoever it was most likely was the person responsible for Cassidy's death.

One way or another, Lacy would stop this.

She couldn't let Rick or anyone else get in her way.

After washing up and slipping on her clothes, Lacy went in search of her host. She had to thank him and somehow make it clear that last night changed nothing about the investigation. She wasn't talking to him…no matter what sort of threat he devised to use against her.

She shook her head. How could she think that about the man who'd made love to her so sweetly and fiercely last night?

The whole situation had turned upside down. She'd made the wrong move at every turn.

Last night was no exception.

Lacy walked into the living room, then found him in the kitchen. The coffee smelled amazing but she couldn't stay, not even to share a cup of coffee.

"Thank you for taking care of me last night." Her voice was stronger than she'd expected. Thank God for that. "I'd like you to take me home now."

He lowered the cup in his hand to the counter. And even that totally asexual move took her breath away. His shirt wasn't buttoned and his trousers hung low on his hips. But it was the day's beard growth darkening his jaw that did the most damage to her defenses. Between the sexy stubble and the tousled hair, she wanted to turn right back around and climb into his bed for the next few days.

But that would be a mistake.

"All right." He straightened away from the counter and started to button his shirt. "There's something you should know, Lacy."

The way he said her name made her shiver. She steeled herself for the impact of looking at him directly. The blatant desire on his face shattered the last of her fortitude. How could she possibly walk away from this man again?

He licked his lips as if remembering her taste and then, as if he'd flipped some sort of internal switch, his entire demeanor took on a professional air. All traces of intimacy were gone. She blinked, certain her eyes must be playing tricks on her.

"We discovered more human remains day before yesterday."

At first his statement didn't make sense, then, suddenly it did. "Another body?"

He nodded. "At least what's left of it."

A premonition of doom enveloped her. "Who?" The word was scarcely a whisper...a breath of sound.

"Pamela Carter."

Lacy grabbed for the closest chair. The conversation she'd had with Pamela's father filtered through her mind like a haunting melody. *She just left for work one day and never came back.*

"We haven't released that information to anyone except her father," he warned. "I'd like to keep it quiet for another day or two."

Lacy gathered her wits. There were things she needed to know, if Rick would share any other information. "Do you know what happened to her?"

"We believe she was shot with a small-caliber handgun."

Lacy couldn't draw in a breath. She had to know the rest. "Have you estimated when this…happened?"

He lifted his broad shoulders and let them drop. "Can't be certain but judging by a receipt we found in what was left of her purse, about ten years ago. Probably the same day she failed to show up for work."

Pressure pushed against her from the inside out as if she might explode at any second. "Do you think her murder is related to Charles's?"

He nodded. "I'm positive of it. The ballistics on the slug we found with her remains was a match to one of the slugs discovered in the trunk of Charles's Mercedes."

Lacy started to shake inside. She prayed she could prevent the tremors from becoming visible but she wasn't sure. "I'd like to go now."

When he started for the kitchen door, the telephone rang.

Lacy struggled to maintain her composure until he'd completed his call. She had to get to the girls. Had to tell them about Pam. This changed everything.

The idea that Melinda had left the hospital the day Charles disappeared thumped her memory, but Lacy refused to believe that Melinda would have hurt either Charles or Pamela. No way.

But someone had.

Someone who had wanted them both dead.

"Thanks, Kilgore." Rick ended the call and settled his steady gaze back on her. "That was one of my men who's been standing by at the lab to relay any information we learn about Pam's remains. There's a new development."

This could only be worse news.

"There's confirmed evidence to indicate Pam was about four months pregnant."

*But her sister, Carmen, the oldest, claims Pamela was pregnant by Ashland. Guess we'll never know.*

"Charles got her pregnant." Lacy hadn't realized she'd muttered the words aloud until Rick reacted.

"Who told you that?"

Lacy hesitated. Why lie? He knew she'd been to see Pam's father. "Her father said Pam told her sister Carmen that she was pregnant by Charles."

Rick looked surprised by the news. Lacy couldn't help wondering why Pam's father wouldn't have shared that bit of information with the chief. It could have been relevant to Pam's case.

Surely Pam's own father hadn't killed her…and then maybe Charles for getting her pregnant.

Or maybe it was about the money.

No, that didn't make sense. If her father had taken the money Charles had withdrawn ten years ago he wouldn't be living in poverty now.

Would he?

"I don't want you to talk about this to anyone," Rick reminded her. "The media has made a big enough circus out of this. Details like these will only hurt Melinda and the children."

Of course she wouldn't tell anyone.

Not even Kira or Melinda...or would that be another mistake that would come back to haunt her?

"If I tell anyone," she said honestly, "it will only be Kira and Melinda."

He pushed his fingers through his hair. "Are you sure you want to tell Melinda?"

Lacy shook her head. "No, I don't want to tell her. But it would be better coming from me than to let her learn it from some newspaper article when it gets out and you know it'll get out."

He nodded vaguely. "Guess you're right about that."

"I'd like to go please." She had to get out of here. She couldn't stand around chatting as if last night hadn't happened. As if every part of her wasn't begging to have a repeat performance.

"Sure." He grabbed his keys on the way out.

When they'd settled into his truck, he unlocked the glovebox and pulled out a weapon in a leather case.

Lacy hadn't ever noticed him wearing a sidearm. It startled her now.

"I don't wear it often," he explained as he hooked it onto his waist. "But today feels like a good time to take precautions."

She wasn't the only one who was worried. She wasn't sure if that made her feel better or not.

Once they were in his truck and he'd shifted into Reverse to back out of his driveway, he said, "About last night." His gaze connected with hers and she felt his heat clear across the cab. "Last night was special to me. No matter what happens, I want you to know that."

They didn't talk any more after that. He drove her home and she got out. She wanted to pretend that life could somehow be normal again, just for a moment, because she had a terrible feeling that might be impossible.

* * *

About two that afternoon Lacy felt ready to face the others so she drove over to Melinda's. She'd had a long, hot shower to wash away the last of last night's memories. And she'd gotten right with what she'd done. She had needs the same as anyone else.

She pulled into Melinda's driveway and got out of her Explorer. She wasn't scheduled to relieve Kira until six. That was the new schedule. Six in the evening until six in the morning and vice versa. Kira had left the message on Lacy's parents' answering machine. She'd sounded calm. Like Lacy, she was apparently trying to make the best of things.

Even if everything felt wrong just now if she let herself really dwell on it.

Shaking off the troubling thoughts, she didn't bother knocking at Melinda's, just opened the door and stuck her head inside. "Hey! I'm here."

When no one answered she walked straight to the living room. That Kira and Melinda stood there glaring at each other took her aback. Clearly, she'd walked into a very intense conversation.

Melinda was the first to recover. She pushed a smile into place and met Lacy in the middle of the room for a hug. "I'm glad you're here." She pulled back. "You okay today? You look rested."

"I'm good." Lacy looked from Melinda to Kira, the undeniable instinct that something was very much amiss tugging at her. "Is everything all right here?"

Melinda ushered her to the sofa, her movements almost mechanical. "I didn't sleep very well last night, but otherwise I'm okay."

Kira wouldn't look at Lacy. "What about you, Kira? Did you get any sleep?"

Kira still didn't make eye contact. "Are you going to tell her or am I?" she demanded of Melinda.

Dread surged inside Lacy. Something had happened. Oh God. What now?

"What's going on, Melinda?"

"Kira received one of those calls last night."

Fear abruptly replaced the mounting dread. "God, what did he say?" Though they had no idea who the creep was it was just easier to say he. In one way Lacy was relieved that she wasn't the only one getting the calls now.

Kira faced her then, fury tightening the lines on her face. "That you were plotting to blame everything on us."

"That's insane!" Lacy couldn't believe what she'd just heard.

"Is it?"

"Wait, Kira," Melinda urged. "You know Lacy would never do anything like that."

"Do we?" she demanded, unconvinced.

"Kira, how can you believe someone like that? Don't you see what they're trying to do?" Lacy urged. "The point is to tear us apart."

"The point is murder," she threw back at Lacy. "Cassidy is dead. According to our wacko caller, one of us is next." She pointed to Melinda and then herself. "He said you were conspiring with Chief Summers to pin the whole thing on us. And, personally, I'm beginning to believe him. You've been acting weird since we arrived."

"Kira, please," Melinda pleaded.

"Where were you last night, Lace?"

Lacy wanted to refuse to answer the question but she knew that any attempt to hide her actions last night would be futile. Kira already knew.

"I was with Rick."

Melinda stared at the floor a moment then said, "Kira called your house around midnight to see if your folks had made it home and to touch base with you. No one answered."

"What did you tell him?" Kira demanded.

Lacy turned to Kira. "I didn't tell him anything, Kira. We had sex. Several times," she added. "We didn't do any talking."

"You really expect me to believe that?"

"He was my first," Lacy admitted out loud for the first time in her entire life. "The summer before my senior year." She looked from Melinda to Kira. "I was the only one who was still a virgin and I wanted to change that. He and I had been flirting…sort of… forever, it felt like. So I chose him."

"I knew it," Melinda murmured to herself, it seemed. "I knew he'd always had a thing for you, now I know why."

Lacy wondered why Melinda was behaving as if nothing bad had happened. Unreal somehow. Delayed shock? Cumulative stress?

"That's also why he's been following you," Kira added, her words bitter. "He thinks you'll be the one to break. Do you really expect us to believe that you shared his bed last night and didn't spill your guts?"

Fury kindled deep in Lacy's belly. "Did you tell Brad anything the other night when you were out with him? Does Brian know you're cavorting with your old lover?"

For one endless beat, Lacy was sure Kira would burst into tears, but she reined in the emotion. Lacy hated herself for stooping that low, but Kira had goaded her into it.

"He would have been my first," Kira said, her voice

wobbly but her expression fierce. "But Charles, the son of a bitch, beat him to the draw."

Melinda swayed. "Why didn't you tell me this?" Again her tone sounded strange, almost monotone.

Kira turned to her, tears rolling down her smooth cheeks despite, or maybe because of, her anger. "I didn't want you to ever know. You were so blindly in love with him. When he found out about Brad and me, he used it to make me do what he wanted. You know how it was then. My folks would have grounded me for life if they'd found out I was seeing a white boy. They would probably have sent me away to boarding school."

Kira was right about that. Ashland was just now beginning to overcome the legacy of racism.

Melinda laid a consoling hand against Kira's arm. "It was my fault. I was stupid for not seeing what he was."

Lacy moved up next to her and put an arm around her for support. "You were in love, Melinda. You couldn't see past that."

"He did the same to Cassidy," Kira said quietly. "He found out about her sexual persuasion and he used it to get favors from her, as well. Brad always thought it was Cassidy putting a wedge between us. He never knew the truth."

Dear God, Charles was an even worse monster than Lacy had believed.

Melinda turned to Lacy. "What about you, Lacy? Did he hurt you like that?"

Lacy shook her head, thankful to be able to do so. "He must have known I wouldn't be able to keep the truth from you."

"Of course not," Kira said bitterly. "The perfect Lacy would never do such a thing. What makes you any better than me or Cassidy?"

Lacy's emotions reeled, bruised all over again by the impact of her friend's words. "Nothing. I just meant I assumed that was his reasoning, since he didn't attempt anything like that with me." At least not until ten years ago, but she wasn't about to mention that morning. Not with the tension already thick enough to cut with a chainsaw.

"Seems pretty convenient that Charles never hassled you, and now that his body is found, the chief of police is suddenly your secret lover."

She honestly thought that Lacy had tried to make them look bad in front of Rick.

"I don't know why you're acting this way, Kira, but I haven't done anything to deserve the third degree. This caller is probably the person who killed Cassidy, why would you listen to anything he said?"

"The caller said you intended to blame all of this on Melinda and me. He was warning me. You have to admit it looks pretty bad for you, Lacy. Especially considering that Cassidy is dead now and she's the one who knew the truth."

What the hell was that supposed to mean?

"What're you saying, Kira? What really happened? What did Cassidy know that the rest of us don't?"

Kira threw her hands up. "I'm finished here." To Melinda she said, "I'll see you at six in the morning."

"Kira, wait," Lacy urged. She didn't want her to leave like this.

When she didn't stop, Lacy followed her to the door. "Don't walk away with things between us like this, Kira. You know this isn't right."

She looked at Lacy one last time before she walked out the door. "I know one thing, Lace. You're going to take us all down with you and I don't think I can forgive you for that."

The door slammed behind her, but the words were still ringing in Lacy's ears.

Kira didn't trust her. Somehow she believed Lacy was to blame for all of this. It was insane.

"Come on, Lacy," Melinda implored with something resembling real emotion. "Let's put this behind us for a while. We can't let any of it get to us. Cassidy would want us to stick together. We have to try."

At least she had that part right.

Kira couldn't recall ever being this angry. Well, except for the day she had found out what Charles had been doing to Melinda. The whole sick relationship had given her flashbacks about what he'd done to her.

Her tires squealed as she spun out of Melinda's driveway. She needed to cool off. She had to think. Why the hell would Lacy lie so blatantly? And if she was honest with herself, she would have to say that Lacy had looked totally shocked. Maybe Cassidy had been wrong about Lacy. Maybe their psycho caller was wrong.

Kira wanted to believe Lacy. But it was hard knowing what she knew. Maybe she should just tell Lacy everything and see what she had to say for herself. But she'd promised Cassidy that she wouldn't ever tell.

What the hell was she supposed to do?

Her cell phone rang and Kira cursed the damned thing. She was sick to death of Brian calling. If this was him she was going to tell him to go to hell…to never call her again. She should have known things would never work between them. He was just too damned possessive.

She dug the phone out of her purse and checked the screen. Blocked Call. Fear fired in her blood. What if it was the one who'd called last night?

Only one way to find out.

Kira swallowed back her trepidation and punched the button to accept the call. "Hello."

"She denied everything, didn't she?"

The caller.

Kira wet her lips and tried to think what she should say to this psycho.

"That's all right, you don't have to answer. I know she did."

Kira looked around the neighborhood as she drove along the street. Who the hell was this freak? She'd demanded an answer to that question last night, but she hadn't gotten anywhere.

"What do you want?" She tried a different tactic today.

"I have the proof you need to protect yourself, Kira. I wanted to give it to Cassidy but someone killed her first. Maybe I should give it to you."

Kira was uncertain about a lot of things, but protecting herself wasn't one of them.

"What do you want me to do?"

# Chapter 15

Lacy couldn't just sit around Melinda's house and do nothing. She had to try to figure this thing out. There had to be a reason Kira felt the way she did.

Melinda was no help. She kept insisting that she had no idea what Kira meant. But Lacy had a feeling she knew exactly what the other two had been insinuating all along.

Every instinct warned Lacy that time was running out for all of them. She had to devise a way to prod reactions that she could ultimately control.

The only option she felt at her disposal was to approach Bent Thompson. She hadn't seen him since the day Rick had told him to stay away from her, but he had to be out there somewhere. Watching.

The idea that he could have been the one to kill Cassidy made her shudder.

Surely he wouldn't have been so blatant about following her, especially considering Rick had caught him, if he'd intended to murder one or all of them. That would be pretty stupid.

She couldn't talk to Rick. He would only use anything she said or did against her.

Lacy refused to consider how real last night had felt. Part of her had been convinced that he had deep feelings for her. But then he'd turned it off this morning just as suddenly as he'd switched it on. No matter what he'd said, his actions had spoken far louder.

She was obviously a bigger fool than even she had known.

"Lacy, you need to stop worrying about the things Kira said. She was just angry. She'll be fine by this evening. You wait and see."

Lacy wanted to believe it would be that simple but she knew better.

"Melinda." She sat down on the sofa next to her friend. They'd had dinner already. There was nothing left to do except obsess on what she couldn't accomplish—finding the truth. "Don't you see how important it is now that we determine exactly what happened to Charles? Our lives may depend on it."

Melinda shook her head. "I wish you would stop. This is just too hard."

Lacy hated that she made Melinda relive the past by talking about it, but the ugly past was back to haunt them. They had to face it head-on. The feeling that Melinda was either hiding something Kira had said or trying to pretend this whole mess would just go away kept digging at Lacy.

"All of us had reasons to want to kill Charles," Lacy admitted. "But how can we be sure if one of us really did when we refuse to talk about it. Cassidy is dead. We don't have to play by the rules she set anymore."

"You should be ashamed, Lacy," Melinda scolded without actually looking at her or infusing her voice with authority. "She was our friend. We trusted her. Why would we change that now?"

"Because someone killed her," Lacy argued. "Because that same someone may be the person who killed Charles." She wanted to add *Pam, too,* but she couldn't do that yet.

Melinda got up and walked away from Lacy. "I'm not going to talk about Charles's murder, Lacy. I just can't."

"What about the money?" she offered. "What happened to the hundred thousand that Charles withdrew that day? What if Bent Thompson did take it? What if he knows the truth and is just trying to make it look like we did it?"

Melinda spun around to face her, her expression twisted with pain that no amount of pretending could veil. "We did do it, Lacy! Don't you remember? Why do you keep pretending we didn't? *We!* Do you hear me? We killed him? You know that. And our actions are the reason Cassidy is dead. It's too late to change that. Let's get past it."

"But we didn't take the money!" Lacy argued still. "Someone else took it, which means someone else was involved."

"He probably gave it to one of his whores," Melinda lashed out. "Are you satisfied now? If I had my guess, he gave it to that tramp Pam Carter. She's probably living it up somewhere on his money."

Lacy had to look away. How could she keep this from Melinda? It would be all over the news by tomorrow.

"He didn't give it to Pam Carter," she relented.

Melinda's head came up. "How do you know that?"

"They found Pam's body...her remains." She rubbed a hand over her face. God, she hated to do this. "She was murdered with the same weapon used on Charles."

Melinda's eyes widened in disbelief. "That's impossible."

The vehemence in her words surprised Lacy. She had no more idea about that than Lacy did. "It's true," she assured her. "They've already done the ballistics on the bullets they recovered from both Charles's Mercedes and Pam's rudimentary grave."

Melinda wandered back to the sofa and plopped down as if she could no longer hold up her frail weight. "This is crazy. I don't understand."

What she didn't know was that the worst was yet to come. "They didn't find any money with Pam's remains. But they did discover one other thing."

Melinda's eyes met hers and this time they were all too alert. "She was pregnant, Mel," Lacy said with an ache in her chest. "I'm sorry, but there's reason to believe it was Charles's baby."

Something changed in Melinda's eyes then. She shut down and drew back into her shell like a frightened turtle.

"I wish I hadn't had to tell you this, but it'll probably be in the papers tomorrow. And even if they don't release the part about the baby's paternity, since it probably hasn't been confirmed, you know there will be speculation."

"I don't want to talk about this again." Melinda stood. "I'm going to lie down now. I'd appreciate it if you don't disturb me."

She left the room in that same daze of denial she'd displayed when Lacy first arrived. Lacy wanted to go after her, but she understood that her friend needed time to absorb the awful ramifications of what Lacy had just told her.

Lacy closed her eyes and rubbed at her temples. "Charles, you bastard," she muttered, "why didn't you just stay buried?"

Feeling too restless to retire this early herself, Lacy tried to call Kira. She didn't mind making the first move toward reconciliation. They couldn't let this thing fester between them. It would only make bad matters worse.

Kira had turned off her cell phone and there was no answer at her folks' house. Annoyed, Lacy hung up. Not that she actually blamed Kira. With the way Brian called, ignoring the phone was the only way to shut him down.

She couldn't help wondering if, when this was over, assuming it was ever over, Kira could go back to Brian and pretend Brad hadn't touched her life again.

Lacy studiously blocked the images from last night and this morning. It would be so easy to wake up in Rick's arms every day for the rest of her life.

But at the rate she was going she would either wake up dead or in prison.

Neither really appealed to her.

But no one wanted to cooperate in fighting the inevitable of one of those two ends.

She had no way of getting to the bottom of this mess if she couldn't get any cooperation.

She prayed Rick would have more luck. As much as she didn't want his investigation to ruin any of their lives, someone had to uncover the truth.

No matter the cost.

She moved to the family room and turned on the television to watch the weather situation. Maybe her parents would be able to head home by tomorrow. If only the weather would cooperate.

Rick stared at the list Brewer had compiled for him.

Right there smack in the middle of a hundred or so other names was Lawrence Oliver.

Lacy's father.

He'd registered a .38 nearly twenty years ago.

The registration was still valid.

Rick rubbed his chin and studied the list as if he could make that one name go away, but he couldn't.

Lacy had had access to a .38 on the day Charles was shot. Whichever .38 had killed him was undeterminable, but the fact remained that she'd had motivation and now, apparently, the right caliber of handgun to commit the crime.

If there was a ballistics match she would have some major explaining to do. But first he had to get the weapon. Since the Olivers were still out of the country, his only option was Lacy. Not good.

The idea that two different weapons had been used didn't make sense. Maybe the poor bastard had had himself two violent confrontations that day. How could both have occurred so close together and why hadn't he sought help after the first one if he were conscious?

Again, it didn't add up.

But damned little about this whole thing did.

Cassidy Collins had been strangled. They were no closer to determining how or why than they were the morning they found her body.

No evidence. None. Not one speck.

Other than the two slugs recovered from Charles's

trunk, basically the same situation existed with his case. Pamela Carter's situation was no better.

No real evidence, plenty of motivation and potential suspects, but nothing concrete.

It was as if a ghost had killed all three.

But that wasn't the case.

Proving it, however, was another matter.

Nigel Canton's movements appeared to be restricted to work and home. Bent Thompson couldn't be found. He'd stayed out of sight since Rick warned him to leave Lacy alone.

Rick glanced at the clock on the wall next to his desk. Nine. He should go home. He was damned exhausted.

The idea that at this time last night he and Lacy had been in his bed drilled straight into his thoughts. He wanted desperately to touch her again. To call her right now just to hear the sound of her voice.

But she didn't want to trust him. She was afraid to risk further contact with him. He understood the problem perfectly. She had something to hide related to Charles Ashland's murder and she didn't want to risk his prodding it out of her.

Too bad she didn't know him better than that. Last night had had nothing to do with the investigation. Whether or not he could convince her of that when this was over, he couldn't say. He'd just have to ride it out and see.

For now, he had to do what he could to protect her. According to Brewer, she and Melinda hadn't left the house. Larson was stationed outside the Jackson home. Kira's folks had attended church tonight, but she hadn't left the house.

Rick rubbed at his burning eyes and decided to call

it a night. Maybe he could drift off to sleep with the scent of Lacy Oliver permeating his sheets.

If he were really lucky, maybe he'd dream about making love with her the way they had last night.

As he turned off the lights in his office the phone rang. Damn. And he'd thought he would get away at a decent hour.

Considering the way things had been going in his town, he braced himself for just about anything.

"Summers."

"Chief, this is Larson."

Rick frowned. Larson sounded unsteady. "What's up?"

"You need to come over here right now, Chief. The Jacksons came home from church a few minutes ago and well...their daughter, Kira...she's dead, Chief. I've already called the coroner."

Rick didn't recall hanging up. The next thing he knew he was en route to the Jackson home. He kept turning over and over in his head the idea of how anyone could have gotten in and killed her with his deputy sitting right outside.

Pure fear trickled into his veins. He pulled out his cell and entered Melinda's home number. He needed to hear Lacy's voice. Now.

Bent had decided exactly what he wanted. He'd set up the big meeting. All he had to do now was make his desires known. He'd waited a long, long time for this.

"Are you ready to know the value I've placed on the rest of your life?"

His reluctant guest stared at him as if he were nothing but a cockroach to be squashed if the opportunity permitted.

But if anyone was going to do any squashing it would be him. Bent had to laugh. It felt so good to be in control. He liked that something as trivial in the grand scheme of things as that pitiful little .38 he'd hung on to for all that time had opened up the same opportunity for him as winning the lottery. He had big, big plans.

"I was thinking," Bent said, dragging out the moment. He so loved this feeling of dominance, "that maybe I would like to—"

"Die?"

His full attention jerked back to the person seated next to him in his old Camaro. He opened his mouth to ask what the hell that remark meant when he saw the gun, and his words deserted him. He hadn't expected this…not in a million years.

As streetwise as he was, he'd screwed up. He'd counted his chickens before they hatched.

# Chapter 16

Rick watched through the viewing window as Jacob Griggs, assisted by a surgeon, removed the slug from Kira Jackson's chest cavity. He hated that this procedure was necessary. The family didn't want an autopsy and, frankly, one wasn't necessary. A single gunshot had killed her. The necessary blood tests could be conducted without a brutal, full-scope autopsy. But a partial examination was necessary to search the body for prints or any trace evidence left by the killer.

And he had to have the slug, which was still lodged in bone.

Jacobs and the surgeon who'd been on call were taking great care not to do any unnecessary damage in deference to the family's wishes.

Kira's parents had called her brother's military unit in Texas to make him aware of the tragedy, as well as any other relatives who lived outside Alabama. Arrangements had been made with the preferred funeral home to take charge of the body when Rick was finished with the necessary official procedures.

He couldn't promise that it would be today, but he would do the best he could.

Kira's nude body had been wrapped in a shower curtain and left in the bathtub of her family's home.

This killer wanted the world to know that he or she was avenging the death of Charles Ashland, Junior. First Cassidy's body had been shoved into the trunk of her car and driven to the lake to the exact spot where Charles had been dumped ten years ago. Then Kira was murdered and her nude body wrapped in a shower curtain in a manner similar to the way Charles had been done.

Whatever the secret Lacy and her friends had been hiding, someone else knew about their involvement. If he'd had any doubts whatsoever, he had none now.

He'd relieved Deputy Brewer from duty and sent another of his men to watch Melinda's house. Brewer was devastated. Larson had been interrogated up one side and down the other and he was certain no one had come into the house on his watch. Since he hadn't set up watch on the Jackson home until after Kira left Melinda's, Rick estimated that the killer could have been waiting inside the house for the right opportunity. There wasn't any way to know yet. Forensics techs were going over the house in an attempt to find anything that might help determine who had committed this heartless crime.

When had living in Ashland become so damned dangerous?

The whole town would be in an uproar as soon as the news was out. The media frenzy would only get worse.

But none of that was at the top of Rick's worries just

now. He had to stop the killer. Two of Lacy's friends had been murdered. That left only Melinda and Lacy.

Griggs motioned to him that he'd gotten the slug and Rick breathed a sigh of relief. Kilgore would rush the slug to ballistics and they'd do a comparison test ASAP.

Right now he wanted to get over to Melinda's and break the news to Lacy. He'd asked the Jackson family not to inform anyone local until morning. They had agreed, or maybe they'd simply been too much in shock to argue. Whatever the case, he was grateful for their cooperation.

Last night he'd ordered his men to maintain radio silence so to speak to keep things quiet, but he couldn't prevent those damned reporters from doing their job. Too many were watching. Two or three had swarmed the street outside the Jackson home, but one of his deputies had kept them at bay. Another handful had picked up on the call to the coroner and followed his van.

The murder would be reported in this morning's paper as well as on the news. Lacy could already know.

To avoid the reporters when he left the hospital, Rick had parked his truck in the maintenance crew's parking area. As he took the elevator to the ground level he decided on a course of action. He waited until he'd made his way through the maintenance division and out the rear exit before he made the call.

There were only so many readily identifiable players in the saga that was Charles's murder investigation. Rick was about to give them all a good shake to see what kind of reaction he got.

When he had Brewer on the line, he asked, "You hanging in there?"

"I'm ready to do anything I can to help, Chief. I've been waiting to hear from you. I need to do something."

That was exactly what Rick wanted to hear. "Okay. I want to shake some trees. Find out if Melinda Ashland's brother is back in town yet and if he is, haul him in for questioning. Same goes for Nigel Canton. Track down Bent Thompson and bring him in if you can find him. And when you've got those three in interview rooms I want you to call Senator Ashland and have him come down to the station."

A beat of silence throbbed across the line. "Are you sure you want to shake *that* tree?"

The whole damned town was afraid of the Ashlands. But Rick wasn't. "Damn straight. I want to talk to all four of them. This morning. I'll be there shortly."

First, he had to talk to Lacy, had to see with his own eyes that she was all right. He should just lock her up and keep her safe until this was over. But she'd never go for it. He'd just have to keep a deputy close to her and even that might not be enough.

Lacy waved the blow dryer back and forth over her hair, causing the long strands to whip around her face. She watched the strands fly around, her mind on last night and the way she'd tossed and turned. She hadn't been able to get back in touch with Kira. Melinda had stayed in her room.

What the hell was happening to them?

Had a lifetime of friendship come down to this so easily?

Apparently so.

As much as she wanted to pretend everything would turn out okay when this was over, she knew that wasn't going to happen.

Cassidy was dead. Nothing would bring her back.

Lacy had made the mistake of getting involved with

Rick again. There was no way anything good could come from that.

She closed her eyes, not caring which way the dryer blew her hair. As much as she wanted to, she simply could not consider what she and Rick had shared a mistake. It was true that nothing could come of it. They lived in two different worlds, and always had. Though society no longer separated them, geography did. Her life was in Atlanta, his was here.

If she survived this ordeal and left Ashland again, she wasn't entirely sure she would ever return.

The memories would be too painful. Her parents could always visit her in Atlanta.

Forcing her eyes open, she focused her attention back on drying her hair. She'd showered and dressed. Melinda would be up soon and she needed to find a way to make amends with her dearest friend. And maybe Kira would show up at six with a whole new attitude and the two of them could mend fences as well.

Lacy frowned and listened over the roar of the dryer. Had that other sound been her imagination? Maybe. She was tired, the only decent sleep she'd had was the night spent with Rick. She shivered and tried not to replay the scenes from that night but her mind had a will of its own.

She ran her fingers through her hair, let the hot air sift between them. The feel of her hair slipping through her fingers reminded her of how it had felt to have Rick's fingers there. He'd touched her in ways she couldn't hope to ever forget. Just the memory made her ache for his touch now. Made her want to hunt him down and—

Pounding on the bathroom door yanked her from the fantasy.

"Lacy!"

Melinda.

Lacy clicked off the dryer and tossed it aside. She jerked the door open.

"Are you all right?"

She first took in Melinda's terrified expression, then, slightly beyond her friend's trembling frame, the man behind her.

Rick.

"What's happened?"

"It's Kira," Melinda blurted, her voice quavering. "She's been murdered."

So much happened in the next few moments Lacy wasn't sure she absorbed it all. Rick was talking to her, but Melinda had fainted and she couldn't focus on his words.

He carried Melinda to her room, placed her carefully on the bed. Melinda roused and burst into sobs. Lacy held her, rocked her like a baby until she cried herself to sleep. Her thoughts whirled frantically. Kira couldn't be dead. But she was. And it all boiled down to the same single, excruciating idea. Somehow, this was all Lacy's fault.

The pain she expected to feel didn't come. Instead she felt completely numb…empty.

She'd had to call Melinda's doctor for a sedative. Thank God the pharmacy was willing to deliver. After she'd tucked the covers around Melinda, she got up to leave the room. Rick waited just outside the door. She didn't know how long he'd been there or even how long she'd held Melinda to console her. Lacy felt nothing at all, not even a sense of the passage of time.

She closed the bedroom door and somehow found the strength to ask, "What happened?"

"Let's go downstairs and we'll talk."

Lacy knew that was the right thing to do. She didn't want to disturb Melinda. But her brain wouldn't function properly; otherwise, the idea would have been hers. It took all her attention to make her feet work right as they descended the stairs. Strange. Now she understood why Melinda's behavior had seemed so odd last night. Shock.

When she would have guided Rick to the living room, he took her arm and tugged her in the direction of the kitchen. "You need some coffee."

She hadn't had coffee this morning, had she? She didn't think so. But she really didn't want any now.

He ushered her onto a stool at the island and set about making a pot of coffee. Her eyes followed his movements, but she couldn't anticipate what came next, as if she'd never watched coffee being made before. Her mind wouldn't move forward on its own, wouldn't wrap around a concept.

The carafe had already been filled and the filters and can of coffee placed on the counter when Rick started. Had Melinda been about to make a pot when he arrived? What difference did it make? That simple question felt so daunting. Lacy couldn't catch up.

The scent of coffee drifted up from the machine before Rick approached the island where she sat.

"Are you sure you're ready to hear this?"

She'd asked him what happened. Somehow she'd forgotten doing so. What was wrong with her? She couldn't hold a thought.

"I want to understand what happened." The words came out of her mouth, but she felt as if she were listening to someone else speak.

Rick braced his hands on the counter. "Kira was

shot. Once in the chest. The bullet tore through her heart, glanced off a rib and lodged in her spine."

His words evoked the corresponding images in her head. Her entire body convulsed at the horrifying pictures.

She'd been wrong. She hadn't been ready for all that information.

"Excuse me," she mumbled as she slid off the stool and hurried to the guest bathroom tucked beneath the stairs. She'd scarcely landed on her knees on the floor when her stomach heaved with such force that had she eaten that morning, all would have resurfaced.

She heaved for several more minutes before the overwhelming, repetitive urge passed. As horrifying as looking at Cassidy the other morning had been, she hadn't thrown up. Now, just hearing about Kira sent her in search of the nearest toilet. Maybe it was a cumulative reaction.

Taking a deep breath, she pushed to her feet, washed her face and rinsed her mouth. She stared at her pale reflection.

Now there were only two.

Melinda and her.

Whoever the killer was, one of them would be his next target.

If Rick couldn't stop him. And she knew he couldn't. It had to be her…somehow she understood that.

He waited for her in the hall. "Sorry," she said in the strongest voice she could muster. "I guess I wasn't as prepared as I thought."

"It's understandable." He looked anywhere but at her for a moment, but when his gaze landed on hers once more, the intensity there made her reach for the wall behind her for support. "We need to talk about this, Lacy.

I don't know if I can protect you and Melinda if you don't tell me what it is you've been hiding all these years."

And there it was...the ugly truth. The cause of death for two of her closest friends. The damned cross she'd had to bear for ten long years.

Suddenly, as if a light had gone on in some deep, dark recess of her brain, she knew exactly what she had to do. So simple, she should have thought of it before.

She would send Melinda to the Ashlands, where their security would protect her and then she'd wait right here in this house—the scene of the crime ten years ago—for whoever thought he or she had a score to settle to come for her.

And then she was going to kill the son of a bitch with her bare hands.

"You're wasting your time, Rick," she said, her voice lacking any sort of inflection. "I can't tell you anything and neither can Melinda. Your efforts would be better spent trying to solve the murders of my friends."

He moved in closer, pinning her against the wall with his nearness. "I know you're lying, Lacy, but I'll cut you some slack right now considering all you've been through. But I'll be back later to talk to you again."

It would be so easy to get lost in his eyes, to trust that he could fix this. But he couldn't. It was too late. Only she could stop it now.

"I won't change my mind. You'll only waste more precious time coming back."

A muscle ticked in his lean jaw. "Don't leave this house, Lacy. My men will be watching."

"Like they were watching Kira last night?"

He flinched. For the first time since she'd heard the news, she felt pain...pain for all that had happened...pain for all that would never be.

He left.

She didn't move. Couldn't.

She'd just stay right here until she pulled herself back together, then she'd set her plan into motion.

Tonight it would end one way or another.

Brewer was waiting for Rick in his office when he returned to City Hall. He looked like hell, but the man refused to go home. He wanted to find Kira's killer.

"Canton and the senator are fit to be tied," he said. "Melinda's brother isn't taking it so well, either."

Kyle Tidwell, Melinda's only sibling, had just gotten back in town from a funeral. His wife's aunt or something like that.

"What about Thompson?" Rick tossed his keys onto his desk.

"Haven't located him yet."

Rick grabbed a file to use as a prop. "Keep looking."

"Will do, Chief."

Rick hesitated. "Follow up on that search warrant. I need to know if Lacy's father still owns that thirty-eight. I can't get through to Mr. Oliver by phone. Looks like he and his wife won't be getting back before tomorrow. I don't want to have to execute a search warrant."

"I'll do that now," Brewer assured.

Rick took the easiest door first. Nigel Canton, former partner of Charles Ashland, Junior.

"Good morning, Mr. Canton. Thank you for cooperating with our investigation."

Canton did not look happy to be cooperating. In fact, he looked mad as hell.

"I don't know what you're up to, Summers, but I've called my attorney and you will be hearing from him. I've had enough of this crap. You should be talking to

Ashland's wife and her friends if you want to know what happened to him."

"Kira Jackson is dead." Rick said this as he took a seat at the interview table directly across from Canton. That his mouth dropped open and his pupils flared indicated that he was surprised by the announcement. "I'm sure you're already aware of Cassidy Collins's murder."

He shook his head, as confusion overtook the surprise. "I don't...why would you call me in to question me about her? I don't really even know her. Or the other one, for that matter. Only that they're part of the group I'm certain killed Ashland." He appeared to recover his composure then. "Not that I'm complaining. They did the world a favor in my opinion. That's the only reason I bothered to pay my respects to the Collins woman."

Rick studied Nigel Canton for a moment before he spoke again. Could this man have killed Charles? Possibly. Even the most civilized man could commit murder in a fit of rage. "How's your wife, Mr. Canton?"

Fury whipped across the man's thin face. "I know what you're getting at, Summers, and I'm not taking the bait. What happened between Ashland and my wife was a long time ago."

"So was his murder."

"I read the papers, Chief. I know Pamela Carter's remains were found. Doesn't that clue you into who's responsible for both murders? Ashland's wife had more to gain than anyone else. Plus, she had the help of her loyal friends. That's where you should be directing your energy. Not harassing innocent citizens."

Rick opened the folder he'd brought with him. It actually had nothing to do with the case, but Canton didn't know. "I know how he made you feel, Canton," he said finally. "Ashland always made you the butt of his jokes. Hell, he fucked your wife. You had every right to hate him. And you gained yourself a sizable profit from his death as well."

A new flood of anger darkened the man's face. "I waited seven long years for that profit," he snarled. "While Ashland's estate got fifty percent of everything I made. So don't try to make me feel guilty for getting what was rightfully mine in the end. I deserved every cent."

Rick pinned him with a warning glare. "Don't leave town, Canton. We're not finished yet."

With that said, Rick left interview room one and headed for door number two, Kyle Tidwell, Melinda's protective older brother. He wanted the senator to sweat a little longer.

Kyle Tidwell was tall, six-three or -four, and solidly built. He'd played football through high school and he'd gone on to college on an athletic scholarship, which was good because that was about the time his folks lost most everything when their business went belly-up.

The Tidwells had been good folks. Rick had often wondered if the parents' untimely deaths had been as a result of the extreme stress. The father had suffered a heart attack days before Melinda's graduation. The mother had passed after a bout with cancer less than two years later.

The family had certainly suffered more than its fair share of tragedy.

Including Charles Ashland, Junior.

"What's going on, Rick?"

Rick sat down at the table with Kyle. Though the two hadn't graduated together, Kyle had been only two years ahead of him. They'd known each other.

"I need to ask you a few questions about the afternoon Charles disappeared, Kyle."

Kyle made a sound of disbelief. "This is ridiculous. You know I have an alibi. I've been down this road before with your predecessor."

"Things have changed, Kyle. We need to reassess that alibi based on the latest evidence."

Kyle's irritation turned to nervousness. "What new evidence?"

"I can't give you the details just now, but I will need to speak to the woman who provided your alibi ten years ago." Rick had followed up on the nurse's statement that Melinda wasn't in her room for a time that day. He'd taken that possibility and worked out a scenario. According to Kyle's statement to Taylor ten years ago, he had left the hospital for about two hours with his girlfriend at the time, leaving his car in the hospital parking lot. If Melinda had gone anywhere, she would have had to have done so in Kyle's car. Rick had no evidence to indicate she had, but he could bluff.

"But I don't know where she is now." Kyle swallowed hard. His mouth worked a moment before his next words came out. "I haven't talked to her in years."

Rick ignored his mounting discomfort. "You're aware that Kira Jackson was murdered last night?"

"I heard the news on the radio. I just got back into town, like an hour ago. I was on my way to see how Melinda is holding up when your man Brewer hustled me over here."

"Where were you last night, Kyle?"

Survival instinct seemed to kick in. "What the hell are you trying to say, Rick? I didn't hurt Kira. You know better than that."

Rick stood. "Go home, Kyle. Try to locate that old

girlfriend of yours and—" Rick paused before he turned to the door "—don't leave town for anything."

"I don't understand this," Kyle argued as he shot to his feet. "Why would you need to confirm my statement?"

Rick decided now was the moment to play his hunch. "I found a witness who saw your car at Ashland's house the afternoon he disappeared. If you were with your girlfriend, then who was driving your car?"

He left the room, closed the door behind him. That should stir a reaction between Kyle and his sister, which was the whole point. Two down. He glanced toward his office, saw Brewer and walked that way. "Any word on Thompson yet?"

Brewer put his hand over the mouthpiece of the receiver. "Not yet."

Rick nodded and moved on to room number three. The senator. This one wouldn't be so easy.

Unlike the other two, Senator Charles Ashland, Senior, was not seated. He paced the room like a caged animal.

"What the hell is this about, Summers?" he demanded with all the pomp and confidence of a battlefield general.

With the senator he opted for a different approach. "We have reason to believe that Pamela Carter was carrying your son's child. Do you suppose that's why Charles killed her?"

The outrage Rick had expected didn't come. Instead the senator smiled knowingly. "I know what you're up to, Summers. You want to solve at least one of these many murders you have on your hands. Well, let me assure you, I won't allow you to clear your slate by slandering my son's name." He strode to the door, but glanced back before opening it. "You're finished in this town, Summers. I've tolerated all the incompetence I intend to. Melinda and her so-called friends killed my son and you haven't done a damned thing about it. Personally, I'm glad someone is avenging his murder."

Rick barely restrained himself from grabbing the man and slamming him into the nearest wall. But that would only get him arrested. Senator Ashland pretty much owned the town and Rick had just sealed the fate of his career. No Ashland ever made empty threats.

But he would take the chance if it meant he could stop these murders. Senator Ashland might not commit murder himself, but he had the means to hire anyone he wanted to do the job for him.

Rick exhaled heavily. Maybe he was grasping at straws here. He damned sure didn't have anything to go on, despite the fact that the bodies just kept piling up.

"Chief."

Brewer came barreling through the door before Rick had reclaimed his professional bearing.

"Yeah, Brewer. Did you find Thompson?"

"Sure did."

Brewer's resigned expression pushed Rick to a higher state of alert.

"He's dead, Chief. One shot to the head. Found him over on Tupelo Pike in his car."

Before Rick could ask anything else, Brewer went on, "That makes five, Chief. Three in the past week. We need to call in the big guns. I'm not sure we can handle this on our own."

As much as Rick didn't want to admit it, Brewer was right. "Call Agent Fowler over at ABI and let him know we could use his assistance."

ABI was the Alabama Bureau of Investigations. They helped out local law enforcement when a case got too complicated.

This one had just gotten extremely complicated.

Francine, Rick's secretary, stuck her head out of his office. "You've got a call, Chief."

What now? "Take a message." Hell, if it wasn't a dead body he didn't have time to take it.

"I don't think you're going to want to do that, Chief," she returned. "It's Mayor Hamilton."

Perfect. The senator had gone to the mayor.

Just what Rick needed right now.

Pressure from above.

He'd known when he'd had the senator rousted from his mansion that there would be repercussions.

Might as well face the music.

With two of Lacy's friends dead, and only one other besides herself remaining, the lyrics were quickly coming to a close on this song. If he didn't nail the perp soon…

He had to make this happen.

Or die trying.

# Chapter 17

The telephone had rung. Melinda had obviously answered it. Lacy stood outside her room and considered whether or not she should go in. But Melinda had told her to go away once already when she'd knocked. The silence on the other side of the door indicated that the call had ended.

What if it was *that caller?*

Adrenaline rushed through her. She prayed it wasn't. The numbness she'd felt earlier had faded somewhat for Lacy. She'd talked to Kira's mom and then she'd cried. Brian, Kira's fiancé, was there. He was devastated. She'd thought about trying to call her own parents, but she didn't want to worry them. They were under enough stress trying to get home to her. She wished for that blessed numbness again.

But she wasn't so lucky.

She'd just have to get through this the best she could.

She knew what she had to do. All she needed now was Melinda's cooperation.

The bedroom door unexpectedly opened. Melinda rushed out, her face even paler, her eyes wide with terror.

Lacy felt her heart sink lower. She couldn't make herself ask what had happened. The call must have been more bad news.

"That was Kyle," Melinda blurted. "Rick just questioned him. He's pressing Kyle to confirm his alibi for that day." She rubbed at her forehead, her eyes wild with panic now. "Rick has a witness who saw Kyle's car at my house that afternoon. Kyle is panicking. He doesn't know how to reach his old girlfriend. His wife is extremely upset."

Lacy stilled. "Are you saying Kyle may have confronted Charles?" Oh, dear God...not Kyle. Surely he wouldn't have killed Charles. As protective as he was of his sister, Lacy couldn't believe he would kill someone.

"No." Melinda covered her face in her hands a moment and shook with the emotions flooding her. "This is all my fault. All my fault," she wailed.

Lacy took her into her arms and tried to soothe her. "I'll call Kyle and talk to him, see if there's anything I can do to help."

Melinda pulled away. "You don't understand." She shook her head adamantly. "It wasn't Kyle. He's telling the truth about where he was. It was me." She slumped with defeat. "I left the hospital, took his car and went home to confront Charles."

A tiny tremor of shock radiated through Lacy. The idea that Melinda had left the hospital had been mentioned, but she'd refused to really believe it.

"Was Charles there when you got home?" Could she finally, after all these years, be on the verge of the truth?

Did she really want the truth? What if Melinda had killed Charles in a moment of emotional desperation?

Melinda nodded jerkily. "I think he'd been with someone. He...he was half-dressed and the covers on the bed were rumpled."

Lacy could hear the hysteria building in her voice. "Just calm down and tell me what happened."

Standing in the upstairs hall, outside the room where they'd discovered Charles's body all those years ago, Melinda slowly told her story.

"I started screaming at him that I wanted a divorce. I couldn't take it anymore."

Lacy didn't ask any more questions, just let her talk.

"He laughed at me, Lace. Laughed and laughed." Her eyes took on a faraway look. "I hit him and he still laughed. He said he didn't care what I did, that he would leave me with nothing—no children, no money, nothing."

Anticipation pounding in her chest, Lacy waited for the rest.

"He told me that he could have any woman he wanted, including my best friend." She looked at Lacy. "He told me how much he wanted you and how much he hated me." She blinked. "I don't know what happened, but something inside me snapped."

Lacy suddenly wished she had been the one to kill Charles. She hated him more now than she had ten years ago. How dare he taunt Melinda using her as leverage. She'd flat out turned him down and he'd known that she would never agree to be with him.

"There was a pistol on the table next to the bed," Melinda said softly, her voice sounding as far away as her expression. "I don't know where it came from."

Realization turned to ice inside Lacy. Her father's pistol. The one Charles had taken away from her.

"I shot him." She flinched. "He stumbled back…fell to the floor. Hit his head on the bedside table."

Lacy's breath left her in a whoosh. Melinda had shot Charles. Dear God…what would she do now?

Melinda's shoulders lifted in an attempt at a shrug. "I didn't know what to do. I got sick to my stomach. I rushed into the bathroom and threw up."

"What about the gun?" Lacy urged. She had to know how it had ended up back in her father's desk.

Melinda frowned a moment as if uncertain of the answer. "I dropped it on the bathroom floor."

That didn't make sense.

"How did—"

"I just ran then," she continued, cutting Lacy off. "I didn't know what else to do. Charles was just lying there so still. This small hole right here." She gestured to her left shoulder. "I didn't even try to help him."

"Wait." Lacy went back over all that Melinda had just told her. "Are you saying you left Charles lying on the bedroom floor?"

Melinda nodded. "Next to the bed."

"And you only shot him once?"

She nodded again. "Just once."

Relief rushed over Lacy. "You didn't kill him, Melinda."

Tears crowded in her eyes. "Yes, I did. I just told you. This is all my fault. Cassidy and Kira would be alive if it weren't for me."

Lacy shook her head adamantly. "No, you don't understand. We found Charles in the bathtub and he'd been shot twice. Not once, Melinda. Twice."

Hope and confusion flickered in her eyes. "Are you sure?"

"Yes. I'm positive. He was shot two times. And he was

nude in the tub, not on the bedroom floor. All the blood was in the tub. There wasn't any on the bedroom floor."

"But he had on his trousers," Melinda argued.

Lacy shook her head again. "Not when we found him. You see, you didn't kill him."

Melinda's expression cluttered with worry again. "Cassidy was convinced you were the one, and I let her believe it to protect myself." She shook with emotion. "I was wrong, Lacy. But I was so afraid I'd lose my children."

Lacy tensed. She'd known that was the case, except for the part about Melinda's actions. "I didn't do it, Melinda."

Melinda looked away. "It was my fault. I let them believe all that time that it was you when I knew it was me."

At least Lacy understood now why Melinda had responded the way she had at times. "But you didn't kill him, Mel. Neither of us did."

She nodded vaguely. "I still don't understand why Cassidy and Kira were so convinced it was you."

Time for her own confession. "The gun you used. The one you dropped on the bathroom floor." Lacy realized then how the weapon had gotten back into her father's desk drawer. Cassidy was the one to clean up in the bathroom. She'd recognized the gun and put it back where it belonged. Tears burned behind Lacy's eyes. All that time she'd been protecting Lacy. She and Kira both had believed she was the one and they'd insisted on the vow of silence, even when Lacy argued, to protect her. "Oh, God." She swiped at her eyes. "Cassidy found the gun and thought I was the one who'd used it."

Melinda frowned. "I still don't understand."

"It was my father's gun."

Any remaining color drained from Melinda's face. "How did it end up on the table by my bed?"

Lacy knew she didn't mean the question the way it sounded. "Charles came to my house around ten that morning. He'd been drinking. He tried to…hit on me."

Melinda's eyes closed in agony.

"I told him to get lost. When he wouldn't leave, I ran to my father's desk and got his gun." She shook her head at how foolish that move had been. "He just laughed at me. He took the gun away from me and left."

"You think he brought it home with him and left it on the bedside table?"

"He must have. That was the last time I saw him alive."

Melinda pressed her fingertips to her forehead. "So many lies. So much hurt."

That was the truth. Charles Ashland, Junior, had damaged many lives.

A new realization crept into Lacy's thoughts. If Melinda hadn't killed Charles…and she hadn't killed him. Clearly Cassidy or Kira hadn't killed him, since both had been convinced that she had. Then who did?

A chill went through Lacy. "Mel, if none of us killed Charles…then who did?"

Melinda had obviously just come to the same conclusion. "Do you think the person who killed Cassidy and Kira could be the one?"

Lacy wasn't sure it made complete sense, but she didn't know what else to think. "It's possible." But why? "I don't get why he or she would lie dormant all this time. Hell, he got away with it. Why resurface now and start killing again? Wouldn't that risk everything?"

"It doesn't make any sense at all," Melinda agreed.

"Unless," Lacy began, "the killer was still here when we moved Charles's body."

"You said you felt someone was watching you," Melinda offered, jumping on the bandwagon.

Lacy walked past Melinda and into the master bedroom. "After we'd gotten Charles's body wrapped in the shower curtain and into the trunk of the Mercedes, Cassidy sent me back up here to make sure we didn't miss anything." Lacy walked around the room, remembering the steps she'd taken that night. "I checked the bathroom again. It was clean. Cassidy had scrubbed the whole room with Clorox to make sure no trace of the blood would be found. I checked the carpet and the sheets in the bedroom. I didn't find anything incriminating. No blood. Nothing. I can only assume, considering what you've told me, that he got up before any blood got on the carpet. He may have just been dazed from hitting his head. The gunshot wound may have been very minor."

"I guess that's possible. You packed the suitcase for him next, right?" Melinda asked, remembering what they had told her.

Lacy walked over to one of the two closets. She drew open the louvered doors on what used to be Charles's closet. "I grabbed a suitcase—overnight bag—from here." She pointed to the shelf overhead. "Then a couple of shirts and trousers from the hangers. I put them in the suitcase along with the shoes and socks he'd left on the floor." She looked around the room again. "And I put the clothes he'd left on the floor in there, along with his wallet."

"But if someone was watching," Melinda wondered aloud, "where would they have been hiding?"

Lacy turned to the other closet. Melinda's closet. "Maybe in there. You can see through the louvers if you get in just the right position. You'd hear everything."

Melinda shuddered visibly. "So you didn't see anything that could have been a clue in the stuff you picked up on the floor. You didn't notice anything about his clothes."

Lacy shook her head. "Nothing." Then she remembered the one other item she'd picked up. "And his wedding ring. It was on the floor, too. I picked it up and put it in the suitcase." She figured the bastard had taken it off while he screwed someone else's wife. It had probably fallen out of his pocket when he took off his pants.

Melinda frowned. "You couldn't have picked up his wedding band." She crossed the room and opened a drawer on her jewelry chest. "Rick gave this to me after they recovered the body. It was in the trunk of the Mercedes."

Lacy stared at the gold band. "Are you sure it's his?"

"Of course." She tilted the ring and pointed to the initials inside. "See. NCA, Jr."

She was right. "Then whose wedding band did I find on the floor next to your bed."

Melinda still wore hers, even after all this time.

"Maybe it belonged to the person who killed him."

Lacy trembled with anticipation. "You're right. It's the one piece of evidence that connects the killer to the murder scene." Lacy turned to Melinda's closet once more. "She…it had to be a she considering what we know now…watched from her hiding place in that closet. When we got rid of Charles's body, as well as the evidence, she thought she was home free. That's why the person who knew our secret never tried to collect the reward. She couldn't…she was the killer. And she was safe until the body was found and we came back. Then she got worried, had to figure out a way to get rid of us before we figured out the truth." Lacy tried to remember exactly what the gold band had looked like. It hadn't looked particularly feminine, but then she'd been terrified.

"It was one of his lovers," Melinda said, disgust tingeing her voice.

Setting aside any lingering reservations, Lacy nodded. "Had to be. She knew her initials were inside that wedding band and we took it before she could get it back."

"But Pam is dead and she wasn't married," Melinda said, apparently going through the list of names.

"What about Nigel's wife?" It had to be her. "You know Charles and his partner were at each other's throat then. What if she wanted Charles to leave you for her?"

"Maybe Nigel came in," Melinda suggested, "caught them, killed Charles but couldn't bring himself to kill his wife."

"We have to talk to her." Lacy suddenly found it strange that she hadn't seen Nigel with his wife since she had returned to town.

"We can't. She's in Europe with two of her friends. They're having some kind of spa treatments. I heard Gloria talking about having been to the same place."

That was damned convenient. "When did she leave?"

Enlightenment claimed Melinda's face. "The day after Charles's body was found. I remember because that's when I heard Gloria talking about it to one of the women at City Hall when we…were there to talk to Rick about what would happen next."

"You mean to tell me Gloria was discussing spas on the day after her son's body was found."

Melinda scrubbed her hands over her face. "You have to know Gloria. She always does that, especially when she feels intimidated or nervous."

Anticipation was prodding at Lacy again. "We need that ring. It's the only evidence that exists. We need it to bring Cassidy and Kira's killer to justice."

"And to protect ourselves," Melinda added. "But what happened to the suitcase? It wasn't in the Mercedes with Charles. You think it's still in the lake?"

Lacy shook her head slowly from side to side. "We forgot to put it in the Mercedes. So I buried it."

The same anticipation Lacy felt lit Melinda's eyes. "Where? Can you still find it?"

"I know exactly where it's at."

Digging it up would be the only difficult part.

"We have to get it."

"No." Lacy held her back when she would have rushed from the room. "This killer wants both of us dead. You have two children to worry about, Mel. You can't take this kind of risk."

"There's no way I'm letting you do this alone."

For the first time in ten years, Lacy felt she had her friend back.

But she couldn't risk losing her again.

Nigel slammed down the phone. Where the hell was she? He sends her off to Europe to enjoy herself and she won't even answer the phone when he calls. This was her fault anyway. If she hadn't crawled into bed with that cutthroat bastard, he wouldn't be in this position.

He'd taken care of everything once, had taken care of her even when she didn't deserve it. And this was the thanks he got for it.

Nigel supposed if he hadn't been so preoccupied being angry with his wife he might have heard the door open to his home office.

But he didn't.

He wasn't even aware anyone had come into the room until it was too late.

# Chapter 18

"Please, Lacy, don't try to do this alone. Call Rick. Let him help."

Lacy held her ground. "I can't do that until I know for sure. For one thing, we can't be sure who actually killed Charles—Nigel or his wife. Or did he hire Bent Thompson to do it? We can't do anything that will tip our hand. No one knows we've figured out this much. We have to keep it that way until we have the evidence in our hands. Hell, I can't even remember if the wedding band was a woman's. I thought it was Charles's. What if it wasn't a woman's?"

"It had to be a woman's," Melinda argued. "Charles's ring was in the Mercedes with him. I told you that."

Lacy nodded distractedly.

Melinda wrung her hands. "I don't like this. You know we can trust Rick. We can't do this alone."

She was right, Lacy did trust Rick. But this had

nothing to do with trust. This was about making sure she didn't screw this up. All she had to do was go to her grandmother's old place and dig up the suitcase. Any additional steps between here and there could somehow ruin everything. His men would have to know and she didn't want to trust anyone else until she had that bag in her hand. And what if she was wrong? She knew the gold band was in there, she just couldn't be sure it really meant anything.

Maybe she wasn't making sense, but she'd lived with this burden for ten years. All four of them had let plain old fear keep them from learning the truth. She wasn't about to let anything get in her way this time. Once they had the bag, then they could call Rick.

"I need to go straight to where the suitcase is," Lacy insisted. "I don't want to take any chances. And I need you to act as a decoy."

"I don't like this, Lacy. I don't like it at all."

"No one will know I'm even gone," she urged. "Anyone who's watching us will follow you."

It took several more minutes to persuade Melinda, but that was okay because there was another hour before dark and Lacy needed the cover of darkness.

When she'd finally gotten Melinda to agree to her plan, they set into making preparations.

First they stuffed a sweatshirt with towels. Melinda dug up a long dark wig her daughter had used one Halloween. A half-gallon milk jug would have to serve as the head. In the garage they put the makeshift mannequin together in the front passenger seat of Melinda's car using a king-size pillow to prop it up.

"That looks like a stuffed sweatshirt and a wig on a milk jug," Melinda commented drily.

Lacy laughed for the first time in days. "Yeah, well, in the dark maybe it'll pass."

"Maybe."

Lacy rounded up the shovel she'd found in the garage storeroom and a heavy-duty flashlight. She patted the pocket of her sweatshirt. "I've got my cell phone. Got the flashlight and shovel. I'm ready." She wore a sweatshirt, in spite of the heat, to ward off mosquitoes, plus it was the only dark long-sleeved garment Melinda owned. She'd always been the one to wear bright colors. Jeans and sneakers completed her getup.

"I'm still not feeling so good about this, Lace."

Lacy held up a hand. "Shush, Mel. We've agreed. Let's not go backward." An ache echoed through her. "Remember, we're doing this for Cassidy and Kira."

Melinda nodded.

"You back out of the garage and drive to the Jacksons'. If you pull up next to Kira's rental, the passenger side of your car will be camouflaged from the street." She remembered that from the other night. She wasn't sure why the rental hadn't been turned in yet. Maybe the family was still too distraught. "Get out and go in at the side entrance, and before your tail can get a good view you'll be inside. He'll assume he simply didn't see me get out because of the bushes."

"Okay. What do I tell anyone who asks about you?"

"Tell them I have a migraine." Lacy hadn't suffered from a migraine in years, but most people didn't know that. They would only remember that as a young teen she'd had a number of debilitating headaches.

"When I have the suitcase I'll call you and then you can meet me at City Hall or Rick's house, wherever he is."

Melinda exhaled a heavy breath. "Well, let's do it then."

Lacy hugged her. "I love you, Mel." She wished she

had said those words to Cassidy and Kira since coming back to Ashland, but she hadn't. She knew they had known how she felt, but she realized now more than ever how fleeting life could be. A person should say what they feel...often.

"I love you, Lace." Melinda drew back, her eyes watery. "Please, please be careful."

Lacy smiled and struggled to hold back her own tears. "Time to go."

Melinda loaded into her car while Lacy quickly loosened the lightbulbs in the garage-door opener—the less light the better. Lacy stepped back into the deepest shadows of the garage as her friend sent the overhead door into the up position and prepared to back down her driveway.

When the garage door closed once more, Lacy rushed inside the house and watched the street from between the slats of the blinds in the entry hall. Sure enough, no sooner had Melinda glided off down the street than a police cruiser lit out after her.

"Worked like a charm."

Just in case, Lacy used the back door and stole her way around to her SUV. She tossed her shovel and flashlight into the back seat and headed for her grandmother's farm just outside town. She stayed on the back streets in hopes of avoiding any police cruisers.

Twenty minutes later she'd parked next to the old Oliver home place. The place where her father had grown up. Where he and her mother had lived the first few years of their marriage. And finally, where Lacy had enjoyed listening to stories told by her seemingly ancient grandmother as she rocked back and forth in her cane-back rocker on the shady front porch.

No one had lived here in fifteen years, since her grandmother had passed away, but her parents kept the place up. Couldn't bear to part with it. Lacy sometimes wondered if they expected her to come back and produce them a gaggle of grandkids. Both her mother and father were only children, and so was Lacy. But they had spoken fondly many times of having a little herd of grandkids.

Rick popped smack into the middle of that thought.

She shook her head to clear it. She had to be out of her mind. Maybe she was still in shock after losing her dear friends or maybe she was just slipping over the edge and didn't know it yet.

The moon, full and round and hanging almost to the ground, lit her path as she walked past the house and across the massive backyard. They didn't make backyards like this anymore. These days, most were scarcely big enough to hold a small patio.

But this—she surveyed the moonlit landscape—was what one referred to as sweeping. An ocean of grass bordered by trees as old as time and as tall as giants.

She'd walked this path a million times with her grandmother and always ended up in the same place, through the woods, across the cornfield and to the stream. Lacy had loved the stream in the woods on the other side of the field her grandmother had leased to a local farmer after her husband had passed away.

Lacy made her way through the underbrush, weaving between the big old trees, until she reached the place where she and her grandmother had buried Trax, her older-than-dirt hound dog. That dog had taken up space on the front porch for as long as she could remember. And when Lacy was sixteen the old fellow had finally died. Two years later her grandmother had joined her beloved husband and hound dog in the hereafter.

The family cemetery was at the far end of the property near a duck pond. Olivers for several generations were buried there.

As much as she loved her grandmother, Lacy didn't want to join them anytime soon.

She stopped at the spot where she'd buried Charles's suitcase ten years ago and stared down at the dead leaves and lush plants that had grown over the spot.

Dropping to her knees, she said a little prayer for Cassidy and Kira. She wished again that they'd realized the truth years ago so they wouldn't have had to live with this horrendous burden. But they'd stuck by their vow to never speak of it again. They'd stuck by one another.

There was something to be said for that kind of loyalty. The sad thing was that in doing so they had protected a murderer. That murderer had almost succeeded in getting away with not one but at least three murders.

Time to stop her once and for all.

But what if the ring told them nothing? Pushing aside that doubt, Lacy jammed the shovel into the ground. It was harder than she'd expected. But it had been ten years. And she hadn't forgotten how hard the digging had been that chilly night.

She shuddered at the memory of the snow falling down around her. It almost never snowed in Ashland, but that night it had.

Getting back to her feet, Lacy put her full weight behind the digging and that helped considerably. Another memory assaulted her. The blisters she'd had on her hands the next day.

"Damn."

She should have thought to bring gloves, too.

"No pain, no gain," she mumbled as she thrust the shovel deep into the ground.

The one other thing besides the icy temperature she recalled vividly from that night was the idea that she should bury the suitcase as deep as possible. She felt reasonably certain she would regret that decision before she was finished here tonight.

But then, if she hadn't, critters might have dug it up and dragged it off. She damn sure hadn't wanted to take a risk like that.

Grunting with each pound into the well-packed earth, she comforted herself with the knowledge that she might soon be able to nail the scum who had killed her friends. She couldn't actually say whether this same person would have been the one to kill Pamela Carter, but there was a good possibility that whoever left that ring had killed Charles and murdered two of her best friends. Lacy wanted that person to pay for killing her friends. Neither Cassidy or Kira had had any idea that they were concealing the one piece of evidence that might lead the authorities to the real killer. So their deaths had been for nothing.

Fury flamed deep in Lacy's gut. She was the one who'd packed the suitcase. She would see that justice was done.

The crack of a breaking branch jerked her attention to the right. She froze. Had someone followed her here? She didn't remember seeing any lights in her rearview mirror.

She grasped the shovel's handle more tightly and drew it up to her shoulder in preparation of swinging it like a bat.

"Lacy?"

Lacy wilted with the withdrawal of adrenaline. "Mel, what the hell are you doing here?"

Melinda cut through the trees into the small clearing where Lacy worked. "I couldn't let you do this alone." She clicked on her flashlight and shone it on the ground. "Why don't you let me dig awhile?"

Lacy released a lungful of tension. "You're here. I guess you might as well." She passed the shovel to Melinda. "I won't even ask how you managed to get away without being followed."

Melinda plunged the shovel into the ground. "I borrowed a car from one of the guests."

Lacy shook her head. "What's a grand-larceny charge after you're sent up the river for concealing evidence in a homicide?"

Melinda hesitated in her work. "I hope that's a rhetorical question, because I have no idea."

"Just dig."

A clunk accompanied the shovel's next lunge into the earth.

"I think maybe I hit something."

Lacy got back on her knees and slowly moved the flashlight's beam over the area. A black nylon corner jerked her attention back to the spot when she passed it.

"That's it."

They both started to dig then, using their hands, anticipation driving their movements.

When they had unearthed the black overnight bag, they sat back on their haunches and caught their breath.

"You poke around inside," Mel said. "If we turn it upside down we might lose the ring in the darkness."

Lacy nodded. "Good idea."

The zipper resisted at first but finally surrendered to her tugs. The sound buzzed in the night like a cluster of dry flies fighting to escape their shells.

She reached inside and dug through the damp, musty articles of clothing. She'd found the ring after packing the other stuff. It should be close to the top...unless it had filtered down to the bottom.

Finally her fingers encountered the cold, smooth circle of gold.

Her heart jolted. "Got it."

She pulled her hand out of the bag and opened it to display the ring lying on her palm.

"It looks like a man's ring," Mel said.

Holding her breath, Lacy took it between her thumb and forefinger. "Hold the light steady, Mel."

Lacy tilted the ring, peered at the inside of the band that represented love and commitment.

"Can you see anything?" Mel wondered aloud.

"I see what might be an—"

"Give me the ring."

Lacy's head came up at the fierce order.

She blinked, unable to reconcile what her eyes saw with what her mind knew.

Melinda spoke first. "Renae?"

Renae Rossman. She stood over them, a gun in her hand.

Lacy squeezed her eyes shut just for a second to make sure she wasn't seeing things.

"Give me the ring," Renae commanded.

Lacy felt her hand moving toward the other woman's.

"This can't be your ring, it's—"

And then she knew. Renae had married the older man for his money, but she'd needed more. A younger lover...one who gave her what her much older husband could or would not.

"Now stand up."

Lacy jerked at the harshly uttered words.

"You and Charles were lovers." Melinda's words weren't a question. Like Lacy, she had just come to terms with what Renae's appearance meant.

Renae laughed hatefully. "We were more than lovers, sweet little Mel. I was his first. We'd been in love for years before he screwed up and got you pregnant."

Lacy slowly got to her feet, the fingers of one hand curled around the shovel's handle. Melinda was already standing and, judging by her stance, was madder than hell. Lacy looked at the gun, then at Renae. Somehow this just didn't fit, but fear kept her from being able to analyze what it all meant.

"If you were lovers, why did you kill him?"

Renae's full attention, including the weapon in her hand, swung toward Lacy. "How dare you ask me that?"

"What about Cassidy and Kira?" Melinda demanded. "Why did you kill our friends?"

"Because you all deserve to die for what you've done," she snarled. "And now that I have my ring back, I won't have to worry about it turning up afterward. That little mistake has haunted me for ten years."

"You won't have to worry about it turning up after what?" Lacy ventured, her fingers tightening around the wooden handle. She had a pretty good idea what Renae meant.

"After you're dead."

Fight or flight zoomed through Lacy. She had to do something or this crazy woman was going to kill them.

"Why would Charles want you?" Melinda countered. "He had all the young, beautiful girls he wanted."

Lacy held her breath and hoped Melinda hadn't just sealed her fate.

Renae glared at her but kept the gun trained on Lacy.

"Fool. We were in love. I was prepared to leave Wes. We had it all planned out. Then he learned you were pregnant and the senator threatened to disinherit him if he didn't marry you."

"If that's true," Lacy offered, easing a half step closer to Renae, "then why all the other women?"

She lifted her chin defiantly. "Charles had a voracious sexual appetite. No one woman could have expected to be enough. But he loved *me.*" She sent a menacing glare in Melinda's direction. "We made love and I begged him to run away with me. I'd even bought him a wedding band to prove I meant what I said. I had it engraved. *Love, Renae.* But he only laughed at me. I swore I'd never let him hurt me again."

Renae appeared to get lost in her memories for a moment and Lacy took advantage of what might be their only chance. She swung the shovel at Renae and screamed, "Run, Mel!"

Rick arrived at the Jackson home as quickly as he could. He'd been stuck in a briefing with ABI. And then Nigel Canton's body had been found, along with a confession typed and left for all to see on his computer screen. He'd admitted to killing Charles Ashland, Junior, and then trying to frame Lacy and her friends.

Everyone, including the mayor and the senator, were relieved to learn the truth. But Rick had a bad feeling about the whole setup, *setup* being the key word. He would reserve judgment until the forensic folks were finished with their work, but this was way too pat for his comfort.

The deputy watching Melinda and Lacy had informed Rick when the two went to the Jackson home. He'd figured that was okay considering, but the longer he thought about it, the more uneasy he'd gotten with the idea. He needed to see for himself that Lacy was safe.

As soon as he arrived at the Jackson home, trouble met him at the street. Deputy Phillips was busy filling out a report on a stolen vehicle.

"I've already put out an APB, Chief." He shook his head. "It's ridiculous when a person can't even visit a grieving family without having their car stolen."

"Are Mrs. Ashland and Miss Oliver still inside?"

Phillips nodded. "Yes, sir." He pointed toward Melinda's car. "I haven't taken my eyes off that vehicle."

Apparently not, Rick mused, if another was stolen right under his nose. But then who would have expected a thief to waltz up to a wake and drive off in a car.

"I'm going in for a minute," he told his deputy.

Not looking forward to the somberness inside, he made his way up the walk and across the porch. Kira's folks were devastated, just as Cassidy's had been. It was a damned shame.

Mrs. Jackson's sister welcomed him and asked if he'd like something to drink.

"No thanks, ma'am. I just need to touch base with Lacy Oliver."

The woman frowned thoughtfully. "Kira's friend?"

Rick nodded.

"I don't believe I've seen her tonight." She called out to another of the visiting family members. "Have you seen Lacy Oliver tonight?"

Dread pooled in Rick's gut.

The other woman shook her head. "But Melinda was here for a little while. She left about an hour ago."

Rick was out the door and at the street in three seconds flat. "How long ago did you call in that stolen vehicle?"

"We got it, Chief," Phillips said. "County just found it over on one-nineteen parked at the old Oliver place."

Terror seized Rick's insides. "You tell County to stay put. I may need them. I'm on my way."

"Yes, sir."

Phillips sounded confused, but Rick knew he would follow orders.

"Dammit, Lacy," he growled as he slid into his truck. "What the hell are you up to?"

The best he recalled, no one lived at the old Oliver home place. It had been empty for more than a dozen years.

As soon as he'd cleared the last intersection in town he floored the accelerator. Ten more minutes. That was all he needed.

His phone rang. He fished it out of his pocket. "Summers."

"Chief."

Phillips.

"County just reported gunfire in the woods behind the Oliver place. They're ready to go in."

"Tell 'em to approach with caution. There may be two victims being held against their will out there."

He threw the phone aside and focused on driving. He had to get there before it was too late.

Lacy ran through the brush, zigzagging through the trees as fast as she could.

Melinda had run in the other direction.

Lacy stilled and listened over the sound of her own breath sawing in and out of her lungs. She needed to make sure Renae followed her, not Melinda. Melinda had kids…she had to survive this.

Nothing. Silence.

Damn.

She had to do something.

"What's wrong, Renae?" she shouted. "Can't keep up?"

The sound of brush being parted grew louder.

A bullet whizzed past Lacy's head, took a chunk of bark off a tree less than a foot away.

She lunged deeper into the woods.

At least now she knew Renae was after her and not Melinda.

Lacy braced herself for the downward plunge as the landscape swept into a meadow. Her right foot twisted on a tree root and she went down in a flailing, rolling tumble. A tree trunk stopped her and pinned her right arm between the bark and her body. Pain seared upward from her elbow to her shoulder. Lacy bit down on her lower lip to hold back the scream of agony.

The sound of running in the distance behind her had her scrambling to her feet. Fire raced up her arm. Broken, she decided.

Didn't matter. She had to keep going.

Holding the injured arm close to her body, she ran harder, faster, and didn't look back, didn't slow for anything. Limbs slapped her face, but she didn't care. A few scratches and bruises, even a break, was better than being dead.

She stumbled again and swallowed the cry that rocketed into her throat. She got to her feet and looked around to get her bearings. Fear snaked through her chest.

Wait. This wasn't right. But she'd been through these woods a thousand times.

The sound of foliage brushing fabric pricked her

senses. Renae was close. Lacy didn't have time to think anymore, she had to run.

She lunged forward, thankful for a second wind and a renewed burst of speed.

She was suddenly in the field. Rows of knee-high corn spread out around her, taunting her in the moonlight.

No more cover. She needed to be back in the woods. How had she made such an error in…

Renae emerged from the tree line. Lacy ran. She had no choice.

The full, low-lying moon she'd admired tonight was now her enemy, tracking her movements like a spotlight.

She ran anyway, her legs heavy and cumbersome like wooden clubs. Pain radiated up her arm. Her lungs burned for more air. She'd never make it to the other side of the field.

Something hit her in the back. She fell forward. Landed on her knees. At first she thought she'd been shot, but Renae had only pushed her down.

She pressed the barrel against the top of Lacy's head. "Three down and one to go."

"Why?" Lacy croaked, her throat so dry. Her heart flailed against her sternum, but she needed to know why. "Why…after all this time?"

Renae jammed the tip of the weapon even harder into her scalp. "For ten long years you let me believe he'd left me. I was certain he'd run off with that little whore Pamela. I hated him for what he'd done to me. But then, when they found his body, I knew. He would never have left me…never. The four of you had taken him from me. Now it's time to pay for what you did."

Lacy squeezed her eyes shut in anticipation of the blast.

The explosion rent the air.

She opened her eyes…wondered if she was dead but was afraid to move.

The sound of footfalls rushing toward her jerked Lacy around.

Renae lay on the ground behind her…a good portion of her skull missing. Lacy cringed.

"You okay?"

Rick was suddenly at her side.

She wasn't dead…she was safe.

"Melinda?"

"Melinda's fine. She's back at the house."

Lacy was alive. Melinda was alive.

"You're safe now, Lacy." Rick helped her to her feet, careful of her injured arm. "It's over now."

It was over.

# Chapter 19

Lacy slept for the better part of two days.

She hadn't realized just how exhausted she was until she fell into bed.

When she'd finally joined the living again, she'd talked to Melinda. Her kids were both home with her and she was finally completely happy.

Lacy's folks had made it home. Thank God.

Kira's funeral had been extremely emotional.

Lacy missed her and Cassidy desperately.

She'd taken a couple more weeks off work. With her broken arm and all that she'd been through, going back any sooner was out of the question. Her parents were taking care of her as if she were twelve again. It felt good having someone take care of her.

The whole town had pretty much gotten back to normal. The news had run constant coverage of the final outcome of the Ashland tragedy for almost a week now.

No one, least of all Gloria Ashland, had suspected the relationship between Renae and Charles. She was, from Melinda's reports, at least attempting to be kind to Melinda. It was a miracle anything made the woman feel guilty. After all Melinda wasn't the one who killed her son or disposed of his body. She'd been as much a victim in this as Charles had. Maybe more.

But everyone appeared to be satisfied that the truth had been uncovered and it was really over.

Everyone except Lacy.

She'd heard what Renae said in those final moments before Rick had put a bullet through her head.

*The four of you had taken him from me.*

*For ten long years you let me believe he'd left me. I was certain he'd run off with that little whore Pamela.*

Renae had said those things. Lacy hadn't imagined a word of it.

She'd told Rick, but he'd chalked it up to shock. She had been shocked, that was true. She'd run for her life, and her arm had been broken. But there hadn't been anything wrong with her hearing.

Renae couldn't have killed Charles.

And if she had, who had killed Pamela? Charles? What happened to the money? Did Bent Thompson take it?

He was dead, Lacy had learned and so was Nigel Canton.

If she believed what everyone else did, Renae had been one busy lady. She'd killed Cassidy, Kira, Bent and Nigel.

It wasn't an impossible feat, just unlikely in Lacy's opinion. And why kill Nigel? Had he learned of Renae's relationship with Charles? She had a feeling Rick wasn't convinced with the scenario either.

Putting everything else aside, none of it explained what had happened to the hundred thousand.

She'd mulled over that detail until her head hurt.

Lacy got up and walked over to stare out the kitchen window. The stars were in full form tonight. Her world felt secure again…for the most part.

She braced her hands on the counter and reasoned out the conflicting thoughts preventing her from moving on.

As much as she wanted this all to be over, something wasn't right. She definitely didn't want to disrupt Melinda's life again.

So what did she do? Forget what Renae had said to her? It seemed like the simplest thing to do.

But part of her would always wonder.

Renae had admitted killing Cassidy and Kira. When she'd held the gun to Lacy's head, she'd said something like, three down one to go. But Lacy was very nearly certain she hadn't killed Charles…or Bent Thompson…or Nigel Canton.

And what was the deal with Canton's confession? Clearly that had been a setup.

That part didn't tie in neatly, either. Even if Renae had killed him and typed the confession, she had to know it wouldn't cover Lacy's and Melinda's murders.

It was as if two different people had been at work in this killing spree.

And then there was the money.

Lacy knew she was obsessing about that aspect of the case, but she couldn't help herself.

She had to talk to Rick about this. She'd kind of avoided him lately…or maybe he'd avoided her. Either way they hadn't seen much of each other in the past few days.

If there was any chance someone else out there was involved, she wanted Rick to look into it.

Surely that wasn't too much to ask.

Then again, she supposed she should be grateful that

the D.A. had decided not to press charges against her and Melinda for obstruction of justice and concealing evidence. A damn good attorney was all that had stood between them and probation.

Then again, that was probably as much Rick's doing as Melinda's fancy attorney.

Maybe Lacy should stop by and thank him.

Lacy hadn't driven since that night. Now was as good a time as any to get back in the swing of things. Her folks were out for the evening.

She didn't bother calling, just drove to his house. As she pulled into the driveway she considered that maybe she should have called. For all she knew he could have company.

She didn't care. This wasn't a social call.

Holding her head high, she strode up the walk and knocked on the door. It wasn't until he answered that she considered how she looked. Her hair was in a ponytail and her jeans and T-shirt were far from appropriate social attire. But it was too late now.

"Lacy." He opened the door wider. "Is everything all right?"

"I need to talk to you."

He stepped back to allow her in then closed the door behind her.

"Would you like something to drink?"

She shook her head. "I want to discuss some details about the case that just don't make sense to me."

"Lacy." He held up both hands in a whoa gesture. "The ABI and my office are still evaluating this case. I can't talk about it with you or anyone outside that investigation right now."

"Then don't. I'll talk. What if someone who wanted to protect the senator killed Charles?"

Lacy might have been mistaken, but she thought for sure she saw a flicker of surprise in his eyes.

"Why would you say that?"

"Think about it," she suggested. "Charles and Pamela disappear at practically the same time. Just before a possible scandal breaks out. Remember, Pamela is pregnant. The volcano on Charles's extracurricular activity may have been about to blow. But someone stopped it. They took the money Charles had withdrawn, for whatever reasons, and hid it away."

Rick listened without saying a word.

"Then, seven years later, the senator receives an anonymous donation to his reelection efforts. A six-figure donation. Wes Rossman was his campaign manager. Doesn't that strike you as coincidental?"

Rick took her left hand in his. "Lacy, I know this is eating at you, but I can't discuss it with you or anyone else. You have to trust me that we're doing all we can to tie up the loose ends."

She shook her head, uncertain whether or not he actually believed her. "Renae didn't kill Charles, Rick. She killed Cassidy and Kira, she said as much. But she didn't kill the others. I'm certain of it."

Rick considered her speculatively. "Do you have someone in mind as a suspect?"

Was he mocking her? Too flustered to care, she answered frankly. "Why not Wes Rossman? He's very close to the senator. Isn't there talk that he might be in line for something big if the senator makes it to the White House?"

"Why not Canton?" Rick countered. "He confessed."

"As far as I'm concerned," Lacy argued, "Renae's participation rules out Canton."

"I don't know if Renae rules him out, but you're

right. It definitely wasn't Canton. His wife broke down and explained the situation between her and Charles. There was an affair. Nigel Canton got her out of the hot seat when her personal assistant attempted to blackmail her about the affair. He paid off the assistant and started paying more attention to his wife. Nothing more."

"What about Bent Thompson?" Lacy prompted. For a guy who couldn't talk about the investigation, he was on a roll.

"We still don't know Bent's role in all this."

Lacy thought about that for a moment. "He could have taken the money...but why turn around and donate it to the senator's campaign?"

"We don't know that the donation had anything to do with the missing money."

That was true.

"That's about all I can tell you, Lace."

She tried not to be affected by the way he said her name. She'd been pretending that he hadn't made love to her again and that she hadn't thoroughly enjoyed it. He appeared not to have any leftover feelings where that night was concerned. Why should she?

"Thanks for...hearing me out."

"You don't have to rush off, do you?"

Her pulse tripped. Was that an invitation to stay for more than conversation?

"I...well, not really."

"I could order a pizza. We could catch a movie and just relax."

As wonderful as that sounded, she was pretty sure where it would lead. This whole standoff thing that had been happening between them had her second-guessing herself to the max. What if he hadn't felt the way she had as they made love? She'd thought that he was as affected as she was, but she couldn't be sure.

He hadn't made any overtures along those lines.

Even now, he had only invited her to eat and watch a movie.

Two different worlds, she reminded herself.

He had his life here, she had hers back in Atlanta.

Her career.

No love life to speak of, not even a real home. Just an apartment and a twelve-hour-a-day work schedule.

Was she feeling sorry for herself now?

She should just go home and take some time to think this through. Spend some more quality time with her folks.

"I should go." She gestured to the door. "My folks will be home soon and they won't know where I got off to since I didn't leave a note. They worry about me after all that's happened."

Rick nodded. "I understand."

He followed her to the door. Said good-night without even touching her then closed the door.

Great.

Well, at least that answered one question for her.

But there was still the nagging detail of who had actually killed Charles.

She couldn't just walk away from this.

Rick picked up the telephone and put in a call to Agent Fowler. It wasn't that late, but the man could be at church. It was Wednesday night after all. Still, Rick needed to check in with him. It was clear that Lacy was getting anxious. He couldn't risk her doing anything foolish again. And he damned sure couldn't risk damaging the final stage of this investigation. They were too close.

When Fowler himself answered the phone, Rick said, "This is Summers. We may have a problem."

## Chapter 20

Lacy parked across the street, as far from the street-lamp as possible. She sat in the darkness and watched the home of Wes Rossman.

It had to be him—it made perfect sense. She couldn't believe she hadn't realized that before. Bent Thompson wouldn't be dead now if he'd been Charles's killer. He'd have taken the money and never returned to town. Canton, well, she couldn't be sure why he'd ended up dead. Unless he'd come to the same conclusion as her.

Her friends were dead because of Renae's need for revenge. The calls had come from Renae. Rick had confirmed she'd used a cloned cell phone.

But that didn't explain who had killed Charles.

It had to be Wes Rossman.

If Wes had discovered his wife's long-running indiscretion he would have wanted to end it. A man of his age and position, married to such a beautiful woman, might very well want to hang on to that trophy wife instead of killing her too. So he took care of things the way a businessman of his caliber always did— discreetly.

Lacy rubbed at her forehead with her left hand. She scowled at the irritation of having her right arm in a sling.

She had to do something. She couldn't just hang around outside Rossman's house hoping he would make a move or a mistake of some sort. She had to prompt one. This man could not get away with murder. Not even the murder of a scumbag like Charles.

She dug around in her purse for her cell phone, then realized she didn't know the number. "Damn." A quick call to information and she had what she needed. She entered the number and waited through three rings.

"Hello."

Lacy tried her best to analyze that one word, but it sounded so cold, so empty, she simply couldn't.

"I know what you did, Mr. Rossman," she said, deciding to try his recently deceased wife's chosen method. Only Lacy intended to let him know just who had his number, literally. "This is Lacy Oliver and I'm going to the D.A. with what I know. You should never have gone that far to protect the senator. He won't do the same for you. Now you're going down." She ended the call before he could respond.

Then she waited, her heart pounding, for him to react.

The garage door lifted slowly, the light pushing out from under it like a convict lunging toward escape.

"Come on, you bastard," she murmured, wanting this over once and for all.

The elegant Cadillac backed out of the garage and then rolled to the end of the driveway.

Lacy held her breath and prayed he wouldn't notice her car parked behind a neighbor's on the opposite side of the street.

He drove away without hesitation.

She waited as long as she dared and then eased out onto the street and headed in the same direction.

The fingers of her left hand clenched around the steering wheel. She told herself over and over she was doing the right thing. This couldn't wait another week or month for Rick or his ABI buddies to decide her theories held merit. Rossman might get nervous and flee the country. He had the kind of money to do that in a heartbeat.

Her pulse fluttered when he took the street that led to the senator's estate.

"Bingo," she muttered as he stopped at the gate. She parked a half a block away, again on the opposite side of the street, and turned off the engine and lights.

He sat at the gate for more than a minute. She wondered what was taking so long. It wasn't that late. The senator wasn't likely in bed.

Then a cold, hard reality broadsided her. How the hell would she follow him from here?

Her stomach lurched.

Her full attention shifted back to the Cadillac. The massive iron gates had started to slowly open to allow the vehicle's entrance to the property.

She licked her lips and tried to catch her breath.

If she didn't get in behind him she wouldn't be getting in at all. Climbing over the wall or the gate would set off a perimeter alarm.

She was out of the car before the thought had fully formed. She crossed the street in a dead run. Keeping as close to the shadows as possible, she lunged through the gate just before it reached the halfway point of closing.

She was in.

Taking a moment to catch her breath, Lacy told herself to calm. She could do this. All she had to do was observe. Anything she heard or saw might be useful to the investigation Rick didn't want to talk to her about. She didn't care about technicalities and search warrants.

Maybe it was a mistake, but it was one she had to make or she would always regret it.

She thanked her lucky stars that the Ashlands hadn't added any dogs to their security as she ran across the lush landscape, staying in the shadows of massive trees. Since the press had left for the next big story, the extra security personnel had been let go, as well.

When she reached the looming mansion, Rossman had already gone inside. His Cadillac sat in the circle driveway in front of the grand steps leading to the front door.

She concentrated hard to visualize the layout of the house. She'd only been there a couple of times—the first on the day of Melinda's wedding to Charles and then for a Christmas party celebrating the imminent birth of Melinda's first child.

Moving around the side of the house, she went to the windows that, as best she recalled, were located in the senator's study. The first set she chose was the wrong one.

She told herself to calm and think.

A rustle of brush somewhere behind her sent her heart knocking against her sternum. A rabbit hopped off into the darkness. Ten seconds passed before she could breathe easy again.

The next windows she chose were the right ones.

Rossman and the senator were in there all right.

She had to bend her knees and hunker down just a little to see through the partially open shutters. The two men were yelling. She could hear their muffled voices but couldn't make out the words.

Rossman abruptly crossed his hands over each other in front of him in a scissoring motion and shouted something that sounded like, "This is finished." But Lacy couldn't be certain that was what he said.

The senator tried to stop him, but Rossman shrugged off his hand and stormed out.

Lacy hurried to the front corner of the house and watched Rossman get into his car and drive away.

What did she do now?

Her pulse started to trip again and the burn of adrenaline urged her to act.

She had to do this.

The senator was primed for this moment. Rossman had reacted to her call. Now she had to see what the senator had to say about his old friend.

Did he realize yet that his right-hand man, his best friend all these years, was likely the man who had killed his son?

Taking a steadying breath, she walked around to the senator's front door and knocked. She firmed her resolve, squared her shoulders and prepared to state her case. He would surely listen to her despite her role in disposing of Charles's body. She hadn't killed his son. The senator had to want the whole truth.

When he opened the door, Lacy almost lost her nerve. "Hello…ah…I'm sorry to intrude, but I…"

Her train of through trailed off as the impact of his cold stare penetrated the buzz of adrenaline no doubt clouding her good sense. What the hell had she been thinking? What if Rossman told him about her call? She should have anticipated that. But then, wouldn't that have risked exposing his own guilt?

"Senator," she began again, but he cut her off.

"If you're looking for Gloria, she's over with Melinda and the children." His tone was every bit as cold as his stare. "Now, if you'll excuse me, I have things to do."

Lacy supposed she couldn't blame him. No matter what a low-life bastard Charles had been, this was his father. He wasn't going to forgive her, no matter her motivation for what she'd done. He wouldn't forgive her any more than she would forgive him for looking the other way while his son abused his wife for five years.

"It's you I need to speak with, Senator. Is it possible for us to speak privately for a moment?"

He looked confused, then suspicious. "I imagine you won't leave until you've had your say."

She shook her head. "It's too important."

He stepped back and opened the door wider. Lacy walked inside. She felt a chill rush over her skin as he closed the door solidly behind her. Summoning her courage, she followed him to the richly paneled study where just moments ago she'd watched Rossman and him arguing.

Massive wood furnishings. Leather chairs. Nothing but the best for an Ashland. Her stomach roiled.

"What do you want, Miss Oliver?" he asked when he had stationed himself behind his desk. He didn't sit, he simply used the desk as a boundary. Perhaps it made him feel superior.

She took off, didn't even slow to take a breath. "Senator, I believe you should go to the D.A. and insist he pursue another aspect of the investigation into your son's death. The murderer could be someone close to

you. Someone who benefits from your political career."
Like Wes Rossman, she didn't say. "Someone you
consider a friend."

Lacy had spent most of her adult life despising the
Ashlands. She couldn't help seeing the irony in the fact
that she stood in the senator's study now warning him
about a possible danger to his family. Maybe she had
already gone mad and no one had noticed yet.

The senator simply stared at her with that same cold
glare for several endless seconds. "Whatever you hope
to gain by reopening those painful wounds, Miss Oliver,
I can assure you I will not tolerate your telling tales.
What you propose is nothing more that conjecture and
is quite preposterous. My family has endured quite
enough. Renae Rossman killed my son and you and
your *friends* disposed of his body like so much trash.
I'm certain we have nothing further to discuss."

Lacy blinked at the harsh words. But she took them
in stride. He was right. What she, Kira and Cassidy had
done was wrong. She'd faced that after ten long years
of torturing herself with that hidden secret. She
deserved his scorn for that. But he had sins of his own
to answer to, like allowing Melinda to be abused.

"You're right. We were wrong. We had no right to
do what we did." She swallowed the lump of emotion
in her throat. "Your son was a cruel, selfish man."
Before the senator could object, she added, "Still he
didn't deserve to be murdered. No one does." Tears
burned her eyes as she thought of her two dear friends.

"That's why you must believe me when I say, Renae
did not kill your son," she went on. "She loved Charles.
I am absolutely certain it wasn't her."

The senator's face tightened with outrage. "I want
this over, Miss Oliver. As you well know, my family is

irrevocably fractured. I would prefer you never speak of this again."

Ice slid through Lacy's veins. *We won't speak of this again. The vow.*

She would not do that again. No way.

Lacy shook her head slowly from side to side. "I'm sorry, Senator. I can't do that. I'll go to District Attorney Alton myself first thing in the morning. This won't be over until the whole truth comes out."

The senator thrust his hand into his desk drawer and snatched out a weapon. He leveled the business end on Lacy. "You should have left it alone."

Confusion roared through her, stunned her. Had the discovery of his son's remains and the subsequent murders pushed him over the edge?

"Senator, I wish you'd put that gun away. I know this has been difficult but—"

"You don't know anything!" His face distorted with rage or something on that order. "You don't know how it is to have only one son. To put all your hopes and dreams in him and then to watch him not only destroy his own life but also to try and destroy yours as well. I had no choice but to put an end to it. Especially after that trollop Pamela started blackmailing the both of us."

"Pamela was pregnant," Lacy said before she could stop herself. She felt...baffled by his words and the gun. Had he slipped over some edge? He had been under a lot of stress. She choked down a breath. The question was, did she run or keep him talking?

"I know," he ground out. "She'd threatened to go to the press with all she knew about Charles, including his illegitimate child she carried, unless he gave her the money she wanted. After she'd taken his money, the whore came and tried to get more from me."

Lacy felt herself go utterly still inside. This wasn't possible...how could... "So you killed her?"

The question echoed in the room, the sound and implication of it surreal.

"What choice did I have? She wasn't going to stop! She just wanted more and more!"

His nostrils flared with the oxygen intake required to fuel his escalating emotions. Lacy told herself to stop right there, to try and calm him, but she couldn't...she needed to hear it all.

"You took the money." She filled in the blanks, her entire body shaking at this point. "The money Charles had given her...the hundred grand he withdrew."

"It was my son's, why wouldn't I?"

The idea of what might have happened next sent denial surging through her. "You confronted Charles." She held her breath.

"The fool couldn't pull himself together. He'd put his wife in the hospital, had gotten another woman pregnant, and still he sought out more mistresses. He was sick. I couldn't have my son behaving in such a way...I had a future to protect."

Lacy didn't dare say more...she just let him talk.

"After I took care of Pamela—" he squared his shoulders, lifted his chin challengingly "—I went to him, told him what would happen if he got himself into trouble again. He'd been drinking. His mousy wife had shot him in the shoulder." He shook his head in distaste. "He'd managed to get up and get himself into the shower." The senator looked disgusted. "And even then, he had the unmitigated gall to laugh in my face." His expression took on a sudden, faraway look. "I didn't mean to shoot…the weapon just went off." He frowned. "It happened in an instant."

The impact of his words rumbled through Lacy. "You killed him."

"It was an accident," he screamed, his face twisting with hatred or anger, maybe both. "I rushed out of the house. Got down the street and realized I might have left something incriminating. I couldn't think. I had to go back and be sure. Only this time I parked away from his house. It was almost dark anyway. I did what I had to do, but before I could get out of the house the three of you came in. I did the only thing I could. I hid in the closet."

His face fell slack again and he remained silent for so long that Lacy feared he'd lapsed into a coma.

Lacy moistened her lips. Did she dare try to leave now? Would he snap out of his intense reverie and shoot?

She decided to take the chance.

She eased back a step. Just one step toward the door. Toward escape.

The senator's face turned crimson with rage. "This whole thing is Bent Thompson's fault," he snarled.

Lacy froze. She didn't dare move a muscle or say a word. The senator didn't actually appear to be talking to her. He spoke to the room at large.

Would he notice if she took one more step back? "That piece of trash tried to blackmail me simply because I asked him to purchase an untraceable weapon for me ten years ago. And then he kept it when I paid him to dispose of it. He was worthless." He said the last with sheer loathing. "After all I'd done for him. I'd paid him far more than he was worth just to watch my son. I should have gotten rid of him ten years ago."

"You killed him?" Lacy bit her lips together. She couldn't believe she'd said the words.

"I had no choice."

Enough. She needed to get out of here before he decided that she had left him no choice as well.

"Senator, you've been through a lot." She struggled to steady her voice as she eased back one more step. "I should go and leave you to come to terms with all that's happened."

He fixed his aim more firmly on her, letting her know he had no intention of allowing her go. "I tried to end it." He lifted his shoulders in a resigned shrug. "I used Nigel Canton for a scapegoat. He'd been abusing my son's memory for years. He deserved exactly what he got. I thought the confession was ingenuous." He exhaled a weary breath. "If I'd only known that Renae was executing her own revenge, I could have used her instead." He made a tsking sound with his lips. "Too bad for Canton."

"Senator, my parents are expecting me back home."

His full attention leveled menacingly on her. "Then they will be sadly disappointed."

An alarm blared deafeningly. It paused and a computerized voice announced, "The north perimeter has been breached." The squeal of the alarm punctuated the announcement.

The senator rushed to the window to look outside.

Lacy didn't waste any time. She ran like hell. She burst into the long hall that would lead her to the front door.

She was out the door and sprinting across the cobblestone driveway before she heard the drum of running footsteps on the steps behind her.

The sound of a gun exploding forced her to glance over her shoulder.

The senator dashed after her, then took aim to fire again.

Lacy cut first right, then left. Her heart hammered so hard she couldn't breathe.

Vivid flashes of that night in the woods with Renae darted before her eyes. Not again.

God, she didn't want to die.

Lacy dove into the shadows of the trees. Let her senses guide her. She'd come this way before…she could do it now.

She slammed headfirst into something hard and unyielding. Her injured arm throbbed.

"Get behind me."

Rick.

Thank God.

Relief rushed through her. It was short-lived. Another blast of gunfire.

"Drop the weapon, Senator." Rick stepped out of the shadows into the moonlight.

She didn't know how he'd known she was here, but he was here and that was all that mattered.

"She's trumped up all these wild allegations, Chief," the senator said. "She has to die or she'll never shut up."

"Put the gun down," Rick repeated, "and we'll sort all this out."

For one long moment, Lacy was certain the senator might just go along with Rick's suggestion, then he shoved the gun against his temple and fired.

Lacy couldn't move. Couldn't blink away the image.

Rick checked to see if there was anything he could do. There wasn't.

The senator was dead.

Lacy dropped to her knees on the ground, her entire body trembling with the receding adrenaline.

She told herself that it was really over now, but she was wrong.

It would never be over. The memories would always be right here, inside her. She squeezed her eyes shut. Two of her closest friends were dead…nothing would ever be the same again.

# *Chapter 21*

Lacy stored the last of her things into the back of her Explorer.

"You're sure this is what you want to do?" her father asked. He and her mother stood on the sidewalk looking a little nervous and maybe a little shell-shocked.

"I'm sure."

Lacy had made up her mind. Nothing anyone said was going to change it. Not that her parents had tried to change her mind. To the contrary, they had always respected her decisions.

"Well," her mother ventured, "you know where we are if you need us."

Lacy hugged her folks. That part was right for sure. They were there for her. This would always be home.

She climbed into her SUV and headed out to get on with her life.

The nightmare decade was over and she had

survived. Thank God, Rick's ongoing investigation had included surveillance of both Rossman and the senator. Otherwise she might not be getting this chance in life. A lot had changed, including her, and she was ready to get on with whatever the future held.

She waved as she drove away. Her parents waved back just as they had hundreds of times when she'd left home.

But this time was different.

Emotion thickened in her throat. She'd visited Kira's and Cassidy's graves yesterday, had said her goodbyes to Melinda.

Melinda was going to be okay. Her children were both back home with her now and she'd made peace with Gloria. The kids were all Gloria had left. Maybe that fact made Melinda more palatable to her.

Lacy shook her head. Some aspects of her hometown would never change.

She'd just turned onto Norman C. Ashland Boulevard, wiggled her nose at the smell of the old paper mill and started out of town when blue lights flashed in her rearview mirror.

Rick. It had to be him.

Sure enough, his truck pulled up behind her when she eased onto the shoulder of the road.

He got out and strode up to her window. She'd already powered it down in anticipation of his doing just that. Her pulse quickened as she watched him move toward her. She did love looking at the man.

"I'm certain you didn't intend to leave town without saying goodbye."

She sighed, couldn't help herself. Truth was she could look at him all day, but that didn't change what she knew she had to do: get on with her life. She had to keep telling herself that or she'd let sentimentality hold her back.

She shrugged. "I guess you caught me red-handed, Chief. I didn't want to make a big deal out of it. Leaving town isn't that unusual for me. I've done it lots of times." She had intended to call him…eventually.

He braced his hands on the door and leaned in closer making her heart skip a traitorous beat. "I guess I was hoping this time would be different."

There was something else that wasn't fair—the deep, rich sound of his voice. As if looking at him weren't enough. Oh well, Rick Summers was like the finest chocolate, too damned good to resist.

She reached into her purse with her right hand. The arm was still on the mend, but she could at least use it to some extent now. She drew out a business card and pen, jotted her home number on the back of the card and handed it to him. "Call me sometime when you're in the big city. I'll show you a good time."

One corner of that sexy mouth hitched up into a smile. He tucked the card into his pocket. "I'll do that."

"Good. I was hoping you'd say that."

She gave him a wink, powered up her window and drove away.

She did look back just once.

He stood there, watching her go, as he'd no doubt done before.

But this time was different. This time she would be seeing him again. Soon.

*Everything you love about romance...*
***and more!***

*Please turn the page for Signature Select™*
*Bonus Features.*

# VOWS
## of SILENCE

BONUS
FEATURES
INSIDE

4  Alternate Ending

9  Southern Girls' Top Five Rules for

Finding Mr. Right

11  Growing Up with Debra Webb

16  Sneak Peek: *Investigating 101*

by Debra Webb

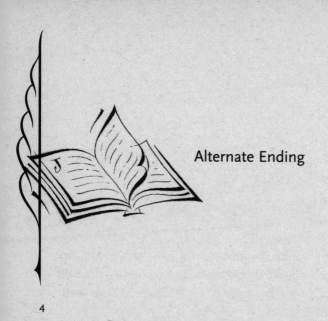

# Alternate Ending

4

After reading Vows of Silence, *did you wonder if the story could have ended differently? If so, read on and find out what could have been...*

## ALTERNATE LAST CHAPTER

LACY STORED the last of her things into the back of her Explorer.

"You're sure this is what you want to do?" her father asked. He and her mother stood on the sidewalk looking a little nervous and maybe a little shell-shocked.

"I'm sure."

Lacy had made up her mind. Nothing anyone said was going to change it. Not that her parents had tried to change her mind. To the contrary, they had always respected her decisions.

"Well," her mother ventured, "you know where we are if you need us."

Lacy hugged her folks, climbed into her SUV and headed out to get on with her life.

The nightmare decade was over. A lot had changed, including her, and she was ready to get on with whatever the future held. No more secrets…no more keeping quiet. From this point forward her life was going to be an open book.

She waved as she drove away. Her parents waved back just like they had hundreds of times when she'd left home.

But this time was different.

She'd just turned onto Norman C. Ashland Boulevard, wiggled her nose at the smell of the old paper mill, and started out of town when blue lights flashed in her rearview mirror.

Rick. It had to be him.

Sure enough, his truck pulled up behind her when she eased onto the shoulder of the road.

He got out and strode up to her window. She'd already powered it down in anticipation of his doing just that. Her pulse quickened as she watched him move toward her. She did love looking at the man.

He tore off his sunglasses and eyed her suspiciously for a moment. "I'm certain you didn't intend to leave town without saying goodbye."

She sighed, couldn't help herself. The idea that she had ignored what she felt for him all those years seemed unbelievable now. So much had happened...so much had changed in the past few days. Except the one truth that she had never really been able to deny, not even after ten long years. She could look at him all day. Still, she'd learned her lesson where Rick was concerned. She couldn't live four hours away and expect to have a real relationship with a guy like him. It was just too much to expect of a mere woman.

"I know your mama raised you better than that, Lacy Jane," he prompted when she didn't readily respond.

Lacy shrugged. "I guess you caught me red-handed, Chief. I didn't want to make a big deal out of it. Leaving town isn't that unusual for me. I've done it lots of times."

He braced his hands on the door and leaned in closer making her heart skip a beat. "I guess I was hoping this time would be different."

The low, husky sound of his voice sent shivers dancing over her skin. Oh, it was different. Very different. He just didn't know it yet.

Maybe she should put him out of his misery.

"You don't have to put up a fuss, Chief. I'm only going as far as one hundred and nineteen."

A frown furrowed across his handsome brow. "One hundred and nineteen? Your grandmother's place?"

She nodded. "I've decided that my future is there. It's where my heart has been all along. I've given up my partnership, but I'll still be consulting for the firm. Otherwise, my only plans are to find a man who wants to worship me and perhaps procreate if things work out."

One corner of that sexy mouth hitched up into a smile. "Do I need a résumé to apply for the position?"

Lacy grinned. "Absolutely not. I'm quite familiar

with your skills. All you have to do is follow me home. We can iron out the details later."

"I'll do you one better than that." He straightened away from her vehicle and before she could fathom his intent he'd skirted the hood and climbed into the passenger seat. "I'll ride along with you, just to make sure you don't change your mind."

"I've been known to do that. But, you don't have to worry, Rick, I won't be changing my mind. I'm not running away anymore."

His eyes locked with hers and she saw the emotion there that she'd felt in his arms the night they'd made love. Love. Unconditional. He reached across the console and kissed her then. Kissed her the way a man should kiss a woman, thoroughly and with every part of his being.

"You know," she murmured when they came up for air, "it wasn't necessary for you to show off like this."

"Baby," he whispered against her lips, "you haven't seen anything yet."

# Southern Girls' Top Five Rules for Finding Mr. Right
## by Debra Webb

1. This first rule goes right to the heart of the chase. If you see a hunk you're interested in, for God's sake call him! Southern girls are never afraid to make the first move. (This is how I snagged my husband.)

2. Once you've gotten past the first couple of dates, there is the all-important "meet the parents" moment. Rule number two is simple: if he can't get along with your daddy and your brothers, he's trouble.

3. Rule number three is another no-brainer. Never continue to date a guy who dares to look at or talk about another woman or old girlfriend while he is with you. This is a sure indicator of a lack of respect or an overdose of self-confidence. (This can also apply to cars. A man

who spends too much time looking at or talking about cars can be problematic as well.)

4. Rule number four is one of the most important rules of all. Every Southern girl knows that spending time with a man's mother is the best way to find out exactly what kind of man he really is. A man who is good to his mama will more likely be good to his wife.

5. Finally, rule number five is the last hurdle. Southern girls understand that there are two tests in particular that a man must pass before he's considered suitable husband material: the sports test and the buddy test. If he'd rather watch the game than go to a movie with you, this is a bad sign. If he'd rather hang out with his buddies at the pool hall than with you at your family's backyard barbecue, you should just walk away. (This rule does not apply to Southern girls who would rather be watching sports and hanging with their bosom buddies as well.)

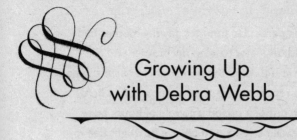

# Growing Up
# with Debra Webb

I grew up on a farm in rural Alabama, a small community called Skyline high atop Cumberland Mountain. I have two brothers and one sister. As kids we had lots of cats and dogs and, of course, a whole slew of farm animals including pigs, cows, horses and chickens.

We only had three channels on the television and those all went off the air by midnight, accompanied by the flight of air force jets and the national anthem. Needless to say, I spent a lot of time entertaining myself with stories and imaginary characters.

One of the scariest times in my life occurred when I was about five years old and at home with my sister and younger brother. My parents and older brother were out on the farm doing what farmers do, working from dawn to dark to make a living. At twelve, my sister was responsible for taking care of me and my little brother as well as cooking the family's meals and keeping the house clean.

This particular summer day my mother had warned my sister to keep my brother and me inside and to keep the doors locked since she had seen a report on the news about a man who'd broken out of a prison a couple of hours away. There was no reason to believe he might flee to our community but my mother was ever cautious just the same.

About lunchtime that morning, my brother and I were playing in the living room while my sister mopped the kitchen floor. I'll never forget that day. It was perfect. There was a cool mountain breeze shifting the ancient curtains on the windows. We sat on the worn linoleum floor playing with the few toys we had, totally oblivious to the idea that we were poor. Suddenly my sister rushed into the room and whispered for us to be quiet. Usually we would have argued, but this day the look of stark fear on her face kept us silent.

My sister ushered us into a hiding place in the corner behind a large chair and side table. I remember her holding us close against her and the feel of her heart pounding in her chest. It wasn't until I heard the screen door creak as it opened that my own fear kicked in.

We all heard the deliberate footsteps as someone came through that back door and into the kitchen.

The intruder walked into the living room and straight down the hall to the bedrooms while we huddled in terror in our hiding place.

As the sound of those heavy footfalls made the journey back toward the living room, I remember being surprised when the salty taste of tears pooled on my lips. I didn't realize I was crying. I wished for my mother and father. I prayed for God to keep us safe. All in those few seconds.

The intruder hesitated in the living room and we all held our breath...our hearts thudding so loudly it's hard to believe he didn't hear the thundering sound.

We didn't breathe again until the danger had moved back into the kitchen. Again our intruder appeared to pause. To listen? we wondered. To reconsider what he had or had not seen? Would he come back into the room and lean over the back of the chair to find us cowering there?

The screen door squeaked loudly, then banged against the wood frame. But we didn't move. I don't know how long we huddled there, too afraid to move...too afraid to speak.

Eventually my sister, being the brave soul she was, moved out of our hiding place and went into the kitchen. She first locked the back door that she had failed to lock earlier. Then she moved from room to room and peered out every window in the house to ensure no one was lurking in the yard. When she returned to the living room to tell us it was safe to come out, we were so relieved that for a moment or two we all considered that maybe we had been imagining things. Perhaps our mother's story about the prison escape had prompted our imagination to run away with us. And then we noticed the footprints on the kitchen floor.

You see my sister had just finished mopping the kitchen floor when she thought she heard something outside in the yard. She'd rushed to hide us in a nick of time before the door had opened. We hadn't imagined anything. Our intruder had walked up the long, dusty road to our house and left his tracks on my sister's damp kitchen floor.

After the initial shock we also noticed that he'd taken the cake of corn bread my sister had baked that morning. We never knew the identity of our intruder. We only knew that he apparently took what he'd come for—food.

That was my first experience with sheer terror. Listening to those footsteps come closer... wondering what would happen next. I'm certain that terrifying exhilaration is at least part of the reason I love writing romantic suspense. My sister's bravery is surely why I write strong, determined heroines.

Watch for my next Signature novel and we'll share another story from those formative years that helped make me the author I am today.

Here's a sneak peek...

# *Investigating 101*
## by
## Debra Webb

*Don't forget to look for my upcoming Harlequin Intrigue book in April 2006 entitled Investigating 101. This story is the newest installment of my ongoing COLBY AGENCY miniseries. If you haven't read a COLBY AGENCY story before, this is an excellent place to start. The Colby Agency is about to hire some fabulous, and very young, raw talent!*

## CHAPTER 1

Victoria Colby-Camp sat at her desk and stared at the neat pile of manila folders Mildred had placed in the exact middle of her clean blotter pad.

It was the same each Monday morning. Mildred gathered the assignment and status reports from each investigator and brought the bundle to Victoria at nine sharp for her perusal. At ten a standard staff meeting would take place in the conference room. New assignments would be dissected and doled out, old business would be discussed. The workweek would continue from there.

The routine never varied.

Victoria sighed, the sound echoed softly in her empty office.

She had no right to feel this way. Life had been extremely good to her for months now. She certainly could not complain…. And, yet, she felt…bored.

Her brow furrowed deeply in denial of her last thought. Perhaps *bored* was not the proper word. She and Lucas had celebrated their first wedding anniversary a few months ago with a long weekend in the Cayman Islands. Her son was happily married and anticipating the arrival of the first Colby grandchild.

What else could she ask for?

The Colby Agency continued to thrive. The cases that walked through reception's doors included the most intriguing and challenging from right here in Chicago as well as all across the nation—ones that no other agency seemed able to solve in addition to those of longtime, loyal clients.

Still, Victoria felt restless.

She pushed up from her chair and walked across the room to look out at the city she loved. A city pulsing with life, filled with magnificent and innovative architecture. A place rich with colorful and turbulent political history as well as vibrant cultural venues.

There was no other city in the country quite like it. No other place she'd rather be.

Dozens of memories filtered through her mind, warming her heart. It seemed so long ago now that she and James, her first husband and the father of her only son, had started this agency. She had known even then that the Colby Agency would be something very special. How could it be anything else? James Colby had orchestrated its creation.

But now, more than twenty years later, something was missing. She concentrated hard in an effort to pinpoint the motivation for the fleeting sensation.

This odd emptiness had started almost one month ago. At first she'd considered that, with her highly trained and efficient staff, maybe she was bored with her level of participation in the business of private investigations. Her right-hand personnel oversaw most of the day-to-day operations. Though she came to the office each and every day and reviewed all activities, she was not personally involved with the execution of assignments.

But her role had always been in oversight rather than execution. Why would she suddenly feel unsettled in that role now? Admittedly, change could be a good thing. With that in mind and much to the dismay of her staff she'd launched a complete overhaul of the agency's decor. A smile tilted one corner of her mouth. Unquestionably the renovations were a nuisance, but she'd hoped that the transformations would lift this sense of lacking she suffered.

The distraction had not worked.

Victoria turned to view her elegantly decorated office. Though the new gold and red tones were quite exquisite, as were the rich jewel tones of the rest of the offices, the relief she'd hoped for had not come.

Nor had the carpet. Her gaze dropped to the beige carpeting on the floor. The contractor had apologized repeatedly for the error. The wrong color had been ordered and, of course, returned, leaving the floor rather bland amid the rest of the opulent decor.

Her attention moved back to her desk and the stack of files there. She really should get on with her Monday-morning review, but the usual anticipation proved glaringly absent.

There was always the chance that her lackadaisical attitude wasn't work related at all.

She'd toyed with the idea of a personal makeover. Nothing elaborate. A new hairstyle perhaps and possibly a color. Victoria smoothed her hand over her firmly coiled French twist. Never one to bother with such trivialities, she'd worn her hair the same way for half a lifetime, never bothering with touching up the multiplying silver strands that gave away her true age.

Was it time for a personal change?

Lucas appeared more than happy with her hair just as it was. She traced the tiny lines accentuating her eyes and wondered why she'd never worried about those either. Most women her age and of her social standing had undergone at least one facelift by now.

No, she decided, that wasn't the problem.

As simple as it would be to pretend a new wardrobe and a visit to a salon would cure her restless feelings she knew deep down that wouldn't help.

Her working life lacked the edge and excitement of the past. Though it was certainly true that the

Colby Agency worked many, many intriguing and exciting cases, that wasn't what she meant.

When she and James had first started the agency everything had been new, including the investigators they hired. One or two had previous experience in the field, but most learned from the master, James Colby himself. Time and experience had honed this agency to a gleaming, precious jewel among its competition.

No more rough edges, no more raw exhilaration.

Affection tugged at her lips when she thought of Trevor Sloan and his untamed surliness. He'd been a man with more rough edges than most and, yet, the best damned investigator any agency could hope to retain. He'd been young and so had Victoria.

On the heels of that thought came an epiphany.

That was the missing ingredient that had her out of sorts.

Youth.

It wasn't that she resented growing older, on the contrary. Her life was everything she wanted it to be and more. This was strictly business related.

And no one knew better about the business of private investigations than she.

Victoria stepped over to the phone on her desk and pressed the intercom button.

"Mildred, find the date and location on that job fair we talked about last week. I'm considering participating." Anticipation surged in Victoria's veins.

BONUS FEATURE

She was onto something here. She could feel it all the way to the pads of her feet.

"I have it right here, Victoria," Mildred said as she shuffled through her calendar. "Embassy Suites downtown, this weekend."

Perfect. "Sign the agency up ASAP. I don't want just a booth, I want a conference room. Get it in tomorrow's edition of the *Tribune*."

"It may be too late to sign up," Mildred warned.

Victoria grinned. "Talk to Lyle Vandiver at the Chamber of Commerce. He'll get us in. Throw out all the stops, Mildred. I want to make a big splash."

"The usual employment requirements?" her secretary asked.

There was no need to mull over the question, Victoria knew what she wanted. "No. This is going to be different. No experience necessary. Drop the age requirement to twenty."

"Pardon? Did you say *twenty*?"

"Twenty," Victoria repeated. That was a far cry from the twenty-five guideline the agency generally used. It had been a very long time since she had considered an applicant too young to have any real job experience. And there was no time like the present to see what she'd been missing.

Still sounding befuddled, Mildred assured, "I'll get right on it."

Victoria sat down at her desk and began to review the case files with a new sense of purpose.

That was what she'd been missing—just exactly what this agency needed—new blood. Young blood. Raw talent.

The unexpected.

...NOT THE END...

*Look for the continuation of this story in* Investigating 101 *by Debra Webb, available in April 2006 from Harlequin Intrigue.*

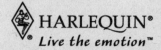